POETIC JUSTICE

Poetic Justice

A novel
by

MARY GRAY

Adelaide Books
New York / Lisbon
2019

POETIC JUSTICE
A novel
By Mary Gray

Published by Adelaide Books, New York / Lisbon
adelaidebooks.org
Editor-in-Chief
Stevan V. Nikolic

For any information, please address Adelaide Books
at info@adelaidebooks.org
or write to:
Adelaide Books
244 Fifth Ave. Suite D27
New York, NY, 10001

ISBN: 978-1-951214-84-5

Printed in the United States of America

1

The poet is a light and winged and holy thing,
and there is no invention in him
until he has been inspired and is out of his senses,
and the mind is no longer in him

Plato / The Ion

GENEVIEVE – the poet

There she sat, all five feet six of her, mostly leg, all one hundred and twenty-three pounds of her, mostly bone, her huckleberry hair pulled back into a low-slung ponytail because another damp jungle-hot Chicago summer simmered outside.

There she sat, all thirty-seven impatient years of her, slumped into the contoured seat of a library chair listening, listening, listening …

Rhythmic music came from a close-by conference room. A thumping hum came from the ventilators. A voice flowed down the heavy oak library table like a rivulet along a forest floor, displacing all other sounds. It carried words poeticizing an act of love.

"… Lying with a woman brings thoughts of mountains … bones rising up out of her flesh … soft wetness, the warmth …" The voice wrapped around the words like soft cotton, "… a snake-like river … uncoiling slowly in the sun …"

The recitation transformed this after-hours poetry workshop into a sexual experience, hardly what Genevieve Dupont had anticipated from the promotional flier's promise of a brief two-session introduction to verse.

"Sweetest is being held by a woman …"

Her body tensed. She bent forward to check out the baritone strains and caught a glimpse, halfway down the table, of a stoic face, intense in concentration, tanned, and patrician, sculpted by years of emotion. His vivid eyes peered over spectacles to read the words he had put to paper. He enunciated each syllable so every ear would absorb the sounds as sensitively as he had experienced the very act of penetration.

"… She takes the seed as the earth takes seed in the spring …"

As he read, the summer evening sun seeped through the elongated gothic windows behind him. His shadow crept across the table, a movement as fluid as his voice. Against the silence of the room, she heard this amorist describe his beloved in lilting tones, his admiration, his lust tripping over each other in lines of unending beauty. "Thoughts of mountains … bones rising out of her flesh …" Genny absorbed that love and pledged that if she could write such poetry, if she could find such love, she would wake up in the morning eager to engage the day.

The class was equally absorbed and offered admiration rather than the expected criticism.

Genny asked him, "Has your lady read that poem?" She wanted him to say, *No, there really is no lady.*

Instead, he answered, "Well, yes, many of those lines I had already written for her."

Damn, she thought, but rather said, "Does she know you're reading them now in public?"

He lowered his head, "I don't think she'd want me to."

Genny sensed his captivity, sprinkled with a bit of rebellion.

The class moved on. Other students followed with a miscellany of adventuresome attempts at wordplay. Genny didn't question the work of any other participant.

"Genevieve Dupont? Genny?" the instructor asked as he checked his sign-in sheet, then around the room. "Do you have a contribution?"

The focus swung to Genevieve DuPont. She muttered her improvised effort, an unsuccessful haiku. Its unattained humor stumbled off her notebook and splatted on the floor. Thwarted, she looked beyond her pad of paper into the dark eyes of the quiet woman sitting across from her, who asked, "Did you mean that to be sarcastic?" The question, though it came from a woman a decade younger, shorter, and frumpier, fed Genny's insecurities – her belonging in a poetry class, her belonging in the city of her expectations, her being unsupported in this quest. Genny had meant it to be poetic.

She felt small and captive in this behemoth of a building knowing she could instead have been out among the more content population, shopping, downing cold beers, delighting in the warm summer breezes.

As Genny approached her thirty-eighth birthday, she cursed her wasted years. Twenty years ago, as the poetry editor of her high school paper, this seminar might have been more apropos. Overriding poetry then were her honors courses in a premier school of the west. Then she played the town bon vivant. Then she made her mark on the local business scene. She breezed through it all. Now, as she took on Chicago, none of it, the honors, the parties, business, none of it worked for her. Poetry she saw as her last chance.

Above her, ceiling lights dimmed, brightened, and dimmed again. It was the library's signal for those using its private meeting rooms that their allotted time was up.

The Mountain Man gathered his seductive papers into his satchel and followed the stream of ersatz poets out the door, taking the damp warmth with him. Slim and straight, tee shirt stretched across his torso, jacket tossed over his shoulder, in him she saw a winning combination of an artist's soul in an athlete's body, a poster boy for a Viva Virility Weekly. Her eyes followed the thinning, tousled hair, blonde blending into grey. Soon he was gone from sight.

She sat in the charged air, lingered over her pens and notepad, and watched him go. Transfixed, she tried to push his lush words out of her mind wishing his words had been created for her, rather than the muse who certainly must share his bed. As she left, she passed by the sign-in sheet and inked "Jonathan Waterhouse" on the palm of her hand.

She envisioned every step he would take – the long journey down the spiraling stairs from the upper floors, slipping through the crowd, exiting onto the street, nodding good-byes to familiar faces. In a fantasy vignette, she would rush to his car, nestle in his front seat, accompany him home, take off his jacket in his hallway, take off his jeans in his bedroom. She would lay him down, kiss his lips, stroke his thighs, make love to him, and leave.

But instead, resigned, she waited at the bus stop with the bustling crowd headed north. The noise of the city drowned out the murmur remaining in her head. She tried to hold onto it in spite of the cars, buses, and trucks that clattered past her. She stood again in the midst of the city's hard surfaces, her flip-flops planted on the cement sidewalk, her back leaning against the glass of a building wall.

Later, in the quiet of her apartment and the darkness of her bedroom, she tried to recreate the flow of love that came from his words as seventies love songs purred from LITE-FM, as silken pajamas slid across her skin, her fingers probing parts of her she wanted him near.

A week later the group came together again. Lenard Lavinski, the poet-on-loan charged with making them into more than they were, stood aloof in the corner of the room waiting for his class to reassemble.

The night was stuffy. The participants sauntered in, bringing the smells of exertion to the closed-off room, and settled around the library table with sticky, bare legs rubbing on wooden chair seats.

Genny was early and signed in again with her name, email address, and phone number. She was tempted to draw a brazen arrow at the entry. The name "Waterhouse" did not appear on the sign-in sheet. She sat alone as she waited for his arrival, cool under an air vent and vitalized by its freshness coming in rhythmic spurts. The bottle of tart lemonade she sipped cut through the dryness of her throat.

Then, standing at the door, the Mountain Man surveyed his options, circled around the table and landed across from Genny. Dissonant voices belonging to boisterous youth and high pitched laughter filled the room. He backed away from it all and settled instead among quieter folk. Like a cello's tones in a Vivaldi sonata, a gentle voice overrode all the chatter. It was all she heard. She raised her eyes and smiled to a distracted face.

Inspiration hit Genny this second time around. A week's effort produced a stirring poem on Einstein, his concept of time and how the unknowing slip through it. She sat back in her chair, studied her words, pleased. She waited through poems by unwashed punks who wrote of erotic pleasures they had never known, by well-padded ladies who wrote of what had thinly filled their lives, by existentialists who made no sense at all, by steely- eyed women who screamed in rage. She rose to read, her voice distinct, as would befit Einstein. Her eyes rarely left the paper, only to see him sitting opposite her, or to scan other faces. Some were attentive. Others' eyes wandered elsewhere – to papers in front of them, out the windows, or inward with their eyes closed.

As she approached the final stanza, she became aware of his eyes on her. The wrinkles in her blouse loomed in her mind like faults in rock formations. Her eyebrows were unplucked, her elbows calloused. Her fingernail was chipped. Was her part straight? She lowered her eyes and sat, not hearing the critiques of the class that delved into the meanings of her poem. He remained silent.

No Einstein for him. He began his recitation slowly, speaking of jasmine. His skin glowed with a sunned luster. He wore a meticulously ironed white shirt, as pure as the petals of the flower he memorialized in the words he spoke. "Extravagant in smell and bloom … A sprinkling of petals … like sparklers … cascading showers of light." His powerful words evoked the silky smell of the flower that filled the gardens of Mexico.

As he concluded, he stared beyond the walls as though waiting for his muse to fill his head with yet another, more eloquent stanza. "Cascading showers of light" settled on a cushion of soft "ahhhh's" around the table.

Humbled, Genny rushed out of the room at the flickering of the ceiling lights, sensing any ties to him evaporating like summer puddles on the city streets. Even with Einstein as her poetic partner, she neither pierced his time and space nor his attention. The intoxicating time she spent around the library table ended, the sessions completed. Without time, she was without opportunity. Without opportunity, she was without hope.

As the first one out, if she waited at the street entrance, could she venture a casual conversation opener? Perhaps a *Hi, your poems certainly do capture an audience. I'd like to read more of them. Have they appeared anywhere?*

... and then what? became her next thought.

Or maybe he would come up behind her and ask which bus she took and could he join her? Or maybe he wouldn't.

But perhaps he could come through the doors with a crowd around him that she could join, slyly slipping in with the group.

But he hadn't arrived with anyone and he left alone. Genny didn't wait at the library doors. He didn't ask her what bus she was taking. She didn't slip in with a group. She left for home by herself surrounded by the hordes of Chicagoans sharing the northbound bus.

2

What may I do to make you glad,
To make you glad and free,
Till your light smiles glance
and your bright eyes dance
Like sunbeams on the sea?

A Poet's Wooing / James Whitcomb Riley

GENEVIEVE – glad and free

"Life is not fair," Genny said as she crossed the room to tone down the air conditioner. Denise looked up wearily from the living room couch.

"Life is not fair," she repeated but Denise had returned to her reading.

Denise was Genny's younger sister. When she turned up in the nursery crib Genny was eight years old and she considered this baby a personal ball of playdough to make into whatever she needed. Genny often needed a friend, a sounding board. That is what Denise became. Now Denise seemed the wiser of the two, the more directed and the more stable, accustomed to hearing such inanities fall from her older sibling's mouth. Her silence bespoke this.

"That poet in class," Genny said, discounting Denise's detachment, "I practically spoke right into his face and he never showed any signs of recognizing my existence. Everyone in the class made some pretty favorable comments on what I wrote and read. Even Lavinski nodded, pretty much what anybody gets from him. But HE sat there, a granite slab."

Genny faced her, intent on eliciting a response. Denise, her eyes still on her book, said, "Maybe he's hopelessly in love with you and can't cope with the emotion."

"Thanks, Denise. I'll put that at the top of my possibilities list."

"Maybe he's married."

Denise's attitude did not alleviate Genny's angst nor settle her restlessness. She checked the street scene beyond the living room windows for distraction. Cars squeezing into rare parking spaces, dogs pooping on the lawns, street lights flickering. As she shuffled about the room, she scanned the bookcases. No title captured her attention. Denise's disinterest did. Being contentedly in love herself, Denise had no mind for those who weren't.

Genny was far from love. A man, a semi-boyfriend, a Brian, occupied time in her life. He was good for an occasional beer and movie, maybe a concert, little else that mattered. He had a circle of friends who pepped up her life and he liked the way Genny kissed. She liked his availability. She liked his law degree. Lawyers were well regarded in the mountain town she had left. Her father would be proud of her choice of beau.

Denise and her David embodied capital "L" Love. Her sister Loved the same boy-back-home-now-grown-up since puberty. Surely she would marry him as soon as he gathered the courage to come from Utah to claim her. They all grew up in Utah, up north in Winton, nestled in the Wasatch Mountain Range. There, Denise and David would marry and procreate and probably die in each other's arms.

Not Genny. She would die that night of a shattered heart. But at least she had enjoyed having Denise living with her in Chicago for a short fling with city life before her inevitable marriage and subsequent death.

Genny sat down next to her, puzzled. "Didn't you ever feel this girlish tingle, this slipping into love when David was first buzzing around the front door?"

Denise was amused. "Tingle? Maybe when I was ten years younger. Not lately. Don't you think you might be a little beyond it too?" she asked Genny. "Whoa, he buzzed?"

"Oh, he buzzed, until he lit on the flower of his life."

Marry the flower? While it occurred to Genny, it must never have occurred to David even after all those years of relaxed courtship. Too comfortable to step forward and admit they were a pair? Apparently. Denise left Utah loving him. She never wavered during the two years she stayed with Genny trying out independence. Brian and Genny introduced her to other men but she responded much as she responded this evening, turning her attention elsewhere.

"Tell me, little sister, what is my next step? Stalk this Mountain Man?" The spoken thought amused her. Genny saw herself in stocking feet, tiptoeing through libraries searching for gangs of poets mouthing lyrical language.

"He did invite us all to visit his Thursday group at the Indie Café in Lincoln Park. I could take up residency there. But then I would have to write real poetry!" She wondered how long it would take for that group to discover her ineptness.

"The most creative thing I do is book a hotel with a Jacuzzi or finagle an upgrade on United Air." Corporate travel, not romantic entanglements, was Genny's primary forte. She worked full days on a computer servicing high voltage business people as they moved from city to city, from continent to continent. Her real world was filled with airlines, hotels, and rental cars. Dependability, not creativity, was the prerequisite for that employment.

Denise feigned deep thought, her head in her hands. Genny was on her feet again, pacing like a caged animal. "I got it," Denise said looking up, her eyes narrowing, "Why don't you just wait for a memory of you to drift back into his consciousness?"

"Like dragonflies drift to water? I don't envision that happening."

Very much unlike Genny, Denise's specialty was waiting. Nothing seemed urgent to her. But then, she was eight years younger. Maybe hitting thirty-seven, with her David not materializing as a husband, Denise might become more practical.

"I take it you're not overly interested in my newly discovered poet," Genny said. "That's fine. There are other people who will gladly listen to the perplexities of my life."

"And who might they be?" Denise asked, knowing Genny's bar-hopping circle.

"There are people in my life who care about how my life is going. I am interested in them and they are interested in me."

"The people in this town are interested in how the Cubs are going, how the Bulls are going, how the Blackhawks are going and maybe if Carson's is having a sale."

"Those are my social people," Genny said. "My other people are a little deeper."

"And who might they be?" she asked again, curious.

"Well, California Stan, my most attentive client at work is one. He always listens to rehashes of my social life." This was a stretch of the truth. Every now and then she would entertain Stan with anecdotes when client calls tapered off.

They knew little about each other but Genny trusted Stan to show her the way out of any jam she might find herself in, as he often had. After all, he was the one who wrote words of praise to her boss when his grandchild broke her arm, when Genny had him on the next plane to be there, to hold her swelling hand. Three questions and he was on his way: where did she live, when was he free to leave, and how was his daughter holding up? His compliment to management set Genny up for a small bonus.

Stan's concern for that little girl broke Genny's heart. He allowed nothing to come in the way of his being at her side. At the time he was on one of his whirlwind tours to solve some problems with manufacturing plants back East, down South, in Canada with several more touchdowns before he could head home. Didn't matter. When his little Betsy fell off her bike the commercial world disappeared. Genny brought the little girl's grandfather to her side.

He was much like Genny's father in times of stress with his ready, reassuring hand at her back, with an optimistic word when grey clouds descended, with a little push when she would have preferred to stay put. Lucky Stan's daughter to have a father like that. Lucky grandchild. Lucky Genny, too, to have men like her father in her life.

"California Stan," Denise said, "uh huh. I can see him as a best man at your wedding."

"Okay, Denise, don't peer into the future with me, but you're missing a front row seat on this suddenly exhilarating ride of my life. The chance to say 'I knew them when …, before they …,' whatever, because I'm gonna get him. Be there at poetry gatherings. Win him over with persistence and unending loyalty. Read lines to him dripping of passion. And then we'll write sensational poetry together. We'll become world-renowned as the foremost love poets of the century. Yes we will."

She stopped mid-step. "But will he ever love me? No. He will only love the words we write."

The smell of ginger from Denise's earlier baking spree wafted into the room. She picked up her book, headed toward the kitchen and asked Genny if she wanted a glass of wine.

"I guess so." Wine could be a suitable ending to her sister's counseling. *Maybe she'll bring me some gingerbread too,* was Genny's consoling thought.

Later that evening her laptop blinked persistently, indicating new messages. Waiting, she suspected, were more enticing ads for a solution to penile dysfunction, more easy mortgage money, more petitions to sign: save the whales, save the trees, save the air. *Why not,* she wondered, *while we're at it, save the world? Or at least, save me.* With a Pavlovian response, she brought up the email.

"From: jonwat@..." it said. Jonathan Waterhouse. The words burred. That's him, the Mountain Man. Her mind rushed to his laptop and deified the keys he had touched to spell out her name.

To: Genevieve Dupont <gennydu@hotmail.com>
Date: Mon, 19 Jul 2004 22:43:23
Subject: Einstein

Genny Dupont,
    You left before I had a chance to tell you how much
I like your piece, both the writing and the reading of it.

You have wrestled with things passing through your life, haven't you? What an eloquent statement of your experiences. You expressed a certain acceptance of the inevitable, which I admire.

It was a wonderful reading. I am glad to know you.
Jon

She trembled while the skies seemed to thunder. More likely it was an airplane flying into O'Hare. "… like your piece … eloquent statement … admire … wonderful … glad to know you." He was glad. The words swirled around her head, dipping and bowing. She logged out of email and turned off the computer, dropping her forehead onto the keyboard, feeling FGHJKL imprint on her skin. Not having enough of it, she restarted the computer and signed in again. "jonwat" was there, still. Yes, really there, still liking the way she wrote and read, still glad to know her.

She went to bed, slept, woke, and moved through the following days like a programmed android. She watched her computer sitting dark and silent on her table, afraid it would disintegrate, taking the message with it.

Two days later she could hold off no more. With restraint, she pressed all the necessary buttons to watch the procedures elapse bringing her back to her email where Jonathan Water-house remained. She pulled him up again to see if the words she relished still sat below his name. Eloquent, admire, won-derful, glad – they were all there; none had escaped.

By now she had settled enough to send a response. Not the primal pleas of love me, love me, love me, me, me, me that rang in her head for forty-three hours. It evolved into this resultant model of dignity and distance.

From: gennydu
To: jonwat
Date: Wed, 21 Jul 2004 18:07:27
Subject: Re: Einstein

Thank you so much — since I am such a fan of
yours the compliment is that much more meaningful.
If I'm free I may stop in on the writing group you
mentioned in class. Thursdays, you said? I suspect
some real writing is taking place there if your
mountain piece is any indication.
Genny DP

There. She had made a move. Thursday she waited for a day of surprises to begin. But the plan made at six o'clock on Wednesday needed an outside nudge. Combed, cleaned, and ready to go, she checked her PC that evening for a repeat invitation that wasn't there. Nothing. She watched the evening that had begun with such expectation disintegrate into dejection while she sat in front of a gibbering television screen, immobile, eating salty, stale peanuts.

Thursday finally ended. Friday, Saturday, then Sunday passed as well. Friday's diversion at a movie theatre with Will Smith in "I, Robot" took her mind away from poetry groups that she had or had not been invited to join. On Saturday she cleaned her room, throwing his email printout into a wastebasket filled with a week's worth of emptied yogurt containers.

Steady by Sunday, she analyzed every word of her July 21 note. "Thank you." Prosaic. Was the "so much" overkill? "No, thank you so much" was gracious. Then she plunged into the core. "Such a fan." Oh my god! She had heard three, maybe four pages of poetry. *That's a ticket to his inner circle? Yes, of course.* She had cast her lot as a fan, a devotee, an idolater. Genny envisioned the general invitation wilting in the atmosphere. Where had her words gone?

As the last week of July frittered away, she looked in on a nearby community college for another poetry class. Her obsession be damned, was it poetry or the poet? Neither brought her much satisfaction. She found a class that concentrated on poetic forms. *That'll do.*

"Wanna join me?" she asked Denise, who clenched her teeth and exhaled.

In the registration office, the clerk, probably a student herself, referred Genny to the syllabus where she pointed out the missed lectures – the limerick, the prose poem, and the sonnet. The classes had begun the first of the month.

"That's OK," Genny said. "What's left?" She took the syllabus to check and noted a handful of other forms yet to be investigated.

The clerk had moved away from her, down the counter to a young man who waited for his share of attention.

"Is the class still open?" she called to the clerk.

"The class is still open. No price discount for latecomers. Down the hall, take a left, room 117. Hurry, it's just beginning. You can pay later." *Enough of you*, Genny sensed the clerk muttering at the end.

The mid-summer weather was at its muggiest, not adding any relief to the dreary college classroom. She snuck into the room from the rear and sat at the closest empty desk. In front of her, heads of hair – braided, blonded, clipped, shaggy. Beyond that, a statuesque woman was writing "iambic pentameter" on the board. *Good, something I know,* Genny thought. *I remember Shakespeare.*

The shift-clad woman turned to face the class. Her eyes glittered with a merriment that the well-schooled enjoy when indulging in their expertise. She nodded a welcome to Genny, the only break in her pace. The students' attention remained forward.

"Now comes the real challenge of poetry," the woman said. Genny would have considered the limerick a challenge, but the class was well beyond that. Many were taking notes with intensity. Genny pulled out her pen and paper, determined to catch up and fit in.

The poetic form, "sestina," was the challenge. "A poetic exercise," the teacher called it. At the board behind the podium, she graphically explained how successful poets played with the form. She diagrammed the accents and word placement schemes to help the class visualize the required patterns.

In a nutshell, the rules were thus: sestinas had six-line stanzas and the six words that ended each line were to be used to end specific lines of subsequent stanzas, six stanzas total. Add to that a three-line finale that included all six words. "This bizarre format has led to some astonishing poetry in the hands of the masters," she said.

Studying the notes on the board Genny frowned. *How hidebound,* she thought. The teacher promised that tackling a sestina would create an addiction, similar to working crossword puzzles, demanding specific words in specific places. "It's a French form," she said. Genny Dupont's Gallic blood started bubbling while she listened to some A. C. Swinburne and some Kipling. She was hooked.

"Think of a serious story to tell," the teacher said while putting some Saint-Saens on her CD player. "Start the narrative in six lines. I'm only asking you for the first six this evening. Give each line five iambic beats."

Studying the distributed samples, Genny unraveled the sestina format. Some enthusiastic discussion followed. Each student rose then, one by one, to test the effectiveness of their chosen storylines on the class.

The heat in the room was debilitating. Genny's palm stuck to her yellow pad. She concentrated on the childhood memory she would translate into poetry. Summers ago, her best friend's father disappeared into the world outside Winton. He just left, like a red-tailed hawk heading north, with no explanation, not to his daughter, and certainly not to Genny. As her friend, Genny shared the confusion, joined by her father who knew the family. They tried to talk her through her loneliness, anger, and guilt. The heat in the classroom was reminiscent of that hot summer when no amount of sympathy could cool down the rage that interrupted her childhood.

Word after word, each one adding to the tale she wanted to tell, spread across the lines to her satisfaction. She began her story with the da dum da dum da dum rhythm of the sestina's iambic pentameter.

"With this first stanza, no rhyming's necessary. With sestinas, just pay attention to the rhythm," came a reminder from the head of the room as they dug into the assignment.

Then one by one again they each stood at the podium to recite their six lines, some tragic, some gentle, some treasured, some mundane. Genny wondered what burning story Jonathan Waterhouse would have attempted. She was sure if he ever read this sestina she was creating he would wish it had come from his mind. But it won't.

3

Dry chafing roughness of cement on my skin
September wind blowing hard against my back
The smell of wet concrete,
The burn of the ax handle in my hand.
These I know.

Work / Jonathan Waterhouse

JONATHAN – September wind

He typed line after line of verse into his computer, deleting each as the words appeared on his screen. Nothing expressed anything of beauty for Jonathan Waterhouse whether he composed electronically or wrote words in longhand on yellow legal pads. Meaningful words were not at his command. He looked around his den, at the books lining his wall, at the stack of meager printouts, to the ream of blank sheets, hoping for some inspiration to swoop over him.

The poetry wasn't flowing as in better times, when he had worn out writing of love he could write of the labor that was so prominently a part of his past. Son of a Pennsylvania warehouseman, he was destined to become one himself, except for his fragile frame and his robust mind – both protected throughout his childhood by his parents and teachers who opened to him a world beyond hard labor, giving him the dream he almost fulfilled.

Neither love nor labor had anything to say to him this morning. Jonathan threw his pencil down and gathered up the papers he had collected at the library workshop. He checked the notes from Lavinski's lectures and reread the poetry the other participants had submitted. The poem on Einstein, poems on city street people, poems on remembered child-hoods, they were easy streams coming out of other people and only added to his frustration. He knew somewhere in his bones were the words he had employed before, putting them together to mesmerize his audiences. Where had his "cascading showers of light" gone?

He checked the class intro sheet for Lenard Lavinski's phone number, remembering the smile of satisfaction that spread across the poet's face while listening to Jon's poetry. Lavinski had main-tained an aloof attitude during the class until his mountain image, his "bones rising out of her flesh" hit his ear. With that, he came alive with anticipation of promise for the class. Jon planned now to reconnect with the practiced poet to provide some nurturing . He hoped it was a reasonable time to call.

As the phone rang, he planned the conversation: *Lenard, this is Jon Waterhouse,* he would say, *from your seminar at the library last month. The downtown library.* He cleared his throat, found his mouth dry and wondered, would he be dismissed as unworthy, did Lavinski ever reach out for help, would he even remember him? His finger hovered to disconnect as Lavinski answered with an aloof voice.

He remembered. With more spirit he said, "Oh, yes. Jon, the 'cascading showers of light' poet."

"Yeah, that's me, and that's probably the last and best thing I've written." He faltered because he had never admitted such failure to another creative mind. "That's why I'm calling you."

As humiliation overcame him the noted poet rescued him saying, "If you never write another line, you can rest proudly on that one."

"And that seems to be the problem, Lenard. I seem not to be able to write another line." The hours of painful probing for expressive words rose in his head. "I've been working on false starts for a couple of weeks, going nowhere, except a little crazy in my head."

"Not an unusual phenomenon, Jon. Give it a rest. Take a trip. Read a trashy novel. Sit through a Shakespeare play – they're all over the map this summer. Relax."

"That's not possible. That word is not in my vocabulary. No words are in my vocabulary."

Lenard said nothing.

"What I thought I should do is follow you around, sit in on another class of yours, or maybe have a private session with you reading things I've written before this drought." His mind flashed *brazen*.

"Oh, I am sorry, Jon. I'm off to London tomorrow evening. I'm about to take in a little Shakespeare myself while I'm there. See? I follow my own advice – a little trip, a little Shakespeare. I don't know what good I could be for you anyway. Plug away. That's what you have to do. Something good will come out of your head, or your heart. Are you in love? If not, a plunge into romance never hurt creativity."

With that, he wished Jonathan the easiest of times. Jon cradled the receiver, picked up a pencil, blinked at his pad of paper and dropped his head onto his arms.

"Useless to try," he muttered, rose, stretched and left the room, the lights blazing, the air conditioner blasting, the computer monitor taunting, the smell of discouragement permeating the air.

Out of his think tank, beyond books and computer, beyond his paper and pencils, beyond a wastebasket filled with crumpled sheets of discarded poetry, his spirits recovered. Once in the hall, no demands on his creativity pressed in on him. In the hall, he could tend to other homey responsibilities, like fixing lunch.

4

In fear and trembling, I think I would fulfill my life
Only if I brought myself to make a public confession
Revealing a sham, my own and of my epoch

A Task / Czeslaw Milosz

GENEVIEVE – fulfill my life

"Lunch?" asked Demetrios from behind his computer, sitting across the pod from Genny. He looked through his banner of flags of all nations, trumpeting to the travel department that he was an elite international agent. It was noon. Genny was shocked that the morning was gone.

"I was thinking of going Spanish. They now have gazpacho on the menu downstairs," he said.

"Lunch? I don't know, Deets. I think I'll skip it. I was hoping to get in some research on sestinas at the library instead."

"How much research does a nap need?"

"Not a siesta, goon bird, a sestina, my poem. You know, school?" His face was so vacant she felt she was talking to a store mannequin.

Demetrios, shortened to "Deets" by those not family, was an expert on allowable plane connection times, airport abbreviations from ABQ to ZYL, knew prices from first to last class and the fees they incurred. Sestinas? Not so much. He exhaled. He dropped his shoulders. He narrowed his eyes and stared at her.

"You'd give up a lunch for a poem? You're heading into deep ..." He didn't state the destination out of courtesy to his fellow workers. Alone, outside the office, there would have been no censorship on his vocabulary. Deets had a passion for vibrant expletives, for the Cubs, he inhaled feta cheese triangles, and devoured the Sunday comics, but had no room for poetry. As conversation, Deets and Genny pretty much zeroed in on Chicago sports and the rest of the above, plus his mother's cooking, his older sister's love life, his latest little brother jokes usually involving bodily functions, and his batting average in the company's summer softball games.

He liked Genny. She knew she was the first real friend he had made outside his elaborate family circle. In their office, he was her best buddy by far. They had a couple client pals, too, who, with their road warrior tales and the adventures they dramatized, added some humanity to the job.

To this friendship she served as a good audience for his exploits, offered him endless opinions on movies, sought or not. She talked about fashion bargains, but her prime knowledge centered on travel bargains, especially involving cities she wanted to visit.

Every time she focused on a favorite, Deets objected by repeating "You want to go to Athens with me, and you know it."

The conversation always ran a similar path: "I'd go to Athens with you, Mr. Demetrios, but you want us to end up in Markopoulos." Markopoulos was a mountain village where his family roots lay, and where snakes came every August, according to his pitch.

"Swallows, maybe?" Genny would ask, hoping she had misunderstood him. No, snakes, on a summer holiday, it seemed. "Who'd want to miss that?"

As an added incentive, he hinted about a delicious second cousin, supposedly waiting for her there. Maybe the cousin was a snake. Who knew? She got confused when Deets started talking about the tangle of branches in his family tree.

When Genny talked about Brian being her weekend playmate, her casualness confused Deets and was probably the reason he wanted to mate her with his cousin. He sensed that Brian wasn't stirring Genny's blood, certainly didn't have the stuff to stir the blood of this Greek.

She had recently introduced the Mountain Man as a casual topic. He was always on her mind. References were difficult to suppress. She thought Deets would approve, in spite of the poetry he brought along.

As he logged out of his computer, ready for lunch, Genny tried to explain the current disinterest in food and fellowship. She was usually available for restaurant outings. They took her away from the mesmerizing glare of her computer screen and into the doings of those she worked around forty hours a week. But she was escaping them all now, into the doings of Swinburne and Kipling from her class sessions.

"There's really no other time I can get at this sestina research," she said. "The poem I'm working on is too complicated. I need to see some perfect examples to get the concept into my head. I'm not above plagiarizing."

Yet the promise of gazpacho's tingle of tomatoes and cucumbers on her tongue almost won her over. Almost.

Deets gave up. "Okay, Miss Muffet, go sit on your tuffet. See," he said, "I can be a poet, too. You're not the only inspired one around."

"Don't be petty, Deets." Across the room the agents gathered. "Sally's getting ready for lunch. Tag along with her. She might even want your trip to Athens." Genny immediately balked at that thought. Athens might be a good getaway for her at some point. She should save it. And Deets with it.

"Or better yet, grab me a salad. I'll need food after my sestina session."

Barely acknowledging the request, Deets moved toward Sally, another agent from another cluster of desks who was assembling a group of lunch mates around her. Genny watched him go with his sprightly step and his trim torso filling his tightly woven cotton knit sweater. *Nice butt*, she noticed, not for the first time.

She called after him, "We'll go to lunch later in the week. OK? Collect all the office gossip and we can have a down deep and dirty discussion later, OK?"

Sally tossed a knowing look. She was the best source of juicy news and would probe Deets on Genny's research. Although seldom reliable, she was a tantalizing magnet for inside information gathered over lunch tables, between client contacts, in the ladies' room, on the elevators, and wherever secrets were shared. Her ears zoned in on conversations. She spread her harvest broadly. Her smile warned Genny that her secrets may not be secure.

Genny trusted Deets with what he now knew about her, her poets and their poetry. None of that would be of any interest to the lunch bunch that gathered around Deets and Sally, who were now moving down the corridor, then out into the summer sun.

No salad would be waiting for her when she returned. Deets abandoned her when she drifted into poets and poetry. But a curiosity about the Mountain Man lingered.

Her headphone, still clamped over her ears, activated with a transferred call from the client the agents termed "chirpy Stan," who now needed a flight to White Plains. Along with the reservation request came the extensive conversation that no one else on the floor but Genny had the patience to share.

Genny's Monday poetry class was a night for odes, from the romantic passion of Keats as in: "My heart aches, and a drowsy numbness pains / My sense, as though of hemlock I had drunk ..." to Dean Young's contemporary passion: "When I saw you ahead I ran two blocks / shouting your name then realizing it wasn't / you but some alarmed pretender ..." What fun to be in love.

In the style of Keats, she created an ode with the Mountain Man in mind and saved it to put in an email as a reminder to him how elegantly she wrote. Cowardice took over early the next morning when the poem went the way of other scratched up sheets, crumpled and discarded.

She settled again into the quiet of her life. Her expectations of surprise messages simmered on a back burner. At the office she and Deets learned about revised international travel taxes, quizzing each other until the most obscure ruling couldn't stump them.

At home in the evening hours she plugged away at her sestina. In the air again electrons bristled, speeding to her PC. Finally, a jonwat email came that watered a withering sprout of hope.

From: jonwat
To: gennydu
Date: Mon, 02 Aug 2004 10:10:55
Subject: Re: Einstein

> *As we passed Loyola University, riding the*
> *downtown bus mid-afternoon Saturday, my friend*
> *Karen said to me that we had missed the Einstein*
> *lectures in Kerry Hall last week and I remembered you*
> *had written beautifully about him. Just as I wondered*
> *if you had attended, you boarded the bus.*

The image of Jonathan on public transportation puzzled her. What had she been doing? Zoning out? Searching for change, for a couple of empty seats? Juggling her purse? Jabbering? Missing an opportunity to connect, that's what she had been doing. Where was that crispy smell of anticipation he always brought with him?

> *That was you, wasn't it? I thought so immediately,*
> *then I was uncertain, but now, remembering your*
> *face from our poetry sessions, I am sure it was you.*
> *How are you? How goes your writing?*
> *When you left the bus you seemed to head down*
> *Michigan Avenue – shopping? We were off toward*
> *Millennium Park to the Art Institute first and then to*
> *the concert.*
> *What a remarkable day it was. Hope you are well.*
> *Jon*

The email contained a discovery, the name of his muse. Karen. Didn't sound much like a muse-name to Genny.

Maybe Celeste or Daphne or Thalia would better suit her role. Not Karen. So, he had Karen and she had Einstein and the Mountain Man's memory of it. Somehow that was not enough.

She considered her next move. Inclined toward caution, her obvious option was a retreat to the safety of a Brian, toward her infertile agenda, toward unchallenged enjoyment. Not the answer. She wanted to return to the poetry where the Mountain Man reigned but was afraid she would overshoot the target with undue enthusiasm. She might hit dead center and knock him down. Or was he a roly-poly that would pop back to bait her again? He was a fluke, Genny determined, an undependable fluke, an undependable ethereal fluke. How could she ensnare that?

> *From: gennydu*
> *To: jonwat*
> *Date: Mon, 02 Aug 2004 22:18:15*
> *Subject: Re: Einstein*
>
> *Jonathan,*
> *If it was 3 pm-ish and if I was with a rather round friend, sitting up front, yes, it was me. Also heading to Millennium. Also heading to the Puccini concert. But instead of expanding our cultural vista, we spent our in-between time drinking gin and tonics and eating salad and pizza outside in the sunshine at the Park Café. Wish I had noticed you. I would have teased Karen about how I lap up your love poems.*
> *My poetry doesn't go. In fact, I am seeking more help. Have started another class - this one on form. Went*

tonight, as a matter of fact, to learn some more about
odes. A good class, you could probably teach it.
  See you soon, somewhere along the bus trail.
  Genny DP

With that sent, Genny shut off her computer feeling vulnerable, exposed. She had referred to a pseudo-muse, slightly overweight. Although she questioned how much inspiration Brian actually brought to her. She confessed to enjoying concerts in the park, to drinking merrily. The undisclosed threats were that she might get in his Miss Muse's face, that she was serious about poetry, that she was serious about him.

All she deduced of him: that he rode the downtown bus – with Karen. That he remembered her face.

What was that face? She saw on the darkened screen of her computer that she needed a haircut. She brushed aside the locks hanging over her eyes. A hint of a grey streak butted into the black, a mark of her thirty-seven years. Beyond the hair, not a bad face, softer than the angles of his cheeks, nose, and chin. Good lips, a hint of a pout creeping in at the corners. An old-soul sadness about the eyes that she tried to disguise with cheeriness. Too many years of hoping for miracles were difficult to disguise. Clear, firm skin, still smooth where he had crinkles about his eyes and furrows across his forehead. But give her the ten, maybe twenty years he had on her and she would be able to match him groove for groove. She wanted those years of his when she too could develop character, depth, and wrinkles, write sensitive poetry stemming from the full life that could break about her when she brought this Mountain Man to her bower.

He was out there, conversing with her. She needed only to push the right key.

From: jonwat
To: gennydu
Date: Mon, 02 Aug 2004 23:53:28
Subject: Re: Einstein

You would not have teased Karen about that poem.
You seem too reserved for that.
We ate inside at the Park Café and drank dirty
martinis (a mistake). Puccini was so full of energy.
Sat way down in front on the right. Where were you?
Millennium Park is lovely but big, a massive loveliness.
I lost you in the space. Didn't see you there and didn't
see you going home. Just one glimpse all day.
No more classes for me. I have enough impetus
with my weekly group. Weren't you going to stop by?
We are meeting this Thursday at the library up north
at 6 if you want to come. I am baking a cake because
a couple of writers are leaving. More reason for you to
come to fill up the ranks. Jon

This was becoming a conversation she had left too soon
the previous night. Genny found his midnight response in the
morning, a sun bursting through her clouds. A sporadic conversation to be sure, it was definitely moving in her direction.
Here we have a poet, she told herself, *who thinks beyond rhyme*
and meter, conversing as though I were in the cult. In the dream
of her adolescent years, as she put fragile poems on the arts
pages of the school newspaper, she would create them forever.
She didn't. Distractions pulled her away.

Is this a poet who will bring me into that circle? I need this
poet. He listens to Puccini; he drinks martinis. He is amusable.
He looks for me in crowds.

He comes equipped with a muse.

Here was her poet with thinning hair and winning face, carved by a life worth reflection, putting him where in the circle of life? He was a poet as distant as a Tibetan mountain god communicating via spirits.

With restraint, Genny moved the stream of casual chit-chat along, maintaining the cool dignity that had proved so successful.

From: gennydu
To: jonwat
Date: Wed, 04 Aug 2004 16:26:37
Subject: Re: Einstein

> *HEY! A poet who bakes? Or a baker who writes*
> *poetry? Or an accountant who does both? What are*
> *you? Can't come Thursday. Working late. Save me*
> *some cake?*
> *Maybe I'd tease, maybe not. I tend to be impetuous.*
> *We sat front left. Crashed a private party, your group?*
> *Were kicked out once and schmoozed our way back*
> *in. Love every part of Millennium, especially "The*
> *Bean"and the serpentine bridge, would like to slide*
> *down its northern banks. We took the Red Line home.*

Hours passed, then days. She fretted with Deets who was as sympathetic as wind is to clouds. She cursed the overtime her job demanded and then reversed her mood thinking of the time-and-a-half it paid. She considered other career possibilities. She drank beers with her round friend, Brian. She waited on the street corner for the bus and scanned her fellow bus mates for the Mountain Man. She saw ladies in espadrilles, old men reading "The Wall Street Journal," and heard wailing fire engines, and the raucous sputter of passing motorcycles. She wrote poems and tore them up. Morning after morning she worked the daily crossword puzzle. She was becoming adept with useless words. No Mountain Man interrupted her flow of life.

Until finally, materializing on her email site she picked up at the office, she found the newest entry. It rankled her with its five-days-in-coming. She sensed no urgency in it, nor any encouragement. She dismissed any importance to the invitation to the Thursday meeting. It was not a proposal of marriage.

From: jonwat
To: gennydu
Date: Mon, 09 Aug 2004 9:27:28
Subject: Re: Einstein

Absolutely, a poet who bakes and that is all I am, having left behind heading up schoolrooms two years ago. I am a little premature at working my way into the golden years — coffee in the sun, reading the paper in pjs and idle thoughts about writing memoirs. Actually attempting some decent poetry, stanza after stanza instead of miscellaneous lines here and there. With a little divine intervention I may create a whole book full of verse. My dream!
You sound like you have a wildness to you — crashing parties, teasing strangers and sliding down banks of bridges, all actions I thoroughly endorse, even if the slide down the serpentine is nothing more than a fantasy with blatant sexual underpinnings.
Enough, it is time to get back to my busy day. Jon

Genny began composing a denial. She weighed the effective options: deny this image, back away, express shock, amusement, gratitude. She spent the day considering its implications and the evening in class writing elegies. Then a late night second thought arrived under his name, wiping away all the skepticism from the morning.

From: jonwat
To: gennydu
Date: Mon, 09 Aug 2004 23:29:38
Subject: Re: Einstein

    Hope my interpretation of your millennium
fantasy wasn't offensive. Apologies if it was.

Apologies already. The man was sending her apologies. Perhaps he was a man with sense enough to realize boundaries, an answer to a maiden's prayer, she with her biological clock reverberating in her breast. Unfortunately, hovering was his muse with her proclaimed luster, her "bones rising up out of her flesh."

Never a muse, Genny was more often a pain in the ass. She could be a strong shoulder, a willing ear, a ride home. But a muse? Never. She brought laughter to the room and donuts to the party. She sent birthday cards and said thank you. She concocted vibrant, vitamin-filled slushies. She had hopes and dreams. She had plans and fantasies. The serpentine bridge at Millennium Park had never been any of these, not blatant, not sexual.

Would that she might have replied: *Now you want to talk sexual, sir, I would take you within "The Bean" and stand with you beneath its apex and kiss your strong shoulders and back and neck and face and watch our images melt into one on the sleek steel above.*

But of course, she shelved that concept on shelves not deep enough to harbor such fantasies. She had too much sense to stack them up and not enough pluck to take action. She decided to spend her imagination on composing proper, enticing responses.

She lived out the week, reporting to her desk as expected, executing her duties, putting her travelers on trains, planes, and buses. Each morning, as she traveled past Millennium Park, she thought of him thinking of her having fantasies with "blatant sexual underpinnings." Or maybe it was just one thought. One was enough for Genny. She filed such impossibilities away with her other hopes. Easily done until:

> *From: jonwat*
> *To: gennydu*
> *Date: Fri, 13 Aug 2004 17:42:12*
> *Subject: Einstein and the mystifying universe*
>
> *I came across your Einstein piece, his mind tumbling, careening through the universe and with no thought of making your mind tumble, decided to send you a poem. Do you know this one by Wm. Blake? Kind of dark but beautiful poem. Best I can do by way of addressing any further need for poetry that you may have.*
>
> *The Sick Rose*
> *O Rose thou art sick.*
> *The invisible worm,*
> *That flies in the night*

In the howling storm:
Has found out thy bed
Of crimson joy:
And his dark secret love
Does thy life destroy.

I might have called poetry the key to my soul as
well. Didn't you refer to it as such in the Lavinski
discussion? Do you read a lot of poetry? Have you read
the Polish poet Czeslaw Milosz. He borders on the
tragic, but I think he's very good.
   j.

Genny realized she was in over her head. She needed poetry but that was her secret. She had relished the cushion of
poetry that her father had provided as she was growing up, his
softness to her mother's iron.

Then the cushion maybe was poetry, but now she needed
a poet. She needed a poet to buy her velvety books of poetry.
She needed a poet to sit at her feet and read her Victorian verse
by candlelight. She wanted poetic lines dropped into her day at
sunrise, at midday, at sunset. It was not the poetry; it was the
poet. Preferably a poet with touches of gray in his sandy hair
who could make pilot announcements sound lyrical. Genny
envisioned spending mornings drinking bubbling champagne
on balconies overlooking blue-green waters, trying to understand his poetry.

She knew she wouldn't understand any of it. Just as she
didn't understand sick roses. It wasn't the poetry she had
grown up with. No worm had found its way into her childhood verses. Well, maybe a couple. She remembered some
Emily Dickinson lines that did in a worm in fine style: A bird

came down the walk: / He did not know I saw; / He bit an angle-worm in halves / and ate the fellow, raw.

That delicious sight stuck in her memory.

Genny didn't remember any name like Czeslaw. That would have been a difficult entry in her father's repertoire. She remembered his deep voice riding the waves of the simple children's verses he would read. She remembered nestling in the crook of his arm, later joined by Denise on his lap, looking at pictures and rocking to the rhythms that she would beat out with her thumbs. With her index finger, she would ride the gullies of his corduroy pants floating along with the lyricism of the poem. She could still recite the "Jabberwocky" without comprehending one word, repeating only the rushes of sound. As a child, she tried to make sense of it. "Two is brilliant and the slimy stoves …" Her dad seemed to know what was happening in all those poems. She tried to understand but gave it up. Sense didn't seem important then. What was important was that his arm was around her.

Often lollipops had come with the poetry, sweet as the rhymes he would read. Sometimes he served up hot chocolate and Madeleine's when the wind was blowing bitter outside their windows. Lemonade or watermelon came in the summer. She wanted to be in the crook of her father's arm forever, but the readings eventually ended. Maybe she grew too large. Maybe he became too busy. Maybe he was tired. Maybe he was old. The poetry stopped.

Yet here again were worms. She hesitated to envision this one that has found her bed. A flying worm yet, destroying her life. Surely, she suspected, there was no one in the world named Czeslaw Milosz. The name was perhaps an unfortunate typo.

Better yet, she had all the knowledge of the world at the other end of a PC cable. She would research Czeslaw Milosz.

She would look up Blake and his rose. She would look up flying worms. Given her determination, there could be no better way to spend the weekend than with a flying worm. Brian, her round paramuse, begged for a slice of it – the weekend, not the worm.

To tear herself away from her screen and such elegant information as worms signifying sexual nightmares would be difficult. Brian merely promised her a movie. Blake's worm promised her shame over sexual passion hidden behind a front of proper modesty. There it was; there she was; there was that wholesome Utah-ness she hid behind. He had found her out. She looked deeper into her urge to slip down the banks of the serpentine bridge at Millennium Park.

Far removed from that urge, Brian and Genny grabbed a beer after the movie. Yet through the evening, she focused on worms, secret, underground, repulsive. They percolated through her thoughts and conversation. They'd fly into her bed during howling storms? Genny needed to know more. She knew where to go.

5

... take a poem
and hold it up to the light
like a color slide
or press an ear against its hive.

Introduction to Poetry / Billy Collins

GENEVIEVE – take a poem

Brian got his Friday movie and a goodnight kiss. As the doors opened for the Saturday morning crowd, Genny found him waiting, fresh as morning coffee, in the lobby of the regional library. The sight of him jolted her into reality after she had been focusing so deliberately all morning on Blake and his sick, wormy rose – as she showered, while she nibbled on her breakfast croissant, while she threw on her Saturday sweats, while she downed a few aspirin to counteract the Friday night beers.

Her less than cordial greeting to him was, "What brings you here? Were we supposed to meet this morning?"

"Well, yes, Genny," he said. "You invited me."

"Brian, I invited the whole bar. Four beers and I get very inclusive." Then the indignity of the rest of the crowd's snub hit her. "And you're the only one who accepted?"

"Looks like it – the only one man enough to protect you from a worm infestation, and probably the only one with a six thousand word article for "Modern Midwest" hanging over his head. I'm here to do research. You're a good taskmaster."

"The worms did kind of take over the conversation last night," she said. "Some good worm jokes came out of it, though." She had especially liked and repeated, "What do you get when you cross a glow worm with beer? Lite ale." Groans had followed that particular gem the previous night and again in the library lobby.

It shamed Genny to think of how lightly she spoke of the Blake poem and of poetry. Brian's friends always brought her into a world of superficiality and insignificance, a comfortable place. Why then, did she want to be somewhere else, with someone else?

"You do have a way of driving the subject matter into the ground," Brian said, "where worms belong, to be sure, but there was a baseball game on the big screen. That would have made for more enthusiastic conversation."

"Maybe so. Good for the boys. But we kinda stuck with worms."

"And that is what you are, excuse the expression, digging into this morning?" he asked.

"That's the plan," she said, "and what is the theme for your morning?" Brian took a deep breath. Something better than worms, she was sure. He had a knack for giving status to whatever he undertook, probably because his law office was lined with books and he had a sofa along the wall with a degree framed in gold hanging over it. He carried that aura of accomplishment with him wherever he went.

"Land use," he said, with a smirk on his face. "So we're both in the same arena. You know dirt, worms …"and waited for her face to light up with amusement.

"That's lame, Brian, but after the flow of the chatter last night, I guess I deserve it. So go to your dirt and I'll be off to my worms."

Normally Genny would make a beeline to the pop literature shelves or the travel books. Today she hit the stacks where poetry lay. Brian shuffled off to the land of law. Sitting alone in the upright puritan church-pew chairs with her piles of anthologies and biographies spread over the massive library table, she felt a vacuum. Brian was by her side so regularly, a suction developed when he was elsewhere. He joined her for lunch. He took her to parties. He drove her to the airport and picked her up after her trips.

This Saturday morning the chair next to her was vacant. Most of the room was vacant so early in the day. Instead of people surrounding her, walls done in an artist's palette of colors that reflected the tastes of the neighborhood – the magentas, rusts, and turquoises of ethnic murals stretching from floor to ceiling – encased her. They distracted her as she delved into the meaning of poetic worms.

Soon Genny piled up her books and found Brian upstairs in his sedate olive and brown-toned legal environment. She settled in next to his chair. So absorbed was he in his dirt, he scarcely noticed she was joining him. As she arranged her collection of things Blake around her, Brian robotically moved books of property law to make room. They were an intent pair, a matched set, inadvertently wearing tee-shirts in harmonious muted shades of earth green, searching with such determination into their separate interests, planted in the overlapping space they had zoned off for themselves.

Genny read to him in a whisper, "Listen to this, 'dark secret love does thy life destroy.' See, I told you to stay away from me."

As she mouthed the words she wondered what dark and secret facets the Mountain Man detected in her cautious email messages. How shallow was she to him, a B-movie in black and white? Now, determined to answer his worm poem in depth, she would know what she was talking about before she plunged into the dialogue.

"It would be easier to stay away from you if you weren't sitting at my reference table," was Brian's quiet response.

He lifted his forearm to the table to cordon off his space. His eyes never left the page. He never openly indicated annoyance at the interruption or any suspicion of any competition poetry posed.

Genny let the chill pass. She was unable to counter his common sense with her illusions. She admired his steadiness, his dedication, his grasp of the realities of life, his optimism, but not enough to adopt these traits. She sometimes borrowed them, wore them for social security, used them as needed as she used his attentiveness and availability.

In the somber atmosphere of the law library, in the sober company of Brian, Genny found Blake more acceptable, sometimes applicable.

"Hey, get this, Brian," she whispered, "here's a guy that says that Blake's worm is shame. That figures, a repulsive, undercover thing. And that all women are ashamed of their hidden sexuality. I say, 'What's to hide?'"

Brian grunted, never giving in to her distractions.

Undaunted, she continued, "If you read this poem and knew beforehand that it was all about sex, would you like it then?"

Having already wasted a whole night playing with the concept of worms, Brian called a halt. He finished the note he was copying and turned full body toward her, a hibernating bear come alive, his eyes questioning.

"Why are you beating me over the head with this stuff, this worm, this poem? What's it to you, Genny? Don't you have anything better to do than chase after a dead poet?"

She could give Brian no answer because it was not a dead poet she pursued. No, in her sights was a very live poet as unlike Brian as a man could be.

Genny had never pursued Brian. He had been an easy snatch. His pursuit of Genny was equally uncomplicated. She had been open season prey, a loner. They were both party pick-ups. An office friend of Genny's celebrated her divorce settlement with a rather large gathering of friends, her friends, and her lawyer's friends. Genny had come as one of the former; Brian, one of the latter.

This divorce celebration carried negative vibrations, not the best breeding ground for a new relationship. But Brian had been charming and appealing that night and Genny rose to the occasion. For a couple of years they continued to be that, charming, pleasant, good company. They fit together. His soft, round features complemented her bony body. He was comfortable. His arm around her was tender. He was pleasant to kiss. Every now and then they bedded down together with a certain amount of excitement. He never asked for more. Genny was aware he was not her future. Comfort was not enough; occasional excitement was not enough. She saw that future now through the prism of poetry.

She remembered him approaching her that evening with her then unimposing small-town aura. She was grateful he came upon her.

"You're not Chicago," was his opening line, insulting had she been a city girl. He was taking a chance. Genny certainly wasn't local and her well-rehearsed response worked, as it did in similar smart-assed encounters.

"No, I'm from Utah where the buffalo roam."

"Then I've got the perfect place for you to hang out. He named an Indiana town just south of the Illinois state line that boasted a buffalo ranch.

"But then," he added, "I suppose if you wanted to hang out with buffalo you would have stayed in Utah." He almost turned away but had had another thought, a substitute for his original. "Well, how about buffalo burgers? I know a couple spots on the north side serving some pretty good samples. That should keep you from being homesick."

Homesickness hadn't been Genny's situation, insularity was. Being not well versed on the subject of buffalo in spite of her western upbringing made continuing this conversation problematic. She could not contribute anything of value to the topic. Sensing this, he moved on to more relevant facts about Chicago and its environs continuing the conversation through the entire evening. Occasional interruptions split them but like a yo-yo, he continued to spring back to her. The man had city friends, knew his Chicago, and further convinced her that she wanted to be a part of it. He had bright eyes, good taste in ties, and savored his beer. If he came along with the city perhaps that wouldn't be such a bad deal. It wasn't until a later phone call did she learn he had himself only arrived in town the previous winter. They had become transplants together.

A picture of Brian with Genny flanked by others at that party, many now gone from the circle, sat on a shelf of her bedroom bookcase. Occasionally when she was dusting the room she chuckled at it, remembering his "you're not Chicago" line.

She in her coordinated pastel pants suit, hair ironed straight and hanging to her shoulders, a "caught in the headlights" expression on her face, Brian must have taken her on as a charity case. She proved not to be what the package indicated. Under his influence, she bloomed in the city.

So with determination, yet with her mind's eye on what she left behind, she proceeded down this chosen poetic path via volumes of poetry, meeting the literary greats right and left in musty, well-bound books. With unflinching concentration, she passed through Blake to other more romantic romantics. Taking notes as she went, she worked through Keats, Shelley, Lord Byron, and Wordsworth. If she saved this material for her Monday night poetry class, she could be the genius of the semester.

Then she returned to Blake. "I'm gonna love you like nobody's loved you … "jammed through her mind in a B.B.King voice. It became her promise to Blake, not an easy call. Her books told her he was into Milton, of "Paradise" fame, so she pursued Milton. Ditto Jeremiah of the Bible. That was it for Genny; that's as far back as she would go. The scholars called Blake a harmless lunatic. Was she bordering on that state? Then in her diligence, she landed upon "The Fly," a poem that spoke to her. More insects to fill her life. She marked the page.

Knowledgeable enough this Saturday about flies and worms and more, she scooted away leaving Brian with his histories of land appropriations that he was working into a piece about eminent domain.

"I've done what needs doing, so farewell, my friend, adieu, mon ami," she said as she left. So she explained away her departure, aware he had probably another five thousand words to go. Her momentary mission: to maintain on the Brian front her ostensible wholesome purity, letting the wormy passion brew in private. She may be destined for the depravity of a fusion with this Mountain Man but at least she was aware of the possibility, even eager for it.

Blake in hand, Genny stopped off in the computer lab and created a message, geared to show off her poetic sensitivity:

From: gennydu
To: jonwat
Date: Sat, 14 Aug 2004 14:02:49
Subject: Re: Einstein and the mystifying universe

Dear Jonathan - you really sent me galloping off to the library to check on Blake. Such a downer poem, I wanted to see the inventory you chose from, and why.

I think I know why. I think you have taken snips of my class writings and arranged them into a collage of me that you are imagining. Remember, my words spring out of my imagination. Who knows what's real?

I am a Leo, burnished sunshine. A lion, nibbling at life. A loping predator, stalking my prey, people to fill in my blanks, experience to give me a lush cushion of memories to retreat to.

If you are doing Blake, a better poem for me would have been:

Little fly,
Thy summer's play
My thoughtless hand
Has brush'd away.
Am not I
A fly like thee?
Or art not thou
A man* like me? *make that maid
For I dance

And drink and sing,
Til some blind hand
Shall brush my wing.
If thought is life
And strength and breath
And the want
Of thought is death;
Then am I
A happy fly,
If I live
Or if I die.

Thank you for sending me to Blake. He's difficult
and different. Gd

Sitting in front of the library computer, surrounded by lit-up screens, Genny was struck by the difference between the world of books she left behind and the hard machinery producing this instant communication. She checked over the message, wondering what ghosts possessed her. What muses, Calliope and her ilk, reached out from Mount Parnassus to redesign her.

She was a Leo, yes, summer born. The rest she created, passing it off as real, one fantasy image following another. From the afternoon breezes, she pulled in combinations of words bristling with brightness to appear on his screen. Fiction, fiction laced with fantasies. She was in truth, harmless. She left no bloody tracks. There were memories, oh there were memories, other loves, painful, nothing she intended to let influence her future. She sent him the preview of this remodeled Genny. What other way to engage him? None that she could design. So that message was the message she sent. She steeled herself for his response, hoping to find out his vision of himself.

As she waited, a thought developed: perhaps she had made herself too impossible.

From: jonwat
To: gennydu
Date: Thu, 19 Aug 2004 10:01:10
Subject: Blake considered

burnished sunshine. A lion, nibbling at life. A loping predator stalking my prey: people to fill in my blanks, experience to give me a lush cushion of memories to retreat into.

Okay, that gives me some understanding. And the fly poem is pretty jolly.

But The Sick Rose is still one of my favorites; the linking together of the sickness and death with beauty, joy, love picks me up. The confounding of expectations that we think are essential; the opening up of unknown possibilities. In the heart of darkness is the seed of light – in melancholy is sweetness. I can understand that. I have found it to be true.

Your capacity and your appetite for experience share a patch of common ground with me. I am fascinated with memories but I don't collect them to hide in. Rather, I will cultivate empty fields as a place of freedom. That's where I go to find me.

Empty fields. He cultivated empty fields. Empty, like alone? She heard the silence.

6

This existence of ours is as transient as autumn clouds.
To watch the birth and death of beings is like looking at the
movements of a dance.
A lifetime is like a flash of lightening in the sky,
Rushing by like a torrent down a steep mountain.

Siddhartha Gautama

GENEVIEVE - movements of a dance

Genny's fields emptied the day after Jonathan's abstruse message arrived. Stan, her favorite traveler, was dead. Tuesday she had sent him to Houston to meet with a Dutch cohort and he ended up dead.

In her workday her travelers continually came and went. She put them on planes in Detroit, in Shanghai, in Buenos Aires, in San Francisco, and they lived to call her again to put them on more planes. They lived.

But Stan didn't call. No "Hi Gennypenny." No "Well hello, gorgeous Genny." No "It's Stan your man." Instead, his office called to have her arrange an earlier plane back to

Amsterdam for Eric, Stan's European business partner. They were together in an auto crash outside Houston, the secretary said. It was raining; Stan was driving. Eric's injuries were extensive, she said. She didn't tell Genny then that Stan was dead. Not then.

She didn't tell her then that his car had skidded in the rain, swerved down off the road, did a one-eighty and hit a tree. Stan was stunned. His rider was out cold. Stan had pulled himself out of the driver's seat and had staggered around the steaming car to get to Eric. Spinning out of control on the wet highway above was a death car, careening toward the same tree Stan's car rested against, smashing into Stan as he attempted to open the passenger door. Stan died. Eric's bones were broken, his insides, a mess.

Once sure that Genny understood the immediate task at hand, the secretary broke and sobbed out that horrid story to Genny's silence. Inside Genny felt the heaving sorrow pushing into her throat. There was not enough room for the greatness of it. She promised the secretary in heavy sour breath pulled out of her chest, "I can arrange Eric's trip home. I'll make it easy, as easy as the airline will arrange. Just tell me when he is free to leave. Oh my God, Stan."

Then she disconnected before the silent sobs started. Deets sensed a tragedy and came to her side.

Stan was Genny's only real client friend. She stayed aloof as a travel counselor. Like a well-programmed robot, she found the times most convenient, the airlines in their favor, the fares the company sanctioned. When she arranged the approved ticketing, client and agent were done. But with Stan, the conversations had been more relaxed. Close to his retirement, Stan had been gleeful over his life. A long, successful life, it had been. He found Genny's to be a lark, more turbulent, and less triumphant.

Their phone conversations were minimally professional: "Well hello, Stan," she would say. "Where're you off to today?" Being summer she would hope for Alaska. In winter, Aruba. Stan mostly went to Seattle, Amsterdam, and White Plains. He had never come to Chicago, keeping their relationship ethereal.

Sometimes when calls were slow, in the quiet, Genny would dream up a trip to his coast. She would wear outlandish clothes, dripping with color, covering her body with style. She would be on a small jet to some obscure private airport in California. Stan would be on the banks of the runway, waving a cowboy hat at the pilot, welcoming him and the plane to his neighborhood. Genny would smile at the sight of this aging man so full of joy at the thought of inland visitors. He looked like her father. He looked like the Mountain Man. She didn't know what Stan looked like. His wife was by his side, thin and tall and aristocratic, smiling at Stan.

In a confidential conversation with Stan, Genny hinted at the Mountain Man. She tried to describe him. "Angular face, weathered. Unruly hair, a little bit sparse. Lean, tall, muscular – toned, like an athlete, y'know." No, Stan didn't know. "But he's an older man, Stan, more settled. Can you believe, he's a poet. Poetry, that's where my writing is going. That's his appeal."

The image drawn of the poet didn't bring a reaction. "An older man, huh?" was what Stan, with his sixty-plus-plus years, had picked up on. "Just pretend you are talking with me," and in a weathered old voice said, "and you will do just fine. We do fine." At that, Genny sensed a slight disengagement because with his next breath he said, "Houston. Houston is where I need to go – next Tuesday. Early afternoon. Coming back late Friday. Can do?"

"Of course I can do. Have I ever not done?" and they moved on to business arrangements – flight, hotel, car, her standard offerings. That was her last conversation with Stan.

No one else at the agency would waste the time it took to get business done with him. After a few months, it became a matter of course that Stan's calls came to Genny. Maybe he would ask for her. Maybe the others just shunted him over to her. She welcomed his calls. Now Stan was dead.

"Stan is dead," Genny wrote on the note sheets she kept by her computer. She traced over the words again and again. Words on paper made death real, easing her pain. She wrote to his wife on company stationery using the proper terms of condolence. More telling words that exposed her grief stayed by her computer. Genny wrote she was sorry. She tore up the note. She was more than sorry; she was devastated, anguished; his death caused a void in her life. But she was his travel agent. Who was she to mourn?

She took out a new sheet. She rewrote the note, again saying how sorry she was. Were she Blake or Keats, she might have the release valve that poetry offers. She was but a stumbling survivor of living and loving, spending weekends in libraries inhaling the bursting emotions of others. She had no gentle words for Mrs. Stan. "I am sorry" was all Genny had. She was sorry, so sorry for her inadequacies.

She addressed her letter to his home office because he never mentioned where he lived, nor his wife's name although she was an integral part of his gleeful life. In conversations she was always "my dear heart." Somewhere in client records, Genny could have found a name, but she wouldn't delve.

Remembering the consolation a Nineteenth Century Lit professor once offered her when she wasn't connecting learning to life, Genny sent what she could not send to Stan's wife on to the Mountain Man. She needed to bring the depth of her sadness to someone. If she had been at home she would have found her father's shoulder; his hand would have found hers. Sitting in her office she looked for that refuge on a computer screen. The quote was not Blake but from the pen of Henry James. Not even close. Jon would wonder.

From: gennydu
To: jonwat
Date Fri, 20 Aug 2004 14:52:55
Subject: Henry James

> *We work in the dark – we do what we can, we give what we have. Our doubt is our passion and our passion is our task. The rest is the madness of art.*

She was pitifully working in a murky dark. Tragedy had created madness in her day. As Stan was being pronounced dead in a distant city, Genny was dwelling on poets and professors who pulled her through struggling moments. Then she envisioned a woman whose life just disintegrated against a tree stump. All this she packaged in an email for a man she hoped could soothe away the discomforts now absorbing her.

Genny's boss called her into her office the moment her corporate liaison contacted her with the news of Stan's accident. Chris stood at her office window. A sun too bright for the sorrow of the day shone through stray wisps of her carefully curled hair. Her back was broad as was her ability to take on the problems of her staff. She turned toward Genny, then sat behind her desk, pulling together papers relative to this client. Her hands were husky, capable. Her face bore a tenderness. She was expecting to learn the details of the arrangements Genny was making for Eric.

"Genny," she asked, "do you need help with Lufthansa? His partner was flying Lufthansa, wasn't he?"

"As far as Stan's secretary ..." Genny could go no further. The sobs came in the sanctuary of her boss' office.

Chris was reasonably perplexed since most of the contact with clientele was over cell phones, telephones, email, Federal Express, and the post office. She wondered where emotion fit in. It had been a long time since she had dealt with traveling clients and forgot that ties developed without face-to-face contact. Over time, conversations exposed personalities even when the curtain of anonymity was in place. Relaxed and formless, Stan and Genny had become close friends, sharing small, safe slices of their lives in extended moments. It happened to others and when it happened it was comfortable, sometimes exciting. The connection was real for Genny, as deep as ties with family and friends. To Genny, talking to Stan was like talking to another part of herself, maybe even creating another herself.

"Genny, do you want to go home? You can. Someone else can take care of this," Chris said. Her attempts at sympathy were shallow, mixed as they were with the need to continue business as usual.

"No, I can stay," Genny said. "I know the situation. I have a call in to Lufthansa to rewrite Eric's ticket. They seem to be agreeable. I can get this done. I have to. I'll stay."

She wanted to leave. She wanted to be alone to reread the books Stan and she had discussed over the many months since they adopted each other. She wanted to tell him of her weekend, of her classes, of her new shoes. She wanted to fly him out of Houston whole and healthy.

Chris continued to be helpful. "As you say. But let me know if you run into any snags. We have some strong connections up the ladder with that airline."

"I won't need them, but thanks." Genny left, somewhat better composed, a challenge ahead of her: to stay professional.

Standing outside the glass enclosed office, she noticed Chris looking back at her, concerned. Her face had taken on some of the grief Genny had deposited with her. Her hand rested on her telephone, ready to call the company liaison, ready to offer her assurances that the details were underway in capable hands to return Stan's injured partner to Amsterdam. Returning Stan to California would be the sorry chore of another agent, one with different expertise.

Genny walked steadily back to her desk with the pressure of others' gazes at her back. Deets began to rise then sunk back into his chair. His face offered consolation but he remained silent.

"Stan died," Genny heard others whisper, "you know, that guy you couldn't ever get off the phone."

He's off now, Genny realized, with an enigmatic message going not to his wife, but to another, alive with the breath of gods.

7

tell me again of the triumph
of stolen crab apples
and the crab apple pie they became
a story spotty and incomplete and full of lies
and masquerades spilling into the wind

Kitchen Tales / Jonathan Waterhouse

JONATHAN – masquerades

"What the hell?" The message Jon studied in the privacy of his den didn't begin with the usual "Dear Jonathan" or "hey jon," didn't end with a Genny signoff, not even a "gd." Where was that party-crashing Genny with her gin swizzling, schmoozing, prancing, and dancing on the Great Lawn of Millennium Park? She belonged with the brightness of the sun and the blue of the moon bouncing off the stainless steel ribbons of the Gehry band shell. Instead, here was Henry James whose stream of consciousness drowned her airiness in his dark prose.

Jon closed her down and rose from his swivel chair to taste the Henry James mood. He found and opened the cover of "Daisy Miller" to read the inscription his mother wrote in this, the book she sent off to college with him: Try to enjoy this and remember to write home. He chuckled as he paced about the room reading random snatches. Genny was as puzzling as Daisy herself.

When Jonathan had written to the inamorata, Miss Genevieve Dupont, coupling sickness and death with beauty and joy and love, he took her into his gray world where murkiness covered all the green sprouts, all the emerging stars, all the shy smiles, all the smells of spice, the sounds of flutes.

Here she was now with him in darkness and doubt when she should be to him sunshine, a lion nibbling at life. Her words promised him that. To look into her eyes would erase the dark words. To see the set of her mouth, the stance of her body, her youthful vigor, he would understand her then.

He glanced over at his phone but dismissed the notion of a call at such a late hour to a woman he didn't know except from sightings across a library table, from the back of a bus, and from bursts of prose and poetry crammed into a computer.

He pushed back his chair and felt stiffness in his bones from the air-conditioned chill of his den. His eyes burned from their concentration on his monitor. He was hungry again, too hungry to consider the enigma further.

Karen tapped at his door disturbing the sleep of Wallace, their shaggy border collie mix, who had planted himself in the path of the cooling A/C. Barking, Wally darted toward the door, jolting Jonathan and providing reason enough to break away from the perplexity that Genny introduced, reason enough to escape the darkness of Genny and his inability to erase it.

"It's safe. You can come out now," Karen said. "The dishes are all done. The counters are clean, you could eat off the floor if you so choose."

Following Wally, Jon was at the door, opening it to a burst of stifling air that made him take a quick breath. "Goddamn it's hot out there," he said as Wally rushed to the kitchen door for his evening romp up and down the yard.

Karen stood stiffly wrapping her hands around the flesh of her upper arms. "and I've got goosebumps just standing here in your doorway. Turn off your electronic toys and c'mon out and suffer the heat with the rest of us," she said; and he did.

Their bungalow retained the ninety-degree heat of the day and she voiced her standard summer complaint. Central air conditioning was not yet incorporated into their budget. In spite of her grousing, the window in the room Jon had appropriated remained the only one to sport a unit. She rarely let him forget it. Now his "goddamn" had made him vulnerable.

She twisted her ample hip into the doorjamb, affecting a come-hither pose to make the invitation into the heat more appealing.

He parried her with "Stop your pouting because you had the kitchen detail. You always forget our deal – when I create the fantasy food, you get to bring the kitchen back into shape. Not so?"

"Yes, so. I just thought maybe I could lure you away from whatever it is that holds you captive in here." Karen knew what held him. His poetry was her prime competition. She reacted to it as such.

"I've unrolled the puzzle on the card table. Want to get at it again?" she asked. "It's been awhile since we tackled that monster. This seems like a good night to do nothing that takes any energy. And the colors are so cooling."

She pulled Jon through the doorway. She was soft and warm with a simple need tonight to spend its remaining moments in some enjoyable pursuit that brought them close. He welcomed her warmth.

Wally circled back between them to make his demands, hopping and whining. In this evening's sedated house, all its creatures had come alive and he would take full advantage.

"Sure, a good night. I'm done in here," Jon said as he walked her away from his space and the allurement that it held, into the kitchen and the commotion the dog was creating. He glanced back into the room and boasted, "Three revisions of the poems that were gnawing at me. Aren't you proud?"

Karen snorted. Not mentioned, but primarily on his mind was the unfinished draft of a note to Genny, another attempt to move in closer to that place where her interests lay, where the darkness was, to explore it, to lighten it, to satisfy her plunge into poetry, to pull off a layer of his persona so she could know him.

The kitchen that Karen had restored to its pristine order still maintained the remnant smells of the shrimp and broccoli stir fry he had created for their dinner. Ghosts of soy sauce, ginger, and garlic seeped from the chopping block and the dish towels. They triggered a late-night hunger brought on by fruitless poetry revisions and clandestine email notes.

"How 'bout a little nosh? – that new cheese we bought at the farmers' market. Oh man," he wiped condensation from his glasses, "what we really need is some fresh air in here." He opened the door and stepped out into the dark with Wally who moved away to begin his stealthy evening prowl around the premises, seeking out the ancient sheep and reindeer of his vaguely remembered heritage, his assumed task in the universe.

Back inside, Jon cranked open the window over the sink, letting in more nighttime heat. "August in Chicago. Sure can't beat it," he said. He spoke to a june bug that flapped against the screen. One swat and it was gone, back into the dark.

He spoke to the night. Karen had moved back down the hall, taking another peek into his office, its space crowded by the oversized roll top desk and bloated upholstered chair he had brought over from his prep school office, a relic of his former life.

At the open refrigerator door, Jon saw a carton of orange juice, leftover roast beef, some plastic-wrapped bread, what was left of a six-pack of a German pilsner. The lit interior resembled the shelves of an inner-city deli. Poking around, he didn't see the package they had carried around the downtown market the previous Tuesday. He saw ketchup, chocolate sauce, wheat germ. No cheese.

"Karen, where the hell is the stuff from the farmers' market? I hope you didn't leave it in the car!"

Karen was on her way to the sunroom and the one thousand pieces of a puzzle picturing the magnificent Cezanne blues, peaches, greens, oranges, grays, and reds. The fractured Marseilles view of the Mediterranean Sea, or at least the parts of it Karen and Jon had managed to put together, had challenged them for months.

"Me? Leave it in the car?" she answered his frustration from afar. "It's you always leaving whatever in the car – your sunglasses, your library books ..." Her voice lost its edge as it moved toward the front end of the house. "... postage stamps, some things I haven't seen in years. They all end up in the same place – usually under the front seat. I haven't even been in that grimy wreck in a week."

That was true. They never drove downtown, especially not to a city market steps away from a bus stop. He remembered the long crowded bus ride home but had no memory of holding the parcel of cheeses whose aromas would have permeated the atmosphere of the bus. Either Karen had taken possession or it never made it out of the Wisconsin farmer's tent. He hoped for the former. It was such a fine selection of Brie, smoked Gouda, some Normandy Camembert.

His eyes gave the interior of the refrigerator one more scan and discovered the unwrapped packages in the cheese bin.

"Who'd put it there?" he said. "Probably me. What else've we got here?" He pulled together samples of the cheese, some slivers of icicle radishes, grapes and found Triscuits in the cabinet, still mumbling to himself, "good enough stuff."

He loaded a platter to bring to Karen as the peace offering he felt he owed her after her exile from his den.

He found her stretched out on the sofa, their ugly green sofa, considered by Jon to be the ugliest green ever allowed on a civilized man's property, ugly when Karen first brought it over from her apartment, probably ugly when she inherited it from her mother, a sickly woman who plagued their lives with her need for attention. Uglier now after being victimized by the sunshine that kept their enclosed porch hot until well into the night, fading everything in its path.

He placed the platter near the Cezanne and bent Karen's knees, planting her feet on the middle cushion then eased himself down, never disturbing the relaxed slouch her body had assumed. Her interest in the puzzle had given way to an Oprah rerun and the problems of the day she was dissecting. Vibrant television colors bounced off Karen's unperturbed face.

"Some crackers and cheese and then to bed?" Jonathan said but his plan elicited no movement from the other end of the couch in spite of the fine presentation of delicacies.

He tried again: "I think that I shall never see a cracker that appeals to me unless it's topped by smelly cheese, a great selection such as these."

Karen looked over at him with a disdain she reserved for any hint that his mind was on poetry. Again, he offered the platter while suspecting that serving women had become his mission: one with pleasures, the other with poetry. His good senses hoped they never met.

The two sat in silence, enveloped by the ugly green, Jon picking at the puzzle pieces with none seeming to belong to the borders they had begun to assemble. The brightness of the turquoise camisole Karen wore clashed with the muted Mediterranean tones of the puzzle and the garishness of the sofa but the soft full breasts the turquoise encased made the clash tolerable. Eventually, she moved her soft, full body over the cushions to pull against his side, nearer to the crackers and cheese. He was damp with the stuffiness of the room and restless with the inactivity. His bare feet ruffled the brown shag carpeting that covered the sunroom floor and he welcomed her.

"What's our lady's problem tonight?" he asked, noting the dourness on the face of Oprah's guest, a famous, glamorous image. He expected no answer from the woman nestling into his side and she gave him none.

Instead, she reached for a radish and made a sandwich of it and a pair of Triscuits, one for her and another for him. She placed it on his tongue.

He wondered how close she was to shutting off the television and moving to the bedroom where they better communicated, when she glanced over and smiled. He watched her eyes move over his damp torso, down his legs to his twitching feet. She licked the salt off her fingers, off his lips. "Go get Wally and let's go to bed," she said.

8

*Were we not made for summer, shade and coolness
and gazing through an open door at sunlight?*

Known World / Seamus Heaney

GENEVIEVE – gazing through an open door

Her Stan sorrow settled down over the weekend as Genny
grew accustomed to loss. Before church on Sunday, she sat
disquieted at her sturdy Jacobean table, a hand-me-down from
her father's side of the family. She had pleaded for the massive
piece of furniture when she left home.

"Too expensive to transport," her father said.

"Why would you want that monstrous old thing?" her
mother asked.

But Genny grew up with that table, long since relegated to
the basement. It suffered noisy family dinners, homework, dress-
making, Girl Scout projects, even ping pong in its later banished
days. Genny resurrected it, broke it down, packed it up and
added it to the truck headed for her new apartment in Chicago.

Her mother's hand-me-downs were better scaled to the
size of her new rooms but it was the furniture that reminded

her of her father that she cherished. As she had planned her escape to Chicago, both parents had willingly parted with many pieces feeling the wood and cloth would watch over her, keep her stable and connected.

She pulled out the sestina, still raw, and turned again to the copied Swinburne pages, her master for this sort of poetic game. She studied him more precisely and asked him out loud, "What was your pain Mr. Swinburne? What put these words in your head? Were your obsessions getting you down? Beware obsessions."

Still unsure of the form, she surfed the internet for more examples of model sestinas. She continued to polish her poem like a moonstone, giving it luster and fire. If it were to become real poetry, it is would be her ticket to the Mountain Man.

First, she needed to undo Friday's sadness, to explain her mood to Jonathan Waterhouse and to herself.

From: gennydu
To: jonwat
Date: Sun, 22 Aug 2004 7:58:03
Subject: forget Henry James

> *Friday was a downer for me, a client was killed*
> *in an auto accident. Henry James was my Friday*
> *mood. But I offer you this Mary Oliver alternative*
> *today, same topic, different view "when death comes*
> *like an iceberg between the shoulder blades, I want to*
> *step through the door full of curiosity … when it's over,*
> *I want to say: all my life I was a bride married to*
> *amazement … I don't want to end up simply having*
> *visited this world…"genny d*

However, Genny felt like an uninvited visitor to a world she craved. For some salvation, she had to claim territory. Could the sestina take her to where she wanted to be?

Letting that rest, she dressed in her somber Sunday finery for her churchly dose of music and morality. Poetry and poets receded in the extravagant rituals of Sunday mass with its soaring organ notes, surrounded by the devout parishioners who frequented her church.

The remainder of the day had other distractions. The laundry. She paid some bills, vowing again to stop using her charge card. The evening ended up in a coffee house with Denise. An icy frappuccino was her treat, charged in spite of her recent vows of frugality. She had bribed Denise to focus on her poem, blatantly buying her attention.

"Denise, did you get the story I am trying to tell in that poem?" Genny was not sure Denise had even read the sestina slipped under the breakfast rolls before she left this morning. She asked the question anyway.

"I read it. I got a little strawberry filling on the second stanza, and yes, I understood the story. I think I remember that girl. She used to hang around our house a lot. I felt sorry for her then and I feel sorrier for her now."

"Good," Genny said, and after a beat asked, "You were moved?"

When it came to "going public" this neophyte was not at all secure in her poetry environment. She felt safest asking the opinion of someone whose familiarity with literature centered mostly on romance novels, like her sister. Denise surprised her by offering a more considered reaction to the theme, and Genny felt more confident that smoothing out the awkwardness would be worth the effort.

Denise stabbed her straw into her frappuccino, stirred it gently and studied the orbiting movement of the liquid. She brought up more memories than Genny thought she would have been capable of absorbing at her little-girl age, still in preschool. Her musing was like oatmeal coming to a boil.

"I remember sitting at the foot of your bed when that friend came over and I remember the tears. I wasn't used to people being so unhappy. I wanted to do something to make her tears go away but you seemed to be doing your best and it wasn't working. I remember Daddy trying to tease her into smiles, but she wouldn't have any of it. I remember saying to myself that I would never let myself be that unhappy."

After a pause, she said, "I am impressed how you juggled the words around. But it's hard reading in some places. I marked them."

Genny was grateful. Denise may not be caught up in her non-romance with the Mountain Man but she was willing to buoy up this creative effort.

Back at home when the day was over, she discovered that her early morning message had plowed up the empty fields of Jonathan Waterhouse.

From: jonwat
To: gennydu
Date: Sun, 22 Aug 2004 22:40:43
Subject: Re: forget Henry James

An iceberg between the shoulder blades? A bride of amazement? Slightly chilling and unsettling. I might find some affinity to that, though I feel less anxiety and more composure than I expected to at this point in my life. Maybe because I accept the inevitable suffering of existence and realize to desire is to suffer, to cease desiring is to cease suffering.

Let me repeat my invitation to join us Thursday. My cake is long gone, eaten to the last crumb. But the writing is always there and sometimes quite good.

From: gennydu
To: jonwat
Date: Mon, 23 Aug 2004 10:25:58
Subject: Re: forget Henry James

Thursdays are bad the rest of this month — it should be enlightening to drop in though. Maybe in September.
September. It's autumn again. Time to pick up the dead leaves and make something of the year before it ends. genny d

The implication was that her calendar was bursting. The reality was that she was full of bullshit. She still stung from the last hollow invitations to his Thursday gathering of poets. Her response was at best bubble wrap to protect her.

From: jonwat
To: gennydu
Date: Mon, 23 Aug 2004 13:23:10
Subject: Re: forget Henry James

well, come for a visit at least by September.

"Smooth," Genny said to the email. He was in abeyance. Better was on its way.

From: jonwat
To: gennydu
Date: Mon, 23 Aug 13:26:14
Subject: Re: forget Henry James

   yes, come in September. I am excited about the
way our writers are developing. I am somewhat
assuming leadership of the group and am happy to
contribute.
   We are now looking into the question of "persona"
in fiction writing, poetry or prose, speaking through
another person rather than being expository. Do you
know the Wm Butler Yeats "Crazy Jane Talks with the
Bishop" poem? Another of my favorites. I hope to use
it to illustrate some of the advantages that a "persona"
can give a writer.
   Regards, Jon

Genny liked the pace Jon was keeping now, more promising than his original unsteadiness. "Crazy Jane" – she liked her too. Any friend of Jon's would be a friend of hers. She would make time to go meet Miss Crazy in the library next weekend. If she could not give herself over to the Mountain Man, she could to his poetry.

In the meantime, she had an evolving sestina and a poetry class that was winding up that evening. Then she would be on her own again, floating untethered in rhythm and metaphor.

The exploration of things poetic was beginning to control her life, to give her a place to be. Notepad and pen were always nearby now. She picked apart and rewrote the poems the Mountain Man had put before her, poems she found on her own and poems from her previous unschooled attempts. She played with words as a substitute for playing with him. She mimicked the swaying rhythms of Blake, matched him rhyme for rhyme and manipulated the sounds reverberating in her brain.

But then Blake's "Never seek to tell thy love, Love that never told can be ..." stopped her cold. She questioned the premise. Silent love was the only possible love? Why was she listening to these people?

Hers would be a love never told, she feared. She was uneasy about it, unsure. She was uncomfortable with the tension, unable to label her feelings "love." So strong and sudden, it required another name. Where could she call it love? Certainly not around the Mountain Man who had used the word only in quoted poetry. If not him, there was no one else to care.

Not Denise. She would never understand the complexity. She who sent love into the background of her life while she remained twelve hundred miles separated from her David. She had the good sense to single out what she considered to be a perfect man dismissing the rest of the world. She knew the game and would win at it, in good time.

Genny watched her younger sister play the game of romance. The periodic visits home to remind David of their suitability. The letters she wrote on scented paper to her beloved, reminiscing about their times together. The letters she didn't answer to create spaces in their continuum.

"Denise?" Genny often asked her, "when does it seem that the search for a mate is over?" Denise had never searched. David had always been there.

Or "What makes you so sure that you and David are so suited for each other?"

Here Denise had a quick response – "Comfort," she said, "pure comfort being with him, secure being apart from him, knowing who he is, knowing what he wants ..."

Comfort and security – would that ever satisfy Genny?

She might have taken lessons from Denise, except the men she had selected to be her game mates didn't seem to be at the same board. She played checkers while they plotted chess moves. Genny jumped rope while they were up in a tree playing hide and seek.

She tried to learn the Mountain Man's rules of the game. His Czeslaw Milosz took her where the high school poetry page never ventured. If her high school Lit teacher had ever bounced any of his lines off her, her mind might have veered off into those unknown directions. She might have begun some serious immersion in poetry just to cloak herself in the likes of him. She might have learned to see her world through a different vocabulary, as Milosz saw it. What were merely green trees to Genny now became Milosz's "emerald essence of the leaves."

Beyond her window, in the park, they came into her sight at last, those emeralds. Instead of worrying over today, tomorrow, yesterday, she followed him in choosing "my home in what is now." *How like A. A. Milne,* she thought, *with his "What day is it?' "It's today," squeaked Piglet. "My favorite day," said Pooh.*

Was this Jonathan's take on his life? She heard the poetry in her head and felt extraordinary. Maybe she could feel at home in this playground, a place where emotions were rolled out into lines and stanzas, to be examined, analyzed, exposed. Yes, she could be comfortable there in the world where the Mountain Man lived.

She would find it.

But where? The college of her choice promised the degree of her choice, but arriving at the proper department intimidated her.

Was she a current student?

"No."

What department did she need?

"Poetry, creative writing, English literature?"

Undergraduate or graduate school? Did she have a degree?

"Yes."

Interested in an undergraduate degree in another discipline or an advanced degree?

Genny's confusion became apparent. "Well, I don't really know. I don't know if I really want a whole degree. I need to talk to someone who can help me out here."

"I'll connect you then with the Master's program. Hold the line, please."

"OK. The Master's program." Her mind wondered what was she doing as the options raced through it: stop being a travel agent to become a poet? Probably poetry wouldn't pay the rent. Being put on hold gave her time to consider the possibility of combining the two careers. If she were as good a poet as she was a travel agent, she could survive.

"Yes, I'll hold."

Being on hold was her problem. She had been on hold for the better part of her adult life, unconnected, fed up now with being at the odd end of a dangling line. She wanted to plug into a reality. But poetry wasn't the reality that travel was. Genny just wanted out – out of sending other people on their missions when she had none herself.

No, working with words was to be her mission. Words were their fun in high school. Finding peers who could manipulate them well enough to put them in print on the pages of their precious publication was their notoriety. The fun of being pointed out as the poet, mostly in ridicule, but good-natured ridicule.

And then what happened? No teachers said to her "There's a little talent there." Maybe because none existed. But what of all the words that mirrored her joys and intrigues and perplexities? Putting them on paper had brought such comfort. To put them on paper had allowed her to see inside herself.

"Hello, this is Marlene Jacobs. Can I help you?" A lilting voice came over the phone Genny cradled in her shoulder.

"I think so. My name is Genevieve Dupont and I am interested in your advanced writing classes. Poetry classes. Do you have any that are open to someone who might not want to get a degree from them, just wants to kind of sit in on the classes?"

As Marlene explained the Master's program, its scope overwhelmed her. She didn't take a note. She lost all the courage she had garnered to get her to this point but repeated her original query, about wanting to sit in on classes.

Marlene suggested auditing as an alternative. The idea struck Genny as a possibility. She felt herself shirking a total commitment in the face of the real thing. Where were her poetic juices? It was one thing to admire poems well done, doing successfully the things that poems do. But to create them, she wasn't sure she had the stuff in her. What was in her? The dabbling she had done to date had released some of the unrest. Those poems she had exposed to critical air were received well. How critical was that air? Some community workshops, some very dear friends, Jonathan, Denise ... Genny wanted a professional to say "Good. That was good. Powerful. You hit it."

"Can you come in so we can discuss what sorts of expectations you might have?" Marlene Jacobs asked. "Right now we are in the midst of the fall registration rush so I couldn't squeeze out the time to see you anytime soon. Would early October work for you?"

They made an appointment. Genny wondered as she jotted the time on her calendar, what would be filling her head in October? Talking to Marlene, she saw herself moving toward poetry with a determined step. What direction would she be taking in two weeks? She thought it was only the Mountain Man that she wanted but as the conversation progressed, she sensed that she wanted more. Maybe Marlene could tell her. She put down the telephone as she studied her calendar.

If visions of Marlene Jacob's vibrating halls of learning had daunted her, they also inspired her. She was aware of new emotions and pleased with the words she found to describe them. She reworked some sophomoric lines from old notebooks and, before she could rethink her actions, she emailed the better of the collection to the Mountain Man without any explanation. She asked for no critique nor for a response. She sent them off into his unplowed ground hoping he would nurture them. She shivered at the consequences.

9

I kissed a stone
I lay stretched out in the dirt
And I cried tears down.

Crazy Jane on the Mountain / William Butler Yeats

GENEVIEVE – I cried tears down

She found Willie Yeats' "Jane" and their persona poetry. What a crush she had on that genius's lanky frame when first they met in room 306 at Fremont High, introduced by a dippy Lit teacher who daily recited Yeats as morning prayer.

"So what's with this Crazy Kate that you are tracking down? Did you fly her into the wrong airport?" Brian was on precarious ground with that comment.

"Her name is Jane, Crazy Jane. It's a poem," Genny's response emerged as sullen as a bumped airline passenger. She was still not able to joke about flying and fliers, not after Stan's accident. Brian let that unsatisfying answer pass. Were "Crazy Jane" and William Butler Yeats involved in a lawsuit, maybe then Brian would have indulged in a conversation. But being a figment of a fertile poetic imagination, no common ground was available.

Genny and Brian were eating Friday night pizza with a couple of friends. Not much of a demand on her imagination. The chatter of the locals distracted her; the heavy air of the pizza parlor comforted her; the leaden load that a slice brought to her gut satiated her. For the moment she was truly trapped in Milosz's "what is now."

"Did you get to the Carson sale?" Genny heard the question from across the table. The conversation was predictably insignificant. She squirmed as she felt the tackiness of her sequined tank top, hooked her thumbs through its straps and confessed that "yes," she had, and had also cashed in on sweaters and tees. "Plus this – four dollars."

The guys made bawdy comments and wished they were on the golf course alone, talking about baseball statistics.

Genny wished she were home, asleep in bed, eager to bring on Saturday. Early that morning the Mountain Man had sent her an email that had cried for a well-designed response.

From: jonwat
To: gennydu
Date: Fri, 27 Aug 2004 07:38:12
Subject: Thank you for the inspiration ...

Back to James – It is a very intriguing quotation – your doubt, your passion, your task – balanced by Oliver – your expectations.

Some of Blake reverberates through James's darkness, limitation, acceptance of doubt as an important source for expression and perception. James's affirmation of the madness of art is provocative. I don't know that there is anything mad about my art. I am really such a balanced, sensible sort of person. What does "the madness of art" mean to you?

79

From: gennydu
To: jonwat
Date: Sat, 28 Aug 2004 11:57:27
Subject: the madness of art…

Egad – now you are asking me to think – not fair.
And in 87 degree temperatures, yet. But for you, I will.
Art is madness? Of course it is. Why else would one
squirrel oneself away in a library to look at words –
as you have me doing. Why else would one wish the
phone remained silent, leaving me alone with words –
as I do. Why else would one read a single stanza three,
four, five times just to taste its elegance over and over
again?
Madness. How seductive I find it. I envy the mad
ones who know how, when and where to create, all
else be damned. I, being sane, still worry about
unmade beds and meals, dust on my end tables, being
at work on time – but less and less, I notice, as I
hopefully slip into productive madness.
But then we are not alone – other madnesses
surround us. Politics is madness. The stock market
is madness. The Sunday comics are madness. Love is
madness. Women's shoes are madness. Escape may be
impossible, pick one and devote yourself to it.
Have a mad weekend.genny dupont

Would he hear her say "love is madness?" To Genny, it
was. She wondered how she escaped being put under careful
watch in a windowless room, each wall padded against vio-
lently spastic movements, while she beat her fists on the floor
in rhythm with poetic stanzas?

No, probably not she surmised as she sipped her morning coffee sitting in the corner of her living room, its fourth-floor window overlooking a tree-laden street, populated by the neighborhood hoi polloi making their happy sounds of summer.

Country French scenes wallpapered the room, all blue and white with peasants in trees picking apples, with cottages nestled among rocky hills. She and Denise inherited the decor with their two-year lease. The walls may have been the reason she agreed to the apartment – so calm, so removed from the city's hustle. She moved to her console desk pressed up close to the picturesque wall she studied while she pecked away at her keyboard. It was a fitting background for the invitation that came after her elaborate reply.

From: jonwat
To: gennydu
Date: Sat, 28 Aug 2004 12:33:27
Subject: Re: the madness of art …

Don't you think we should have coffee together or something and talk? Do you ever have mornings free during the week? Do you know this Dickinson thought?
MUCH madness is divinest sense / To a discerning eye; / Much sense the starkest madness / 'Tis the majority / In this, as all, prevails. / Assent, and you are sane; / Demure, you're straightway dangerous, / and handled with a chain.

"Don't I think we should talk?" she asked the words on the screen before her. "Don't *I* think we should talk? Don't I think we should *talk*! I am afraid to talk to you, with your madness is sense and sense is madness."

Once again, he mouthed what others wrote, pulling her through some misty territory. She tried so hard to keep up with all his poet-people's thoughts. At least now she was getting to know his William Butler Yeats, with his "Crazy Jane."

Were you aware, Mr. Waterhouse, she also has a mountain: "*Last night I lay on the mountain ... I lay stretched out in the dirt and I cried tears down ...*" *It sure doesn't sound like a good thing to have.*

"Okay Yeats, enough of you. The Mountain Man wants to meet and I have to bone up on madness and check my wardrobe for some sensibly 'mad' clothes to wear."

She felt the madness but "much madness" was someone else's territory. She chose to ignore the whole dance, let her whirlwind mind settle, then answered his invitation "straightway," as "straightway" as she dared.

From: gennydu
To: jonwat
Date: Sun, 29 Aug 2004 07:27:42
Subject: Re: the madness of art ...

Indeed I do.

With nothing else to say, "indeed" was the extent of her reply. This assent made her sane, according to the poets. Maybe sane Sunday, August 29, but as Sunday blended into Monday, Monday into Tuesday, into Wednesday her sanity diminished. Her prompt and eager "indeed" went unnoticed.

Beyond Wednesday, her home PC stayed dark. Instead, she had brief conversations with Brian and read up on Emily Dickinson. She made a couple of noodle dinners and slept, hoping not to dream. At the office she concentrated on booking flights and hotels, avoiding the urge to slip into her email.

The weekend arrived. Her curiosity erupted leading her to what had sat in limbo for a day:

From: jonwat
To: gennydu
Date: Fri, 03 Sep 2004 8:51:00
Subject: Re: the madness of art …

> *You are assenting? Glad I don't have to handle you*
> *with a crazy lady chain. I don't, do I?*
> *I think I live a couple miles north of you. Half-way*
> *between us is that idiosyncratic beachside café on the*
> *lake. I could meet you there. Or I could meet you*
> *in the coffeehouse a couple blocks west on Broadway.*
> *Then there is a third choice halfway between the two.*

The air around her vibrated like downed electrical wires; it resonated with sounds like the giggles of children; it brushed past her face like snowflakes. Genny took a deep breath.

From: gennydu
To: jonwat
Date: Sat, 04 Sep 2004 09:15:09
Subject: Re: the madness of art …

> *I like the beach café. The Broadway place is fine*
> *but it is inside and I feel like outside this week. In*
> *case my madness breaks loose. The patrons of choice*
> *number three sometimes scare me. They look possessed.*
> *Your crazy lady kind of folk.*
> *Time? Yes, mid-morning is good. Your call.*
> *Wednesday is good next week – every week – I work*
> *10 hour days the other days.*

Do I have a chance at being straightway dangerous?
Wouldn't I love that on my resume. Genny Dupont

From: jonwat
To: gennydu
Date: Sat, 04 Sep 2004 16:32:30
Subject: Re: the madness of art …

The beach at 10 on Wednesday then!
You want dangerous? Well I guess there is always
that possibility when one lives within the limits of
a tidy, balanced, sane life and then adds to that the
open admiration of madness. But then I don't know
you at all, so this is mostly just wordplay, isn't it?
I'll see you Wednesday. Let's have fun.

She was stepping into his real world. Would she fit? "Are
we a fit?" she asked the monitor. The answer it offered was
Jon's "Let's have fun."

Maybe face to face the words that seemed so easy would
no longer move between them. They had become quite adept
at the hesitant pace they had set for their correspondence.
Genny saw his words before her, they settled in her mind, she
reacted, responded on screen, reviewed, paused, reconsidered.
Then off the words went, monarch butterflies finding their way
home. How could she make it work in real time?

She spelled out again a one-word acceptance, already
choking. Nothing more than "indeed." Indeed she would meet
him Wednesday at ten. Indeed he didn't know her; she knew
so little of herself. Indeed she would do her best to have fun.

10

The air is like a butterfly
With frail blue wings.
The happy earth looks at the sky
And sings.

Easter / Joyce Kilmer

GENEVIEVE – the happy earth

It was a quiet meeting. The earth was quiet. The sky was quiet. Genny studied the lake, afraid to face the park he would be walking across to meet her.

She was dressed "careful-casual" with her faded ivory-toned jeans, clean and creased like campus khakis. Printed across the front of her cotton knit blouse, a butterfly added dimension to her chest. Its wings were splashed with turquoise and rose and outlined with touches of gold. Tawdry? No, it was a carefree butterfly, ready to have fun.

Then, at her back he quoted a line from her Einstein piece, "the minutes on the sand never stretch out long enough." The voice had the same resonance that sent her spiraling in that hot conference room on the seventh floor of the downtown library.

Genny could not turn around she was so fearful of making the wrong sound or the wrong move. He came around to stand in front of her, azure eyes focused on her, close enough that she sensed the heady smell of musk on his skin. He was the same man she saw making his final retreat two months ago, all muscle, vein, and bone. He was taller than she remembered, and tanner.

"I see you do have a face," he said.

"Same face I had on the bus that you weren't sure you recognized. Only this time with eye shadow, and lipstick," she said, surprised at her honesty.

"All that for me?"

All that and more, she didn't say – a Victoria's Secret Angel bra and boyshorts, shaved legs, lemon-lotioned arms, shoulders and neck. He wouldn't find any of that in an email.

"All that for you."

He glanced behind her with distaste. Genny turned toward the café and understood.

"I think I have made a bad choice of eatery," she said. "Do you want to stay here for coffee? Looks like that's all they have, if that."

The café tables outside were empty and rusting, with dried bird droppings on the peeling enamel. Crumpled napkins had joined the first discarded leaves of fall swirling around the scrolled iron legs. Inside was as desolate. Genny didn't want to stay. Neither did he.

"I really need some food," he said. "Let's find a real restaurant for eggs and orange juice. I never got around to eating this morning."

"Why no breakfast? Are you a bed lounger? I can't sleep like that in the morning and it's a good thing because my job begins at seven. Corporate travel agencies are all-day, all-night operations."

He was puzzled, as though he had come in on the middle of a conversation. Yet she continued babbling while he attempted to follow her thoughts.

"That's what I am, a travel agent. When I first started I was night-shift – worked until six in the morning. Believe me, the night people who travel are a sorry lot. The travel problems that come in the middle of the night from the international travelers are challenges. Lost passports, lost luggage, lost spouses …"

He stopped her there, butting into her ramble. "How do you lose a spouse? I'll bet a raft of guys out there would like to know that secret."

She shot him a quizzical glance. Maybe he'd like to lose a muse, she hoped; maybe she could help. Her answer was far removed from her thoughts, "I don't really know, never had one to lose. I guess meeting at the wrong airports or taking mismarked buses. I'll have to ask next time the problem comes across my desk."

"What do you do with your afternoons then, if you start at seven?"

"I don't have an afternoon. I begin at seven, put in a ten-hour day with an hour for lunch and go home at six. Exhausted. But, I get Wednesdays off to recuperate."

"So tell me then, what do you do with those Wednesdays?" he asked again.

What did she do? Genny couldn't think of one tantalizing adventure that had engaged her free Wednesdays. Last Wednesday she took in a matinee. The Wednesday before that was a major grocery run.

She lied. "I guess I write poetry. What do you do with your Mondays and Tuesdays and Wednesdays and …"

"Look for lovely ladies that I can walk the beach with."

Was she now advanced into the category of "lovely lady"? One of many? She would settle for that.

So they walked and talked along the park path with Genny giving away more than Jon. He drew her words in, contributing nothing that exposed his life. At this point, Genny knew more about him from his poetry than from this conversation. Were his poems his life or his fantasies?

"Every day, on the lookout for lovelies?" she asked to put the focus back on him, hoping for some essence beyond the smoothness of his voice and manner.

"It's the privilege of the retired."

"Retired?" She tried to get a fix on his age.

"From classroom teaching …" He at last opened up and drew closer to her. "A little Midwestern lyceum that cut back its programs because of budget restraints, eventually cutting me out as a permanent solution. Me, on the faculty of a small, privately funded prep school – unfunded I should say – with a dwindling enrollment. Can you picture it?"

Genny replaced the greenery of their park and the gravel path under his feet with the ivy covered walls of Victorian buildings and cobblestone walks. The chirping birds and buzzing bugs remained as part of the scene she was creating.

Bugs. He brushed a ladybug off her shoulder. She twitched at his touch. Bugs and worms, he was a man of the earth. He caught her reaction and his eyes twinkled in amusement.

"Goodbye ladybug. They are a sign of good luck, you know. We should have counted the spots then you'll know how many days will pass until your wishes come true."

"I guess we blew that – no time to make a wish much less count spots. That lady's long gone. Would you have wished for a seven-figure endowment for your school?" Genny asked. He was her wish, well beyond the power of ladybugs.

"Nah, that school is long gone," he said without remorse. "What I want is to see my name on the cover of a book of poetry. To be on a coast to coast speaking tour reading its lines. To sign a contract for translations into fourteen languages."

"That'll have to be one mighty huge ladybug."

The merriment didn't last. Seriousness took over and another layer emerged. Genny devoured it.

"An endowment would have made my future a little more predictable. But the money wasn't there and without it I couldn't hang on any longer. I left them to their own monetary misery and decided to live off my investments. Now, I have the leisure to write a little poetry. The plan is to get discovered and rich at the same time."

"And how's that working out?" she asked, putting him in a late-fifties age bracket. She calculated that his retirement left him too old to start fresh and too young to give up on achievement. Male menopause was her diagnosis. She had seen her dad move through this discomforting period, to the family's great enjoyment, adding a black Mustang convertible to their treasures, and a couple of cruises on her mother's calendar. Then he had settled down.

"I haven't decided if it will work. I am writing some poetry. Reading more than writing, I guess. Submitting some things. But I have yet to be discovered. Obviously, literary riches are not flowing into my cup."

Maybe they were, maybe not. Genny couldn't tell. He was wearing a pair of scuffed Ferragamo sneakers. She noticed the Golden Fleece logo on his polo shirt.

"The investments are doing better than the poetry," he said. Either that or Genny judged he was very good at covering the resale shops. "and you?"

Impressed by his confidence, she realized she was out of his league. She could not compete on either level – no portfolio of funds nor poems. She was a traveler though, much more than a travel agent. She tried to match him with what she was.

"I have airline tickets aplenty," she said, "to places hardly on the map. Hotel rooms and rental car deals do more than make up for the travel business's slavery salaries."

She sounded satisfied and she should have been. Travel had been good to her so she told him what she did and where she had been, stories that perhaps would charm him.

She began the litany. "I've traveled down the Sepik River in a houseboat, flown Aeroflot Airlines with trepidation to Saint Petersburg, danced the Highland Fling in Scotland. I have bathed in the Mediterranean Sea." These were the stories she told. It did sound enticing – but enticing enough? She added Australia, Paris, Rio, England, and Wales to the mix.

Already hungry, her mouth tingled when she recreated memories of Sally Lunn's Eating House in Bath with its cloud-light buns slathered with lemon curd and clotted cream. Not to forget the formal haggis dinners in Edinburgh or the Rhone red wines from Southern France.

"But you never wrote about those adventures?" he asked.

"I am not a real writer, I do fussy female stuff," she said.

"And yet you created all that poetry you sent to me. Looks like a writer at work to me."

The reference stunned her. He had read her poems. *Looks like a writer …*

"I do better at traveling than writing," Genny said. "I read on the road but I don't write. I always think I'm too tired. Or too well fed. That library workshop was a throwback to my high school days – the last time I did anything seriously creative. But y'know, I'm beginning to think I am ready to do it again. Maybe even do it well. Why not? Nothing says I need to stay on the same path I'm on right now."

Pausing at that admission, she continued, "Poetry has taken a back seat for too long a time."

"A closet poet," he said and then fell silent again.

"It wasn't very important – for a long time," she said, just to fill in the quiet.

At her confession, his eyes turned dark with a hurt expression. "Not important," he said, bewildered by the concept. "How sad that you were with the wrong people for such a long time. You should have been hanging around with me. I spent my life with poetry. It began before high school with 'Gunga Din,' I think, with its pounding rhythm – how I loved it. And T. S. Eliot's 'Macavity' was so much fun. I never stopped digging into poetry and ended up teaching it to kids the age I was when I discovered it.

"Somehow I never found a 'me' in the next generation. Poetry doesn't seem to have the appeal that hip-hop does to these kids. But I guess they call that poetry, too. Even though it's not quite Robert Frost."

His voice trailed off into an echo as he recited some Frost. "For I have had too much of apple-picking: I am overtired of the great harvest I myself desired ..." and a sadness took over.

"I can be your lost students. I'll write your adolescent poetry for you." It was the best offer Genny could make but he wasn't encouraging. Had he spent too many years pushing kids into poetry without any payoff? His dismissal of her efforts to become what he was prompted her to be more careful of what she exposed of herself.

When he changed the subject she welcomed the digression.

"Let's forget the food and check out the beach. I'll quote sandy rhymes to you and we'll have fun."

The talking became easy again. Walking side by side she was not distracted by his facial reactions. They had shed their shoes and were kicking sand while a wispy breeze off the lake provided a cool contrast to the heat of the morning sun. The sky was an essential blue beyond the fading green of the trees, a hint of the coming burnished tones of fall. In the distance they saw a lone runner beating the asphalt path with fearsome steps, a cyclist, head down and intent, an old man, strolling, at ease with his pace.

At last, they were taking turns revealing enough of their pasts to keep threads of their lives twining around each other like the strands of a rope. He had an older sister to match Genny's younger Denise. He was educated in the East to her Western degree. He drank tea to her beer. He quoted poets from every literary period to her "Chicago Tribune Book Section" familiarity with literature. His youth had revolved around the Vietnam War, lava lamps, "Annie Hall", moon landings, "All in the Family", the war on poverty. Genny grew up with the collapse of the Soviet Union, Kellogg's Crispix, Sally Ride, "The Cosby Show", Simon and Garfunkel and poppers. She searched for some common ground there and found nothing. The gravitational pull she felt was that he had nothing in common with her. That he was different from her. That he was what she wanted to be.

When he turned to face her she stammered, mid-sentence. "… then I was trying to count out some coins – I never could figure out how much they were worth …" When he turned to face her the blue of his eyes reflected an impatience that she read as *is this chatter necessary?*

Without cause or reason, he then leaned over; his lips brushed across hers. Like butterfly wings. Genny lost all train of thought and the flow faltered.

He picked up the conversation she had dropped as easily as he had kissed her. Now, silent, she learned about his contentment.

He was Buddha-like with his contentment, the peace he found in the choices he was making. How he avoided disruptions. He lulled her into his patterns. She walked slower, talked softer. The world beyond her, the sand, the waves, and the sun reaching its overhead height, formed a bubble around her.

He kissed her again, so delicately, it was a memory before it ended. He broke the stillness with, "Will I see you tomorrow night – at my writers' group? It's Thursday and September. You promised you'd come."

"I will come." The past disappointments had been wiped away by two delicate kisses.

Later that afternoon he followed up their morning with an email while Genny was following up with more poetry.

From: jonwat
To: gennydu
Date: Wed, 08 Sep 2004 16:32:30
Subject: Indeed

Well I had fun indeed!
Fun indeed to be on the beach with you and the wind and the sunlight. To do that again would be good – even though I never had my breakfast. It felt like a reasonably safe encounter. So hold off on adding "dangerous" to your resume. Safe is important. Aware of the risks. You understand all that of course.
I puzzled over your literary fate on the bus ride home and concluded that your plan to reinvent yourself is a good one. Listen to the Buddhists – the self does not exist – freedom is to forget it – with no self you can go anywhere. You are free.
Indeed. Jon

To: jonwat

I promised you adolescent poetry. Here are more preliminary attempts:

Genny hesitated. She didn't send the email with the poems she had chosen. Had it been a safe encounter? It was not safety she felt. It was risk. It was being on the brink of the cliffs of Moher, about to soar into the skies or dump into the Atlantic. These poems were Genny. Alone, she wondered who he was; what was at his core. Would she be at home there?

Instead, she printed out the poems and folded them into an envelope she addressed to him. She wanted him to be able to run his fingers over the words as he studied them, to put them in a book he was reading. She wanted them to be with him wherever he went.

She selected a blues poem, an elegy, an ode, all written for class, judged by her contemporaries to be good first attempts, and a twenty-year-old poem from high school that indicated some talent.

Yet the envelope remained on the front hall table the next morning. The bewitchery of Wednesday morning had dissipated. She could not risk losing his respect. It was all she had of him right now.

11

I only know that summer sang in me
A little while, that in me sings no more.

Sonnet XLIII / Edna St.Vincent Millay

GENEVIEVE – summer sang

In the early fall, the cruel indications of winter pierced the air. Chill winds swirling down from Canada said they are almost over, these splendid days of summer. Genny tried to ignore them. She tended to ignore denouements and their ultimate endings. On the street she ignored the crispness of the air and the chill on her neck and fingers. She ignored the recalcitrant sun casting an eerie wash over the land.

However dubious her Thursday felt, the previous day's culmination of two months of sparring with the Mountain Man, bringing him into her orbit, to her side, even bringing his lips to hers, had provided all the shimmer she needed for this chilly day. This evening she would be across a library table from him again, together as part of a larger whole. What he wrote would provide intense conversation. He would hear her writings again, perhaps admire them again. More strands would intertwine.

For the evening Genny wrote a subdued poem about the sun, how it heated their souls. She made it tender, lyrical, hoping it would bring back memories of their Wednesday morning together in ways meaningful to him and her alone.

She rushed home from work, bathed, tapped her neck and arms with citrusy scents and dressed in an unimposing skirt and shirt. Only he would notice her, no one else.

Eagerness splashed across her face as she entered the library room where the group met. Seven faces looked up at her in puzzlement. Genny recognized none of them. Not one of them. She felt a rush in her head like a down pillow exploding.

"I'm here as a guest," she said to their curious faces and they welcomed her. They had begun a reading and she slipped into a chair to listen. No one asked her name. It didn't seem to matter why she was there. She contributed minimally. She didn't absorb what they were reciting nor hear what they said in response. Eventually, someone asked whose friend she was. She named Jon.

"Where is he tonight?" someone asked.

"I dunno," someone answered. "He's a little sporadic. Did he say he was coming? Was he supposed to meet you here?" Genny shrugged her shoulders, not committing to anything.

"Don't know how he could," another said, "he's taking Karen out for her birthday."

"Oh yeah, that's right," they all acknowledged. "But we're glad you could come."

It was a rebuff, bringing her here where she expected him to be. It was a more casual invitation than she suspected. Did he remember nothing of yesterday? Yet tonight he must have known where she would be. Genny was there; he wasn't.

The cold and dark attacked her as she left the library. A Canadian front had enveloped the city and she was disinclined to protect herself from its chill. She rode the bus over to the library but walked home, filling up the rest of the night. She tried to make the meeting meaningless – to join in on a group, not to be with him. She joined in, contributing minimal comments on others' writings. She read a poem and expressed gratitude for the suggestions it received. It could have been considered a successful evening, had poetry been her primary interest. A poet was her primary interest; she was not his. Genny vowed to forget about Thursday poets. In time she would forget, would regain control.

An email had sprung into her laptop while she was gone. Not knowing it was there, she crawled into bed.

Genny buried the humiliation of Thursday, or tried to, and resumed her normal social life with Brian. On Friday he was relaxed and thirsty as they returned to her apartment. She grabbed a couple of beers from her fridge. Denise walked into the kitchen, grunting a greeting at Brian while Genny made it three beers and placed an unopened bottle in Brian's hand.

His response was, "Make it two, it's so stuffy in here. When the hell are you going to get a ventilation system that works?" He took a bottle opener from her and followed Denise into the living room, took off his suit jacket, threw it over the arm of the sofa, threw himself on the opposite end and took a slug of beer.

Juggling the two remaining opened beers and glasses for Denise and herself, Genny followed him snarling "When I move into the Ritz-Carlton. You'll take your one and go home." Thursday night's mood prevailed. Denise took a bottle from Genny's grasp and moved on through the living room. The conversation was unappealing.

After a tiring day with traveling clients, she had met Brian at Cyclone's on Michigan Avenue to celebrate his win in court. She told him, per her upbringing, how pleased and proud of him she was. So proud she even proposed a toast, "… this is the law of the jungle – as old and as true as the sky; and the wolf that shall keep it may prosper, but the wolf that shall break it must die."

She thought she quoted Kipling. What child wasn't weaned on "The Jungle Book?" Her father had taken his daughters beyond the children's stories into Kipling's poetry. How they had giggled at his attempt at dialect: "So 'ere's to you Fuzzy Wuzzy, and the missus, and the kid …" The words crept out of her childhood.

In truth Genny didn't celebrate court victories; she celebrated instead Kipling, Blake, Yeats, and Dickinson, and the rest of their imaginative gang. That's the way her conversations went now since she had rediscovered poetry. Each had a different focus from anything Brian had on his mind. She wandered in the middle of poems, sucking up delicious words. She invented herself and a life surrounding her. Nibbled at life? Reality was barely there for her. Who stalked prey? She stayed inside herself, bringing the poetry to her, craving it. She thought in rhymed couplets, putting colors and motion to every thought she had. Everything swayed in rhythm, words undulated. Similes and metaphors attached themselves to everything she saw.

Brian had brought up his victorious legal case – "People v. Harbour Inn" – and she searched for the tragedy in the tale. She found a beauty in the word "harbor." In her mind, she plotted opening lines that blossomed into the most meaningful poetic message coming from another's woe – this prosaic woe being a property snatch by a developer. Otherwise, the topic had held no interest for her.

She could not carry on a reasonable conversation anymore, perhaps because she was not having reasonable thoughts. Her Mountain Man thoughts were beyond reason. But she tried. She looked over at Brian slouched in the curve of the sofa, nursing his beer and thumbing through a magazine. A book of poetry was on the table before him but "Travel + Leisure" was in his hands.

"Brian, if I became famous, what would you think of me?"

"Is that a real question?"

"It's a real question. I am thinking of going whole hog into poetry. I'm thinking I just may be good. I should give myself to it."

Brian's practical response was, "I don't think poets go 'whole hog'."

"Oh, you know what I mean."

How could he know what she meant? Brian had probably never read a poem in his life that an English teacher hadn't assigned. But she continued, "You know, give up everything, plunge into living and writing. Probe the meaning of everything. Put it all down."

Genny was convincing herself that such an existence was possible. She was not convincing Brian.

"And you were drinking *what* tonight? I thought it was wine – and a very expensive wine at that," Brian said.

Undaunted, Genny said, "I guess if I became famous, you wouldn't believe it," imagining herself drinking French champagne in tribute to her extraordinary achievements instead of Brian's plebeian choice of wine – expensive or not.

"Just show me the money and I'll believe," he said, drowning Genny's thoughts of champagne.

How practical was Brian. The money – she had forgotten about the money. Kiss goodbye her two-times-a-month paycheck. Her annual raises. Tolerate starvation in some ghetto apartment.

Brian, who required a certified lady on his arm, would disappear. It would be hard to look the lady in second-hand clothes.

She doubted the Mountain Man would have continued interest in a struggling poet eating meals in food kitchens. She saw herself gaunt and ghostly, the smell of urine and stale makeup enveloping her. Surrounding her were bearded scarecrows and obese women with hanging breasts. Genny needed another image of her future.

She tried then to be sociable, apologetic for the wasted evening, an evening that she was throwing away, along with Brian. She surrendered, "OK, Brian. I'll stick with travel."

"Stick with whatever you want. It's obviously not me."

"What are you talking about? I was with you and you alone the whole evening. And many evenings before." Genny tried to control the damage that she had been creating over the past weeks: letting her mind wander in conversations, focusing on poetry in conversations, letting meaningless conversations govern the night, avoiding conversations.

"Who is it, Genny? There is someone else invading your life. Shoving me aside? If you want out of our twosome, you go. I am a big boy. I can survive."

For a moment she felt she should protect the ground she stood on. It was solid and predictable. Brian was reasonable and would overlook her past distractions if she could commit to some kind of loyalty. But the ethereal, the inevitable, the nonsensical were the muses that called to her.

So she confessed to the existence of the poet and his hold on her. Tears threatened.

Brian put down his unfinished beer, gathered his suit jacket and stood tall, facing her. "I'll let you pursue the poetry, have at it with the poet, without any opposition. God forbid great genius should be constrained."

She moved toward him but he put up his palm in a halting gesture.

"This was expected," he said. "I've been shoved aside too much. There's not much about me that interests you anymore. And there's not much room in your head after all this poetic gibberish has taken over."

"There's room," she said, although she didn't know where. No room in her mind. No room in her days or nights. No room in her emotions. It was all taken up by poems and poets.

Unsure of the consequences of her inclinations, she said, "This is not a good night to end us, you with your exciting day in court. Let's talk this out. Wanna go someplace less stuffy? For a walk?" she asked in an attempt to revive their former camaraderie, trying to be friends again, needing time.

"I think I want to go home."

Brian left, maybe for home, maybe for a friendlier bar. Unless Genny changed, she didn't think he would be returning. The thought brought no regrets even though this ending left her with only an empty seat at a library table. This weekend began in a ditch and continued on its downward plunge.

What she discovered in a couple of later emails didn't brighten it any.

From: jonwat
To: gennydu
Date: Thu, 09 Sep 2004 6:09:02
Subject: tonite

I forgot another commitment — can we postpone tonite?
Jon

From: jonwat
To: gennydu
Date: Fri, 10 Sep 2004 13:32:30
Subject: yesterday

> *I do badly with schedules. When I invited you to come to the group, I did not remember that I was not going to be there. I am sorry I missed your visit, but I trust that you were treated well. Did you go? Did you read? How were you and your work received? I want to hear your impressions. and what you read.*
> *Jon*

Did you? Genny thought not. Not sorry, not interested in hearing her impressions, not wanting to hear what she read. It was colder still today than the day before. Darker. Sadder. And Brian was right, stuffy.

12

There is only one happiness in life, to love and be loved.

George Sand

GENEVIEVE – one happiness

Something electric was happening outside Genny's bedroom door. Denise was shrieking, then giggling, then purring. It must be David-inspired. No other being evoked that kind of reaction from her normally sedate composure. Genny went to her door, but then hesitated. She suspected the news and hoped she was right.

When Denise hung up the telephone she shouted, "Genevieve. Genny. Genny," who sauntered out as though she had been lounging on the bed, engrossed in a book. Denise stood immobile by the phone, her hair dripping wet, her terry robe secured around her body. She glistened on the outside from the hot shower she left to answer the phone, glistened from within from the phone conversation.

"Genny it's, he was, he's, I'm ..." Genny waited to hear what her sister would tell her as soon as she regained her vocabulary.

"It was David. He's been promoted and they're transferring him to Denver. And, and he bought a diamond and he's coming to Chicago to show it to me and he wants to know if I want to get married this Christmas and I said 'yes.' I said 'yes' Genny. I said 'yes!'"

Genny held her breath through this outpouring of joy. It was the happy news she hoped to hear, that they were setting a wedding date. She wanted her little sister to know forever the joy enveloping her now like shower water. Genny waited. Denise blinked tears from her eyes, and cleared her throat, and swallowed. She threw her arms around Genny, hugging her with her dampness soaking Genny's tee-shirt, her tears moistening her cheeks.

Genny joined her in triumphant tears, sputtering soft happy words. Tears of hopelessness fought with the joy Genny felt for Denise. She wanted to be in her sister's skin now with her uncomplicated love where a David could be a suitable substitute for a Mountain Man. She knew that to be impossible, as impossible as a Brian had been.

David was coming to Chicago with a diamond. It would be a stone worthy of the wait he had put Denise through. David was a geologist, graduated from Utah State University, with honors. At home with stones, he probably had found the most exquisite gem ever mined out of the earth. He probably would have mined it himself if he could have chiseled it out of the foothills of the Wasatch Range. Eager to see its luster did not begin to describe their anticipation.

Then a realization set in. "At Christmas?" Genny asked. "Married this Christmas?" A mere season away was too soon for an event that should follow Genny's by many years according to their mother's plan. With the chosen season, Denise had time and distance working against her and needed her wise older sister to throw her a rope. So Genny prepared to do so, but the date jarred her.

Again she asked, "Christmas? That's not a little too soon?"

"No, we can do it." Denise was so sure. "It's only September; we've got three months. Oh, please, Genny, help me." Denise's pleas became more desperate when she noted how unsure her sister was.

"Not here," she said. "Maybe in Winton. Certainly not here. But sure, it should be in Winton anyway. Mom and Dad would want it there. And I'm sure things aren't so booked up as they must be in Chicago."

Genny filled in calendar squares in her mind with "to do" entries. No wonder Denise hung on to her. In these first moments, she provided a necessary steadiness even though she wanted the excitement of a wedding romance to be hers.

"What an adventure we'll have," Denise said. "We can pick out everything here – the dress, your dress. You'll be my maid of honor. Maybe Mom can fly in to help. and maybe Brian can be in the wedding ..."

"No, not Brian," Genny said. "I don't think I could bear to share a wedding ceremony with Brian. I really don't think he will be around by Christmas anyway. He's just not making it, Denise. He just doesn't have what I know I need."

Genny hadn't seen Brian since their "me as poet" discussion. She was busy. He may have been out of town. He wasn't on her doorstep.

"Well then, how about the Mountain Man," Denise asked. He can come to Utah. He seems to be topping your list with all those messages going back and forth between you."

She turned back toward the bathroom to finish dressing. "By the way," she said, "I mailed that letter to him that you left sitting forever on the table. It was there for days. I thought you forgot it."

Genny froze. Delivering the poems to him made no sense now that she realized how unimportant she was. Denise didn't notice blood rushing from Genny's cheeks. Maybe her face wasn't ghostly white. Maybe her chin didn't jut out, her eyes open wide, her forehead compress into corrugated paper. But Genny felt the contortions. Denise continued talking from a distance and her voice came back into register, "… I can just see him in Utah. Wouldn't that be a grand trip for him."

Some things about men-women relationships Denise would never understand. She and her David – one man, one love. She wouldn't learn that all things don't come to those who wait. She wouldn't learn that for every man there isn't a woman. She wouldn't learn that a good man is hard to find. These were from Genny's curriculum, hard-learned and painful.

One slice of wisdom Genny learned with twenty years of playing at love was timing, that moment when two loves are interwoven intricately enough that the cloth can be unveiled without shriveling under attention. Timing – the moment when love comes under a judgmental glare and stays solid. Bring on friends and relatives then, bosses, pastors and bartenders, passersby on the streets. Hold the banner high saying "this is my love" without fearing it will fizzle into the sky like a deflating balloon.

The Mountain Man was not at the loom yet. Love was not a woof or warp of their cloth. They had no cloth, no banner, yet.

No one, man or boy, had been there with Genny. As a child, she balked at the term "boyfriend." Witnessing some socially precocious child walking her home from school, her mother would greet her at the door with an eager, "and who is your little friend?" "Little friend" soon graduated to "boy-friend," making Genny grimace with distaste. The term was so stifling, so confining, so stuck. To avoid it Genny leaped into fiancé-hood. Even that term laid heavy on her. She rejected being coupled with another for public consumption. She needn't have worried. The other half of the couple had soon rejected the idea too.

The Mountain Man was worth shouting about. Genny envisioned someday holding him high. But not at this wedding.

"No, not Jon either, not now," she said after dismissing the thought. In fact, no one at this moment had earned the privilege of sharing this wedding.

Her dear buddy Deets might have made an attractive entrance but he belonged with her when she was away from the intricacies of doting father, bereft mother, and focused sister. Someday when they all were settled into the people they wanted each other to be, Deets could come hang around, being who he was.

The concept of the Mountain Man in Utah remained in her head. In Genny's mountains, where she pictured him belonging, standing with her in "the most lovely and enchanted valley of them all ..." Thus had gone the words of Thomas Wolfe, recited to the townsfolk at every Winton pageant, every ceremonial gathering. The words were true, "beauty ... grandeur ... sweetness and familiarity cupped in the rim of bold mountains."

Genny's fantasies had no part in the challenge before them. She moved beyond it. A December wedding became her focus.

"When is David coming in?" she asked at the bathroom door, looking around the apartment and noting the scrub-down it needed.

"Tomorrow night. He'll be in Denver with the big guns and will fly out from there. Pray there's no storm," Denise said over the noise of her hair dryer.

"Good god," Genny said. "You know Denver is the least favorite airport of the seasoned fliers I deal with. Chicago following a close second. Winds, rains, snows, delays, cancellations. If Denver doesn't get 'em, Chicago will. Time for some praying," she said. "But let's call Dad ..."

"I'm going to call Mom first. She'll still be at the office. Who knows where Dad is."

"He'll be at his desk to write the checks," Genny said, bristling at her sister's remark. He had always been there to underwrite Denise in spite of her dropping out of college, knocking around town for too many wasted years, and following Genny to Chicago without a plan. Lately though, he was on the other end of the line for her younger sister.

Denise picked up the phone and began dialing from memory.

"Oh sure, of course. Mom." Genny didn't want to be in her mother's head when she heard that the baby sister was first down the aisle.

They, her mother and she, had stood at the kitchen sink that spring afternoon, the two of them, with Genny's diploma, her mortarboard and gown thrown across the enamel table where they ate their breakfasts and lunches.

"And now what do you intend to do with your precious, useless degree?" Genny's mother's voice was hard like the tempered blade of a knife. She expressed no pride in the degree in spite of her daughter's graduating with honors. Add also the commendation for a senior treatise on French immigrants in America, focusing on the creative contributions they had made to the developing U.S. culture.

Her mother's words maintained a sharpness like the thorns of a rose and as invasive. "It was an M.R.S. I was hoping for you. I guess a B.A. will have to do." Such was the graduation praise from a mother who had no degree. She didn't understand why Genny had craved one.

"All the opportunities you had. Why you tossed them aside. Too busy with your books. Too disinterested. You tossed them aside. Why? I'll never know."

The "opportunities" her mother referenced were the parties Genny had been invited to and sometimes attended, the college boys she dated, the weekends away as the guests of the college crowds of other campuses, the get-togethers with family friends whose sons were growing up strong and handsome. These were supposed to lead to a marriage proposal. Some almost made it. None did. The boy/men seemed unfinished to Genny, a single woman now with a college degree and a life to create and a mother who worried about her daughter's future.

Genny wasn't worried. She lived in a thriving town, small but thriving with a newspaper full of job offers and "career opportunities." A future was hers to create. It was just a matter of plucking a possibility.

She had taken some travel/tourism courses and found herself very plugged into the world. She edged toward that as a career. A job, offered and accepted, with offices on the main street of town, reasonable hours, unreasonable salary but rubber band escapes out of Winton, travel far (cheap), rebound home (balking). Taste the country and the world, with a secure bed and meal waiting at the finish.

"Just think," she said to Denise who sensed her sister's eyes on other territory, "I could be stuck in an office in town and you'd never get any exciting postcards. and I would never see New Orleans, or New York, or Newcastle. Just old Winton."

Travel worked for her. It annoyed her mother.

"If you stayed in town some, maybe a couple of the men who live here could catch up with you," she often said.

"I don't want to be caught," Genny as often answered, "if 'catching' means 'settling.'" She could never accept capture.

She could have said, *I don't want to be you, with your predestined life.* But seeing the disappointment in her mother's face, her actual response was, "The world is bigger than Winton, Mom; there are other people out there. I want to find it, and them."

What she wanted was a new, more promising terrain. What she needed was territory free of the disapproval surrounding her in the presence of her mother. She wanted to live beyond the gracious mock Georgian home with enough in it to satisfy them all. Bedrooms aplenty, a great space combining kitchen and family room, a basement for raucous teenaged parties, a toilet seat for every butt in the house, closets to spare and a hideaway in the attic. Genny, her mom, her dad, Denise – the house had absorbed them all.

Even her father's cheerful attitude of "keeping her here as long as we can" became oppressive. When she hit thirty, Genny began pecking her way out, checking the cities she flew into as the guest of hotels and airlines eager for the clients she sent their way.

At first, few destinations substituted for the comfort that surrounded her. In Winton she saw majestic mountains just by opening her bedroom blinds every morning. The air she breathed invigorated her lungs. Her job, her friends, her family demanded little of her beyond her mother's desire to marry her off. She was burrowing into the landscape.

Until she landed in Chicago when she took its "Mayor Daley Welcomes You to Chicago" personally and said, "Thank you very much," to the banner over the expressway and to the cab driver who took her under it.

She walked down State Street and pressed her nose against the windows. "Thank you, thank you," she called to the mannequins in gratitude. She walked down Michigan Avenue and smelled the caramel corn, blinked at the gem-studded jewelry in fortified displays, smiled at the comfortable mix of tourists with cameras hanging off their necks and natives in spiky heels. "Thank you, thank you," she whispered to it all.

In a serious quest, she searched for employment on that street and found it, escaping family pressures in a new big town, a new big office with a new big future.

Since his arrival, David tended toward a comatose state. Previous weekends in Chicago were more carefree. This weekend was dedicated, purposeful. Prior to this visit, David was a tourist. Now he was in town as family with his free will manacled by the urgency of the engagement and pending wedding.

The diamond needed to come out of his coat pocket, into a setting befitting its elegance. It was elegant. Genny knew it would be. She estimated it to be more than a karat but was too polite to ask.

Denise was giddy over its size, its cut, its brilliance, so also the diamond specialist in the Jewelry Center. The four together picked out a setting to show it off.

Item one checked off a list they composed as they clipped along. "No, David," was a common retort. "No time to stop for a ..." Genny or Denise filled in the blank – cup of coffee, sandwich, beer, men's room break ...

They stormed the bridal shops. David too, defying custom. They could have parked him in a local bar but Denise wouldn't let go of his hand. He melted at the visions of her in flowing ivory tulle, in creamy velvet, in chiffon, and in lace. Bewitching beyond necessity, Denise already had enchanted David. They gathered designer and store names, prices, checked availability and delivery. Denise's mom had asked the bride to wear the veil she had worn, a cascade of ivory netting that erupted from a jeweled cap, a fitting halo to the fluff of a dress Denise chose.

They could do this. They were doing it.

They found a neighborhood printer and promised him wording for the invitations within the week, or two. They had nothing now to put on the invitations except Denise and David's names, no church, no date. When they realized without them they had reached an impasse, the sisters passed the responsibility to David. He bravely accepted the assignment to lock those elements up as his first solo task back home.

Next project was the invitation list. They bought a couple bottles of Korbel and headed back to the apartment to begin sorting through relatives, friends, and significant acquaintances who would be on the A-list for this long-anticipated celebration.

They still had Sunday. They filled it with decisions about china, silverware, crystal. Not a difficult task since Denise had been scouting designs over years of waiting.

"Where are we going to put all this stuff?" Denise asked an overwhelmed David, lounging on a loveseat in Field's furniture department. "We don't have a place to live if we are going to Denver."

"Details," David said. "I'll rent an apartment that you can fill up and after we are legal we'll look for something big enough to handle it all." He threw out his arms as if the whole showroom were heading toward Denver.

Genny had seen David's apartment in Winton and shuddered. To him, housing was not a priority. He had been holed up for the past couple of years in a compound whose designer probably had a resume that included penal institutions and post offices. Denise and Genny had often raised eyebrows at the thought of her sharing David's apartment.

"Gen, you don't have to visit us until we move into our spacious mansion in the mountains," she said. "You did promise me that, didn't you, David?" David didn't flinch. His life was now in Denise's hands.

They ended Sunday with a trip to O'Hare to deliver the pumped-up bridegroom-to-be and then took a weary ride home.

Once they had chosen her bridal gown and sent David on his way, the following days focused on Genny's bridesmaid dress. Denise was having no other attendants. She had been out of hometown circulation too long.

"The choice is up to you," she said to Genny.

"I would like to be in plaid. It's a Christmas wedding. Plaid is very merry."

"Plaid, Genny? Don't you think that is a little up-stagey?" the bride asked. "I still haven't forgiven you for graduating from college the same week I graduated from grade school."

Her voice held no trace of humor. Genny had forgotten all the indignities perpetrated through the years. Being the older sister was a trump card she often played, but not any-more. Now, since Denise had come to town, Genny was a nurturing eagle, protecting her from the indignities a big city can throw around, treating her to downtown dinners when loneliness struck.

"Let's get serious".

"I am serious," Genny insisted. "I think plaid would show Winton that we are now big town Chicago, on the cutting edge of fashion."

Denise was not after a Chicago look. She was a bride, had wanted to be a classic bride since Barbie dolls showed her what a bride might be. She wanted a maid of honor to look like a member of the wedding. She wanted tradition to reign.

"OK, serious," Genny settled into the conversation. "What's your favorite color?"

Even though Genny tended toward purple where Denise would be lavender, crimson to her rose, emerald to her peridot, she would conform to Denise's more subdued tastes. She was right. This was her day. Genny asked, "How 'bout something in the burgundy family? Or some of the midnight colors — the dark, dark blues, or chocolate browns, or pewter grays?" Genny ran out of suitable colors that she would wear. "Better yet, since I am the only attendant, let's go see what the stores for real people have. We'll find something that shows off your ivory satin."

That decided, Denise and Genny trousseau shopped — bras, panties, nightgowns, peignoirs, teddies. The choices were all froth, like cotton candy on a slender cone.

Genny disowned her guilt over the poetry she abandoned as she soared with Denise through the bridal stratosphere. No inspired words came to her. As a poet, she was more productive in sorrow than gaiety.

13

In my brain, buzzing and confusion
pushing and pulling leaving me blind
lost
breathless

Bees / Jonathan Waterhouse

JONATHAN – buzzing and confusion

Karen returned from her every-now-and-then beauty session that sent her home glossy and glowing, smelling faintly of peppermint. From the brightened strands of her auburn hair to her sandaled feet, smooth as a newborn's, she had been pampered and perfected during the better part of the morning. She came through the door as pleasant as the day.

Fingering through the day's mail delivery she asked, "Hey Jonjon, I wonder if this is good news or bad," handing him a fat number ten envelope. He noted the return address with an unsettling twang in his gut before he tossed it aside on the table adjacent to the front door. The refracted afternoon light sneaking through the beveled glass highlighted the name "Dupont on Sheridan."

She put her hand over the envelope, patted it and, with a hint of encouragement in her voice, said, "Looks like maybe some of your poetry submissions came back. Open it up – see what they said."

Karen's voice hinted at the kind of hope Jon lived with, that his peers approve of him. Perhaps she understood how he craved a measure of success the academic world denied him. She did not indicate any suspicion of the contents of the envelope.

To sustain her ignorance, his offhand reply was, "Can't be anything good. It's too soon for any positive response from the editors who got my last batch." He reached for the rest of the packet of mail and drew attention instead to the soulful face on the cover of the just-delivered issue of "Time Magazine."

"C'mon, Jonjon, open it up. Good things come in fat packages." She wiggled her torso to emphasize the point, then reached toward the table to pick up the discarded envelope.

Tearing it open, she pulled out a folded sheet and read out loud, "'No longer will you look on baby years ...' This isn't your stuff, is it; what is this? I don't remember you writing about babies." She flipped to a second sheet, waiting for Jon to react to her question. She checked for a name, finding none, she rescanned the first poem again, then the next.

"'Where did she come from this child of the beach all bubbles and beauty and bounce?' Jonathan, really, what is this junk?"

He tried to cover while Wednesday's conversation returned to his mind: Genny's willingness to write adolescent poetry for him. The lines coming from Karen's mouth were just that, adolescent as promised.

"Who's it from? What's that return address?" He asked the question knowing the answer, wishing the bills and mailers that accompanied Genny's envelope could divert attention yet realizing nothing will relinquish its fascination until a satisfying answer to Karen's question emerged. His stony face masked a high-speed brain. He was racing on a six-street intersection. Which way out?

"There isn't any," Karen said, "just Dupont on Sheridan. What is that, a publisher?"

At the third sheet, she read, "'Tall red ice boozy snoozy vodka …' What is this stuff?" Moving further down the page, her mouth tightened. "Who is she Jonathan? Another doting devotee? What are you doing for her? She can't get her rhythms right? Are her metaphors too trite?"

She shoved the papers into his belly, her face contorted into the caricature of a crone, her shoulders shaking as she continued her accusations, "Or is she another Emily Dickinson just waiting for you to discover her. And her body." This last phrase Karen tossed over her shoulder as she stormed out of the room. All the glossy nail polish, all the fragrant oils, every colored strand of hair was for nothing; her man was roaming again.

He followed her down the hall with an embryonic response sputtering out of his mouth. "She's a kid who's just getting into poetry. She's pretty stumped and she thinks I can turn her stuff into silk purses. She assumed I would help her …"

Exasperated, Karen said, "Send her to Columbia College then. Or Newberry. Or send her to Berkeley, yeah, that's good, send her far away. She's using you, buddy. When will you get that into your head? They want you, not your poetry. Try to remember who you belong to."

The bedroom door slammed shut, leaving him alone with Genny's poems, four more transparencies to her mind.

"She's writing up a storm," he muttered, wondering where the creativity would take her, rushing into it like a child discovering salty ocean waves. He hadn't taken her as a serious poet even though the first batch had whetted his interest, not so much for the poesy of it but the eagerness, the uncommonness and the exuberance of her.

"Whatever she becomes, I want to be part of it," he promised himself.

Replacing the poems in the envelope, he walked the sheets back to the dining room, standing paralyzed at the table trying to find a refuge for the contraband, considering every cranny the room offered. The envelope must be out of sight before it incited further conversations. Satisfied at a decision, he squirreled it away behind stacks of china in the breakfront. His singular thought was this was not the time to review Dupont on Sheridan poetry.

Better yet, now was the time to serve a cooling salad for lunch, with a little Riesling plus, plus, plus a decadent chocolate sweet to put an end to her anger. He always depended on his culinary skills to ransom him from quagmires. Genny had now flung him into one of major proportions, so he stuffed his wallet into his jeans pocket and headed down the hall to tap on the door.

"I'm going out to find us some lunch," he said and left for the grocery store when there was no answer.

Out of the house, heading for his salvation, he didn't feel secure. He could imagine Karen hearing the front door close and moving off the bed she had probably pounded into dust clouds. From the window, she could watch him move down the street toward the shopping center at the end of the block. The moments he was out of the house gave her time to reconstruct his movements with the package of poems to determine where he would have hidden it. If she found it thrown on his desk she could deduce it was too unimportant to put away, and relax. But she wouldn't find it in the open; nor would she find a Dupont on Sheridan envelope at all.

The name "Dupont" triggered no memories here, not the names of any poets who entered Jon's conversation, not the name of any struggling bard he wrote with, not the published names he begrudged. It was a name hidden in the quiet of his den, never to be mentioned again if he were to maintain the peace he sought in his house.

Genny Dupont was an interloper, unexpected and desired, who never moved in any of the circles Jon and Karen shared. She wasn't a part of any of the gatherings he dragged his resisting Karen to, attempting to bring her into his poetic world although she had no serious inclination to work with words.

"Full of vamps," so she besmirched her competition, when he tried to include her in the invitations he received. And then the accusations erupted. Primary among them was "Doesn't a wedding ring mean anything to them?" He wasn't wearing a wedding ring, complaining of swelling fingers with the advent of the summer softball season. Karen had forgotten.

He chose his groceries with discrimination, planning his menu as he scouted the aisles. A cold soup recipe came to mind as he scanned the vegetable bins – tomatoes, zucchini, yellow and red peppers. He needed fresh basil and tossed a sprig into his cart. A salad, a Cobb salad – for that he collected bacon, prepared turkey breast, romaine, goat cheese, avocado. The rest he had in his cupboards.

For a finale, he designed a dessert to guarantee a mood reversal. Berries were on display – raspberries, strawberries, blueberries, even some gooseberries. He would layer them into a compote, cover with brandied cream and top the creation off with shaved almonds. In the candy section, he spied white chocolate bark embedded with red-hots for a splash of fun. She would tolerate him for all that.

Returning to his kitchen, Jon prepared these selected ingredients with ease, knowing their goal: peace in his household.

The lunch was elegant; the challenge brought him to a culinary peak. The vividness and garden fresh smells of the cold soup played off the variety of wholesome and healthy ingredients in the Cobb salad. Jon presented the refreshing dessert like a bouquet of mixed flowers.

During the meal, he avoided any conversation about poetry, made no mention of an envelope from Dupont on Sheridan nor any other element of his wordy world. The splendid autumn weather he had just walked through, a diversion in itself, was worth noting as were the striking tones of Karen's hair, overlooked in the pressures of the early afternoon. Where else could his conversation dwell to remove the danger of Dupont on Sheridan?

With his mind on the mellowing colors of the trees, he suggested a getaway, guaranteeing a long run conversation. Karen craved time away from her nine to five existence as right hand to a greeting card executive. Its seasonal stresses, juxtaposed against the relaxed perpetual holiday agenda Jon pursued, opened her to the idea of escape. His talk of a welcomed vacation kept the subject matter under his control.

The talk blossomed into a plan.

"It might be good to drive east and check in on family," he said. His only sister, living in upstate New York, provided a logical destination. She shared a complicated childhood with him and welcomed him for the memories he resurrected. "Janice's home is a good stopping point after a relaxing drive around the lake."

They both agreed the trip would be beneficial – to distance Karen from stress, Jon from incriminating return addresses.

As soon as he could break away from their lunch clean-up, he moved toward his desk with Karen following him into his den, an entrance not allowed under normal circumstances. She plopped into his massive study chair in the far corner of the room, pushing allowable behavior in his office to its extreme. An unneeded spare bedroom, it was his domain, filled with everything to promote comfort and inspiration, including the very chilled air she resented in these hottest days of summer.

She buried herself in the "Time Magazine" that had wrapped the day's disruptive mail. The Republican convention and the terror attack in Russia prompted occasional comment from her distant post and he glanced over his computer screen to notice she had quieted down, her interest diverted. He wanted no more mishaps. He could keep the lid on if he could confine Genny to weekdays when Karen was tucked away in her office in the suburbs, busy and fulfilled. There she was not focused on what occupied him, trusting his activities to be solitary, domesticated, and controlled. He watched her from across the room and, taking advantage of her momentary interest in current affairs, he began the email:

From: jonwat
To: gennydu
Date: Sat, 18 Sep 2004 15:17:15
Subject: poetry

> *Genny – your poems arrived. Such a surprise – you're so productive. I hadn't expected you to plunge in so wholeheartedly. You – our next laureate? Thanks for sending them. Next time – better if you could mail*

*them to arrive in the middle of the week – more time
then – I can concentrate with a clearer head. Weekend
chores take a lot of my time. I'll look at them soon
– tell you what I think and how we can make them
better if needed.*

    *Don't let them get in the way of our fun, though.
Want to discuss them against a backdrop of sand, and
sea? I can meet you and your poems Wednesday at the
beach – didn't you say you have Wednesdays off? How
unique to not have to report anywhere in the middle
of the week. And still get paid. Your work schedule
does mystify me. As do you.*

"*As do you,*" he said out loud before he caught himself but
wondered, *why the mystery, why don't I just leave you alone and
avoid complications?* The answer was in his lingering images of
her – the contour of the bones in her face and shoulders, of the
wild dark hair hanging in her eyes. He thought of her tentative smile when amusement surprised her, how it turned into
a laugh involving her whole face, a face so fresh. He wouldn't
leave her alone because he read love developing in her messages.
Love would be good for him.

    Karen, he realized, loved him proprietarily with a love
he guessed worked for her. He studied his proprietress, now
distracted with the pages of "Time," noticing features not so
classically defined. She was pretty in a wholesome way, the
kind of woman who wore her clothes comfortably to disguise
flaws, who didn't impose her tastes on her surroundings but
rather blended into them. But she was "used up" from tracking
his peccadilloes so tediously, and it showed. Jon felt a chronic
loyalty to her, maybe a pity for her sometimes joyless life. It
didn't hamper him.

He sent the message off his screen, knowing Genny would be there Wednesday; yes she would.

"Jon, I think we can carry this off," Karen said on Sunday, bringing up the trip. By Monday morning they realized the challenge would be to find a free week in Karen's schedule. His calendar was unencumbered by responsibility – he drank his coffee anywhere, watched the stock market anytime, and penned his poems whenever he chose to prod the muses.

She called a little after ten with her triumphant news: "We're in! Norris agrees that our major project is wrapped up and we all could use a breathing spell. It was a magnificent sell job, I must admit. 'Mr. Norris,' I said, 'before we get involved with another blockbuster, can I have a week at the end of the month? Just a puny little week?' Then I added, just to prick his literary conscience, I'm so smart, 'Jon and I need a break. His poetry isn't flowing well and I think he needs some clear air.' That was all right, wasn't it, to lay it on you?"

"And he said?"

"He went right with the flow, calling me a patron of the arts. I think he was teasing me. I don't think he takes you seriously. But he pulled out his PDA, right then and there and plunked in my name for that week. 'You're good to go,' he said. We did it!" Jon heard the smugness in Karen's voice. "Then he threatened to work me to death through the fall. But he'll be doing that anyway."

"So what dates are we talking about? Is that the twenty-seventh?"

"Yes, Monday. I'll need the weekend to get ready. The twenty-seventh through Friday and then we'll have the weekend at the other end. Can you pull us together by then?"

"You certainly work fast. I wasn't prepared to move with such jet speed. Maybe a paddle boat is more my style. But

I can rev it up and the twenty-seventh – Monday – I guess that would be a good time to be on the road." He paused; she waited. "Good. I'll get on it. I'll check with my sister – see if she's open for house guests."

"Not too many days with her, please," Karen said, "we only have a week. She's good for about twenty-three hours."

Karen overestimated the amount of time her sister-in-law welcomed her. She never forgave Karen for splitting up Jon's first marriage, wobbling though it was. It was more convenient to let Karen carry the blame rather than share with his sister the details of the doomed marriage and how little Karen had to do with it. With Karen the demon, sibling relations were easier, putting less pressure on him to explain himself and his proclivities.

"Next Monday, then."

He calculated he had a mere week, a mere seven days to nurture what he began on the beach. He stood settling the phone in its cradle near the breakfront that harbored Genny's envelope. He slipped it out from behind the stacked dishes and moved to the kitchen to find a stored grocery bag.

From there to the den, where he turned on his computer to open a new file. He began typing in Genny's batch of poetry, by-lining each with his own initials to keep her name out of this file, out of his conversation, out of his house. He needed a label, one that told no tales choosing 9-18, September eighteenth, the day the poems arrived. His finger traced on the calendar on his desk the days back to the date when her face shone in the sun's reflection off the lake water, when a kiss underscored what her email messages had been implying. Nine one eight, nine hundred eighteen, innocuous enough, a number that shouldn't incur any curiosity.

Word by word, line by line, he copied the current poems and transferred also what had come before by email, removing their authorship. The file became bloated with Genny poems.

"No longer will you look on baby years ..." *What a bad beginning to this exercise, too strained a beat.* In his mind he recalled the poems submitted by his young students, the restraint he had used in critiquing them; how gentle he was then. He slipped into that mode again. *Bad beginning,* he thought, *not a criticism I can suggest at this tender point.* He dug deep to find words that sounded honest enough to keep her spirits up.

He scanned the page for something valuable – "... brilliant, sun-washed focus ..." *okay, some good sounds.*" He was intrigued by her topics, jumping from childish dreams to youthful pranks to a father's love. He read into the lines a tenderness that centered on her father, sensing the affection that existed between them. *Is this my competition,* he wondered?

As he read through the remaining poems he became heartened. At the final line of the final poem "... to soften what the daylight bares," the steady rhyme pattern layered on the theme worked for him and provided some promise, some hope.

The promise of hope – what more can I promise that isn't already used up by Karen? He could promise her hope.

With old and new poems locked away in the 918 file, he tore up the day's originals, put the scraps into the grocery bag with the destroyed envelope and walked out to the trash dump in the alley. "There. We're rid of that potential time bomb," he said to the squirrels. "Jesus, Karen, you know I'll never leave you. I'm too tired."

Out of the house on a day that invited activity, he decided to stay with the sunshine and breezes and wondered if a softball game were going at the park. He brought his "grimy wreck" out of the garage to realize with dismay how accurate Karen's appraisal of it was. He could wash it, but wouldn't.

He reconsidered the ride to the park but instead swung toward the Music Box Theater to check whatever foreign film was on the early screen, something sensual, he hoped, something obscure. *A flick and a beer, that's what I need today.* He needed daylight, and Wednesday, and Genny, but that would be another day. As a substitute, he pulled "The Reader" off the back seat for its movie listings. To his satisfaction, he found "Cet Amour-la," knowing its focus on love and death would suit his mood like a rose on a grave.

Karen beat him home and was working on dinner as he pushed open the front door to find mail scattered over the front hall table, inspected and deemed non-threatening. He checked the pile, pushing the sales announcements off to the side. As he separated out the bills, a brazenly colored postcard caught his eye.

"Well, I'll be damned," he said. "Slipping into Third" in bold red letters first attracted him but, more astonishing, beneath the title, a subtitle, "poetry on the shutouts of life," and the name Lenard Lavinski, he who led the poetry workshop at the library last summer where Genny first appeared. "Lucky bastard, got published again."

"Karen," Jon shouted from the front hall and followed the smell of garlic into the kitchen where she stood, spoon in hand, stirring a pot of soup, the steam flushing her face and curling tendrils of hair at her forehead and neck. "We are invited to a champagne reception honoring Lenard Lavinski next Saturday afternoon."

She shrugged off his wispy kiss on her neck. "I would be more excited if I knew who Lenard Lavinski was – and where were you that kept you out 'til now?" she said with more interest in the swirl of the oil on the surface of the soup than in wispy kisses or his real whereabouts.

"Lavinski. He's the guy from the library class last July. The one who was surprised that I didn't have a book of published poetry out yet. The guy who was so impressed with my readings in class."

"Oh yeah. That got you far."

His enthusiasm allowed him to ignore the comment. "Let's go to this party. It would be wise to connect with him again. And if his agent is there, it would be better to connect with her – or him. Better yet, if the publisher shows up, dynamite."

"What day did you say?" She gave the soup another stir. "Saturday? We can't. Josie's baptizing her baby that day. You know what a bash that will be. It'll probably go into the night. I told you we were going." She turned around to face him as she asked, "Have you forgotten?"

"Maybe we can squeeze the reception in between the church and Josie's. I should be hanging around these people if I ever hope to get any attention. Lavinski seemed to notice me."

Karen wasn't impressed. "I can't go. I don't belong there. I'm not much good at promoting your poetry, anyway, mostly because I don't understand it."

Her expression was commiserative. As her resistance melted she said, "Can't you stop in by yourself? There would be a little time after the baptism. And then meet me later at Josie's? I can wait for you there. You won't be long, will you?"

"That would work," he said with a calculating smile.

From: jonwat
To: gennydu
Date: Mon, 20 Sep 2004 21:07:14
Subject: Champagne

Lavinski's book signing – did you get an invitation? Will you be going? Say yes.
Don't forget Wednesday. Same beach, same time.
Jon

From: gennydu
To: jonwat
Date: Mon, 20 Sep 2004 22:31:01
Subject: Re: Champagne

Yes and yes

14

Oranges and lemons,
Say the bells of St. Clement's.

The Bells of London / unknown

GENEVIEVE – oranges and lemons

"Would Vogue have any suggestions for literary gatherings?" Denise called down the hall. "Anything vaguely similar to what you own in your closet – or mine?"

"I don't think I've found an outfit yet they would applaud," Genny shouted back.

"Just how many sweaters do you plan to parade in front of me?" Denise was becoming weary of giving her studied opinion on the effect of the clothes Genny modeled for her approval.

The answer came from deep within a bedroom closet, "As many as it takes to find the one that makes me feel luscious."

Genny walked into the living room, a silk skirt swirling around her legs, topped by a lacy, loose knit sweater. Up to now she had tried electric blue, empire green, Chinese red, florals, and stripes. Nothing distracted Denise from the base-ball game on television.

Finally Denise's eyes were on her and she gave a thumb up. "That's it," she said, "stick with fire." Genny stood before her, neck to knees in vibrant orange out of Denise's closet. How the color flattered her surprised Genny.

Forgetting gratitude, she said, "I like this better on me than on you. I'll trade you a trip to Las Vegas for it." Genny always found free airline companion passes to Las Vegas when she needed a bartering tool.

"Won't you please come with me?" she asked again. "You would have such a better time."

"A better time than a weekend holding a lid on the hor-mones of twenty-six raging teenagers?" Denise stayed firm. "No, I can't. I promised Sr. Rosa months ago that I would help out at the youth retreat this weekend. I'm actually looking for-ward to it. I've grown kind of fond of that geeky group." Gen-ny's pout didn't sway her. "Spending a weekend in Wisconsin with them tain't the opportunity a city gal ignores," she said.

"And of course you are so wild and impetuous. They need that kind of enthusiasm so desperately," Genny said.

Denise ignored the sarcasm. "No, but I'm really into that 'Dance Dance Revolution' thing. I'm almost able to get through a whole song without falling on my ass."

"So you'll let me fall on my ass instead in the midst of the local literati. Okay. On my ass in silk and saffron it is. And a lonely entrance into a roomful of people I don't know talking about things I've never heard of. Thanks, little sister, for your loyal support when I need you most."

Genny upped her plea. "This is my Saturday debut, you realize. It's not the middle of the week. Remember I'm not his bus friend that he takes out for birthday dinners. I am not that friend who fills up his weekends, with bones rising out of her flesh."

"Are we overdramatizing a little here? Maybe you're not all that, but 'The Man' will be there and the bones won't. He will look after you, tell you what to say. Or better yet, don't even open your mouth. Just continue adoring him like you are some kind of ethereal being, hovering there only to inspire," Denise said as her eyes returned to the television screen.

"Some kind of muse," Genny said. "Sorry, that job is taken."

"Genny," Denise shook her head, "you are so ludicrous. It's a book promotion, a groupie gathering. He'll be there. You'll be there – and glowing in that outfit. If fortune shines on you, *she* won't be there ..."

Genny couldn't bear to hear any more so she asked, "When do you leave?"

"As soon as the buzzer sounds."

As she walked from the living room, pulling the sweater over her head, she wished she had turned down the invitation. No she didn't. While Denise suspected the book launch was an insignificant event, and it probably was to the world that turns television channels rather than pages of poetry, to Genny the evening was a scarce opportunity to embed herself in Jon's social schedule. She grasped it.

Down on the street a car honked and kids yelled. Denise jumped to the intercom at the first blast and confirmed she was on her way down. Genny was on her own. A saffron muse.

15

... a plaintive theme enters quietly, serenely pleading
for the quiet of the night
for the tranquility of some summer sky.
This acre of peace, this field of emptiness, is all there can be

Peace / Jonathan Waterhouse

JONATHAN – the quiet of the night

"Remember Jon, Josie's at six," were Karen's last words to him as they left the church following the baptism, words that wore the tones of a plea rather than a threat. She took the baby from Josie and followed her to her car, ready to help the new mother with baby-tending and party-giving.

Jon found his way to the reception in the Poetry Chamber of Cinders Book Store on Ashland Avenue, into a space filled with musky incense and elegant books of verse, a sequestered section designed to hold affairs such as this. The room had a masculine feel of leather and canvas supporting the spotlighted author's sports-focused title, "Slipping into Third." Jonathan was comfortable in the backroom atmosphere even though it was filling with faces he didn't recognize.

Lavinski arrived with an entourage of devotees, none looking to Jon like an agent, nobody looking like a publisher. But then, could he spot a publisher, he wondered, having rarely been in their company.

As the crowd grew, he moved in to present himself but the stream of well-wishers remained constant, forcing him into meaningless conversations with strangers waiting outside the circle, most with intentions similar to his.

The initial flurry died and a face-to-face encounter rewarded Jon's patient watch. "Hello, congratulations on the book. I'm Jonathan Waterhouse from your library session last summer."

He would have continued with his minor credentials but Lavinski's congenial response interrupted him. "Yes, yes, nice to see you here ..." Whatever additional words followed faded into background noise as Genny, walking through the door, disrupted Jon's concentration.

"Another of your disciples," he said, nodding toward the swish of fiery orange appearing on the perimeter of the room.

Together they watched her flow into the room. Jon said, "I'll go bring her over." He moved to her side, holding out to her a slender flute of champagne picked off the tray of a wandering waiter.

"A toast," he offered as he approached her, "to the success of Lenard Lavinski and incidentally," hoisting his glass, "to your particular beauty – bewildered beauty. Genny, you look like Alice in Oz. You haven't been to many of these book signings, have you?"

She smiled at his conflated reference to her favorite storybook characters. "Never," she said. "This is the real thing, isn't it? Your dream?" She relaxed after hearing his chuckle welcoming the champagne he offered. "A toast."

With escalating giddiness they drank to Lenard Lavinski each time the trays of champagne passed by, into the late afternoon, through the readings, through the discussions, toasting the bookstore, the publisher, the printer, the library, every appropriate element that had brought them to this moment.

"To Gutenberg, and his movable type."

He raised her one, "To the Baskerville font."

"To Amazon dot com."

"To Powell."

"Who?" she asked.

"Bookseller."

"Okay. To Funk and Wagnalls."

"To Roget – thesaurus," he said.

"I know."

"To "The Pilgrim's Progress."

"Why?"

"Because I've never read it."

"To "Pilgrim's Progress," she echoed.

"Why?"

"Because I never will."

He never left her side. He delighted in her energy, in her happiness as the champagne flowed freely down their throats and ultimately, due to the unsteadiness it fostered, down the front of Genny's swirling skirt.

"Oops, oops," she said, surveying the splash that added a bronzy stripe to the bright saffron silk, "that's not pretty."

She grasped the skirt in her free hand and ambled through the crowd asking anyone not engaged in conversation for directions to the ladies room. Her floundering gait enticed Jon; *so vulnerable,* he thought, taking his plans beyond the Poetry Chamber into other chambers.

Soon she was back coming toward him, clutching her empty glass, the splotch on her skirt spread wide with the application of water. With accomplishment written on her face, unaware she had increased the damage many-fold, she came up to him giggling. Proudly brushing her skirt, her arms streaked with the lotion she had lavishly spread over her skin after the wash-up, she had added another layer of stain to the skirt and spread the tanginess of lemon groves into the musky air.

"Sniff," she said to him when she returned. "That whole ladies' room is yellow and lemon. Lemon soap. Lemon lights. Lemon lotion. Lemon, lemon, lemon. Fat juicy lemons."

"I think it is time to go," he whispered as she chattered on about a lemonade stand of her distant childhood.

"... fat and juicy lemons, fresh from the market." She closed her eyes, inhaling, filling her lungs. "I smell like a lemon. I smell plump and juicy."

She took her juicy palms and cupped Jon's face in them, wiping them gently down his cheeks, her fingers resting on his lips. "Now you smell juicy too."

He took her hand, turning her to follow him out the door with no inclination for good-byes to Lenard Lavinski. But then, had they even said hello?

He was still at her side as she found the lock on the door of her apartment building, now behind her, his hand planted at her back as they entered the elevator. There, he stood in front of her, his hand at the small of her back pulling her close. No butterfly kisses now, he drew her into him with a fierceness that tightened her mellowed muscles. She stood limp at its end, flat against the cabin wall. He pulled her away and led her out of the elevator, down the hall taking the keys from her hand to open her apartment door. He led her bony boozy body to her bedroom.

From: jonwat
To: gennydu
Date: Sun, 26 Sep 2004 03:07:14
Subject: Re: Champagne

> *I like drinking champagne with you. A thousand*
> *bubbles – a thousand kisses.*
> *Jon*

From: gennydu
To: jonwat
Date: Sun, 26 Sep 2004 12:31:01
Subject: Re: Champagne

> *I like making love with you.*

Karen's words in the morning were harsh. "Jon, will you pull yourself away from the computer and help me with this packing. For god's sake. I can't do this alone." Karen passed by Jonathan's office door again and again, her voice penetrating the fuzz surrounding his brain while he sat staring at the screen he had returned to after a restless sleep.

"What clothes for you? Do you want to look degenerate? – cool? – professorial – irresponsible ..." Karen proposed the options in spite of her displeasure with his no-show at the baptism revelries. She continued to harp about the literary reception and whatever follow-up she pictured him and Lavinski indulging in that lasted too far into the night.

"Good thing you aren't the godfather to that child. You surely would have been relieved of that responsibility before the evening was over. I was about to relieve you of me. Or rather vice versa." He sheepishly glanced up as she added, "Yah, that mad."

Throughout the morning she attacked him with complaints, grousing about having to make repeated excuses for his absence, topping off her lament with a whine about falling asleep alone in her bed. "How do you expect me to relax when you are gone god knows where? Me all by myself in that big bed. Did you even try to call me at Josie's?" He was never prepared with answers to such tirades; none were expected. She didn't wait for any.

"You know, I did wake up once, it seems. Sometime in the night, I remember the moon being bright. What was it, three, four when you slithered in beside me? Slithered," enunciating the word, making sure she had his attention. She did. "Lying motionless with that ghastly moon lighting up your face. Motionless – like a zombie. Like a scared rabbit. A sure sign of guilt," she said. "You disgust me. You stunk like sour lemons. What were you drinking? Where were you drinking it? In a citrus grove?"

He *had* slithered into the bed and sensed her wakefulness but had remained still and unavailable beside her, trusting that she hadn't been fully awake. He knew she had fallen back into a deeper sleep when she turned her back on him. Non-combative. He was safe for the moment. She hadn't stirred again until the morning, now more rested than he, more ready for the battle.

"Do you have any idea what the weather will be like? Can you please do something constructive for this trip?" she called from the bedroom. "Or are you too pulverized?"

"I'm checking it now, dearest," he said as he ran the cursor down his contact list to plug in "gennydu@ ..." His fingers fidgeted, knowing the challenge would be to hold onto the rush of last night throughout the week as he toured the East with Karen. While he would be distracted with family, with the furtive Vermont poetry festival he added to his itinerary, with loping around back roads, would her cushion of memories preserve their bond?

He wrote: *What I didn't, couldn't tell you last night is that I leave to go on vacation tonight. Remember freedom. We are free. Free to do. Free to be. You to be you. Me to be me. Precious freedom. Let's hold on to it. To the fun of it. You feel so safe, it is so good to be with you.*

He hesitated and put the message in the draft file, holding it for another perusal before he sent it off to Genny, then Googled WEATHER for a quick answer to Karen's question, knowing she would soon come in to check reports herself. The longer she stayed down the hall, the more time he had to compose himself.

Karen didn't wait, but charged toward the den reviewing Jon's wardrobe in an exasperated voice that catapulted Jon back into the morning. "If we're leaving tonight instead of tomorrow morning, you really need to get a move on. I think we'll need to shop before we go. You need socks, underwear – are you gonna wear pajamas? You need something more presentable in your sister's house. She'll think we're a couple of street people."

He assured her, "I'm not parading around in my underwear at my sister's house. It's good enough, as good as yours."

"No, but I will be parading around you, and that's the whole point – I need new stuff too. We should swing down State Street on the way out of town and treat ourselves."

"That sounds like a helluva way to start a trip."

He turned back to the computer as the weather site appeared and announced "The skies look clear this afternoon and tonight, all the way to the Atlantic. Not that we're going to the Atlantic, but I thought you would like to know that." He raised his eyes to see Karen unamused, standing stiff, framed by the door jamb, dangling a pair of rather ratty briefs off her pinkie, a relic from the depths of his underwear stash.

He minimized the web screen to keep her from seeing the actual report, one forecasting rain in the East, not the sunshine she would appreciate. In doing so, he re-exposed his email screen with its listing of current mails, all the "gennydu'" correspondence hidden away in another file.

Coming into the room she said, "Lemme see, Johnny. What's that weather look like? I'm not driving into the dark if it's not a perfect night. Why do we have to go today, anyway?" She was at his back, noticing the screen. "That's not the weather – don't waste time on email now, Jonathan, we really don't have a moment to spare unless you want to wait until tomorrow morning to leave. This is your idea, you know, this immediate departure, this 'get up and go' launch."

"It's really best to leave today ..." He portioned out his words, giving himself time to think his plan through. He had no reason to start out that day except to remove himself from "Dupont on Sheridan" ASAP, keeping apart the two worlds he was caught up in. Last night's late arrival into Karen's bed remained contentious, sure to become a repeated discussion moving into the core of the situation. Being far from Chicago and distracted would help dissipate the issue.

Trying to be agreeable, he said, "We should go as soon as we're packed. What's left to be done?"

"The packing," she said, "you've got to finish it up. I can't do everything."

"Okay, okay, okay. I'm on it. I'll get us going. It's such a beautiful day now – a good time to get on the road. With an early start today maybe later in the week we'll have time to drive over to Vermont as long as we're in the neighborhood."

He chose this as the moment to present his side trip bonus, unearthed during the week as Karen was negotiating with her boss.

"Vermont! Buffalo is not in the neighborhood of Vermont. Last I looked it was in New York."

"Precisely," he was quick to respond, "Upper New York, across from Upper Vermont – where the leaves turn first. They should be blazing by the time we arrive. I found an inn in Addison that you will like, quaint, simple colonial décor. Pretty little wreaths hanging all over with potted plants overflowing with flowers. Food to make you envy the cook – Johnny cakes, pumpkin pudding, brown bread and clam chowder. Are you salivating yet? Best of all, you will like the price, not too expensive."

"Haven't you been busy? All right. What's the new plan?"

He opened a blank screen making notes as he talked. "If we are out of town by four we can probably get to Toledo before our eyes glaze over."

"Toledo!" Karen said, showing her usual impatience, "That's so romantic of you. What happened to blazing leaves and cozy inns?" Jon interpreted her sarcasm as disappointment in his plans. He tried to recoup with continued hyperbole.

"A romantic overnight in Toledo at a Motel 6, then we are on our way to some follow-up romance at my sister's house in Buffalo. That's Monday and a lively night it will be with her full complement of teen-aged kids."

"This is getting too exciting," Karen said. "What day are we on now? Is it time to come home yet?" She took a deep breath and heaved the air out of her lungs. Her limited patience approached a blow-out point.

He ignored her to continued his preview, "Let's see. Sunday night in Toledo. Monday and Tuesday nights in Buffalo. That should put us in Vermont by Wednesday night. That'll give us Thursday and Friday to wander among the trees, through the covered bridges, drinking wine and maple syrup. Separately, of course. We'll leave Saturday morning and drive two hard days – or three soft days if you can pull off another day at the end."

Converting his itinerary into a romantic adventure taxed his imagination. To keep track of the days challenged his concentration. He entered notes into the computer as fast as he talked, putting in black and white a tight schedule, one he didn't want to design again.

Karen left the room resigned saying, "I'll have us packed in about an hour – since you are not moving very fast in that direction. Plan on going by way of Filene's. Underwear, you know Gotta have it. I think they're open 'til six tonight."

"Filene's underwear and Motel 6," he muttered, "what a splendid life." He rescued the draft to Genny and sent it on. Jon and Karen were now as good as gone with a haphazard plan on paper plus a packet of printouts that outlined his escape from danger.

He drove around the block, but seeing no one waiting at the curb, stalled a moment in front of Filene's, moved around the block again wondering if the driving would ease with time and distance, wondering if his muscles would loosen, if his eyes would cool, if his physical misery, evident even before he had driven three miles, would ever lessen. When he studied his haggard face in the mirror he spotted Karen emerging, approaching the car from behind, bundles in hand.

"Well, that was productive – finding silk boxers on sale makes my day." Karen slid into the front seat of the car implying she had shopped well, her forte. She always shopped well when she was on a mission. She shopped exquisitely in fact, with inexhaustible determination. Shopping made her happy. In less than an hour, she had outfitted Jon's under-layer wardrobe from neck to toe, mostly in silk, in colors to rival the leaves of Vermont, and had done as well for herself.

"Thank you, m'dear," he said as she waggled the shorts in front of him. "The cotton industry is quivering at all that silk you are wrapping me in. I quiver too at the thought of the bill. It was ...?"

"Don't worry, I got paid Friday and I intend to spend it all on you. That's what you get for taking me to the woods. So cool," she exaggerated a sigh. "Being in the woods with you. Just where I want to be."

Karen's newfound cordiality set a better mood for this trip in spite of last night's disappointment. When Jonathan was not within reach she sensed their ties loosening. Tightness was uncomfortable for Jon but she pleaded for it whenever he slipped into another groove. Today, she recaptured her hold at Filene's check-out counter. He would wear the silk boxers and sleep beside her for the week and her world would return to normal.

Well into Indiana, he passed her his researched travel papers including the maps, routes, hotels, and restaurant listings, and notable historic sites, and towns along the way. Through the week he had pulled the information off the computer, the pages now all clipped together in order. After the Buffalo family visit, the days following were noncontroversial until the final weekend with its unannounced Otter Creek Poetry Festival, its seductively colorful information splashed across the final pages of the packet.

As the landscape sped by, he switched from talk radio to the CD positioned in the slot. Rachmaninov thundered from the speakers. Karen bolted to an upright position calculating out loud the dozens of hours they'd be sharing the confined spaces of their tight little coupe while Jon sensed this energy of Rachmaninov might run counter to his attempt to avoid a storm.

"There's not enough room for Rachmaninov, me, you, and all the baggage I've thrown into the back seat. Please, sweetheart – maybe a little Hootie & the Blowfish?" Karen asked. She rummaged in her tote bag offering, "Let's try this, their 'Cracked Rear View.' Can you believe it's still around? I picked it up at the checkout counter. Look at the price! And ten percent off that. Darius must be losing it a little to go so cheap." She began delicately unwrapping the protective cellophane, not wanting to appear assumptive, waiting for permission.

"He never had it," was Jon's grudging response as he accepted the disc. The sounds of "Hannah Jane" reaching his ear were less imposing, less pained, less complex, less soaring than the Rachmaninov they replaced – and more monotonous. The lesser music bored him, but he reacted with a simple "Whatever pleases you, dear. This is your trip, your time." Your distraction went without saying.

Karen hummed along, the ten-year-old lyrics still vibrating in her brain, until "I Wanna Be With You" began when she belted out the words, "… there's nothing I can do, I only wanna be with you." She leaned over to nuzzle her nose into his cheek bringing a contented smile to his face knowing his plan was operational.

But Karen hadn't read the travel packet yet. And Genny was reading the email.

16

Tell me, what else should I have done?
Doesn't everything die at last, and too soon?
Tell me, what is it you plan to do
with your one wild and precious life?

The Summer Day / Mary Oliver

GENEVIEVE, JONATHAN - one wild and precious life

Genny read Sunday's email. She didn't understand. Yes, she did.

From: jonwat
To: gennydu
Date: Sun, 26 Sep 2004 14:32:06
Subject: Off to the East Coast

What I didn't, couldn't tell you last night is that I leave to go on vacation tonight. Remember freedom. We are free. Free to do. Free to be. You to be you. Me to be me. Precious freedom. Let's hold on to it. To the fun of it. You feel so safe, it is so good to be with you

*oh my god oh my god — "I leave to go on va-
cation tonight" — what is happening here — oh
my god talking to myself that won't work I need
to talk to you jon — you've left me here, alone
— where did never again go genny genny genny
— I'm talking to you where did never again go —
never again never again — that eternal promise
of never again would you be left alone — oh yes
oh yes oh no*

"I don't know about you, Jon, but I am overly ready for
real food," Karen announced as she finished her second energy
bar and sent the crumpled the wrappings to the car floor. He
agreed and pulled up to a diner outside Fort Wayne that offered a meatloaf and mashed potato supper as the specialty of
the house with coffee and dessert extra.

They ate it all.

Taking advantage of the quiet, Jon bypassed Toledo
without any outburst from Karen.

"Oh I'm sorry love," Jon said, "but there goes Toledo. I
know I promised you a Super 8 but would you settle for HoJo?
There's one advertised – four miles off the highway. I'm going
for it; I am tired."

His foot pressed down on the accelerator.

"If that's as good as it gets, okay. Maybe I'll have the energy to absorb this tonight," Karen said referring to the travel
material that she had left on the seat of the car. The plan for
the ensuing days was what they could have been reviewing
with their country meal instead of how the trip was tiring her.

He pulled into the lot of a ma-and-pa motel closer to the
highway and glanced over at her. She shrugged, nodded in
agreement and they walked into the bright lights of the tiled
lobby that accentuated their weariness – weary faces and weary

bones. He would be eager to turn over the driving to Karen in the morning. The office smelled of disinfectant, an odor they tried not to notice thinking only of the need to stretch out in a bed they hoped would be clean.

okay okay genny take a look at you — what are you doing now wallowing in the same old muck — wallowing wallowing in the same old pain — it hurts so much

While Jon readied himself for a shower, Karen slipped off her shift and sandals and pulled her cosmetic case from the suitcase to arrange her nightly facial scrub paraphernalia. The trip packet spilled out across the bed. Catching her eye was the exposed last page, an autumnal scene serving as background for the words "Otter Creek Wordfest." From the bathroom Jon watched her fixate on the graphics. As the truth of their vacation became evident, he turned on a stream of water and stepped into its cascade, prepared for the inevitable reverberation.

he's gone you know that don't you, left — gone, genny, gone — who knows where and who knows when he's coming back you don't even know if — you've only got an I go on vacation tonight — I meaning what — I meaning we — where is the gennyjon we?

"A writers' conference," she spat out, the words penetrating the flow of water. "This isn't my trip. This isn't a look at 'leaves turning'. This is a trip to a goddam poetry conference," she yelled into the shower, "A goddam writers' conference! And what am I supposed to be doing while you cavort around with all those poet freaks?"

"What are you screaming?" Jon asked as he shut off the shower and grabbed a towel to wrap around his dripping body, shocked at her outburst, more scorching than he had anticipated. He stepped out of the stall to see the "Wordfest" papers crushed in her fist, her jaw set tight, her hand shaking the sheets in his face.

"Oh, that was my surprise. I found a hokey little B&B on the internet so I booked a room for us for a couple of nights." He remained composed, that being as always his only defense in the face of her furious indignation.

if he's coming back — when he's coming back — who knows I know — yes you do you know — you can see his muse hovering like a shadow behind him before him at his side holding him fast — cut him out cut her out cut — and you you sit here alone staring at I go on vacation tonight while he stares at her with those eyes — those eyes the color of evening — those eyes that pick out the strands of auburn hair in this mop of black — those eyes that spot a quiver under your skin — those eyes — cut them out cut

"A couple of nights — we drive halfway across the country so you can stick me in some crappy B&B while you discover all you don't know about poetry. You are a goddam groupie. You'd rather be around those people than me."

"Karen, please. This town has coffee houses where we can sit, interesting people we can watch. All the trees are changing colors right now, you know, and you can shop your butt off for all the quaint little things you surround us with. You'll — we'll have a good time."

do you remember — no I don't — are you re-membering to take care of number one if there is a number one — who is where is number one — sitting alone collapsing — remember you were going to be a little smarter next time — but was there going to be a next time — please dear god let there not be a next after a first love no never another — but there is here it is

Karen's expression didn't change. "I've already done enough sitting in your crappy cramped car with another day of it driving to Buffalo. Then, of course, all that topped by a day with my oh-so-sympathetic sister-in-law." Karen turned away from his dripping body, then turned back with a condescending scowl embodying the chill that had developed in her in-law relationship.

"But we mustn't forget what we really are looking forward to," her voice hardened, "the wondrous destination you have chosen for yourself. Let's be honest – yourself!"

Surveying the room, she saw now drab walls the color of city squirrels, a lumpy floral bedspread harboring who knows how many bedbugs and how much leftover semen, the spotted brassy lamps over the headboard.

"I don't want any part of this," she said. "When we get to your sister's I'm flying back to Chicago. You can have your damnable turning leaves. Keep your dismal poets. Some vacation! I want out."

that first love — so young — we were too young I was too young to be so in love — yes cut him out cut — and then red convertibles and speed rides down highways distracted you — you and your weakness for scarlet streaks — for hair flying arms flying words flying love flying — whatever your senseless heart required so red so fast — another never again moment — cut him out cut cut — yes in the final moment a never again moment yes — until came the deep pocket good times — good expensive times good well-dressed handsome times — no sitting staring at words there no — good times turned into sitting on front steps waiting for an elopement to begin — still waiting aren't you yes — cut him out cut cut cut

Jon stood before her, his towel draped around his hips knowing only one way to quiet her. He reached out to enclose her in his arms while she snarled at him and pulled away.

"So who's going to be there this time? Katherine? Or maybe Melanie will come back to you, fool that she is. Or Lavinski? Maybe you are into men now? Or Sandra — ooh yeah, Sandra. She never left did she?"

Sandra, Jon's blindsided first wife, dumped on her ass in favor of Karen, referred to in fear by the vixen who now raged around the room not hearing him protest her litany of his past loves. These words could have filled the fight she should have had the night before when he brought in the freshness of lemon or the fight she might have again and again until the name of "Dupont on Sheridan" became the acknowledged center of her anguish.

"Those women are gone, Karen. Can't you get rid of their ghosts? Every one of them. Gone." Gone, as Karen might someday be gone. As Genny someday …

Karen had been one of those women once, a woman on the prowl, a woman past her prime with a wandering married man in focus. Just five years ago she pegged him after their meeting in a neighborhood grocery store, at the meat counter where the butcher had been little help with the cut of beef she was requesting. She looked to Jon, standing by, to translate her request and he had complied in his poised, knowledgeable fashion, so willing to share his expertise, so uncomfortably married.

"What I think you're looking for is a beef fillet strip." Turning to the butcher he said, "You cut me a hunk of tenderloin last week. It was prime. I sprinkled it with lemon pepper, braised it in a little wine and roasted it smothered with some sautéed morel mushrooms. We thought we were eating at Antoine's."

The conversation transfixed her; she was totally unequipped to enter it. He had managed to keep drawing her into it with his eyes, nodding her way as if, of course, she knew the experience.

He carried her bags of groceries home that afternoon through a dusky sunset turning her street crimson as they walked toward her apartment. Romance bounced off the cement. He was catching it below the belt and arranged the bags to free up an arm that he moved around her waist. He left her with a kiss she said was so delicate she couldn't remember the touch of his lips, only the flush that had sped through her body.

Yet she later remembered a telling phrase he had used at the meat counter, "'We thought we were eating at Antoine's.' You are part of a 'we?'" she asked. He never answered her because he was, in fact, a "we," he and a tiresome wife of many years whose discontent with him and his disillusionment with her contributed to nights of anger or silence.

The question was never asked again. Ultimately she succeeded in moving into the "we" seat, devouring beef, devouring him while others who had tried to dislodge him from his discomforting marriage were less successful. Some were less pretty than Karen, some less aggressive, some less financially secure, some had less sex appeal, and more emotional baggage. Some had lingered but Karen had won.

Now he expected her to wipe the slate clean as if the surface with all his transgressions written, one over the other in colors found in a box of children's chalk, could vanish with the swipe of a felt eraser. All that chalk dust, floating in the air, choking her.

"Karen. Karen. Karen." He pleaded in ascending tones. "Look around you. They are all gone." She wasn't listening. "Gone. I've told you over and over again. They are all gone. They never were part of me. No one will be as important as you. You are my chosen."

no promises to me at all but try try hard enough and maybe you can read magic into our time in the sunshine – fun indeed to be on the beach with the wind with you – our times together how delightful each – no no no no no no nonono come back my lady to the real – the winds of a thousand kisses have swept you away – steadysteady there steady now hold fast – steady steady like Brian steady like Denise I am that steady I am – like a butterfly yes like a butterfly – not steady, free – remember we are free like a butterfly – we are so free – like a butterfly – he is so free – like a butterfly – cut

Karen stared at him, credulous. "I want to believe you, Jon, but you make it so difficult with your secret life, with your people who I don't understand, with all your freedom. Are they gone? Really gone?" Karen's tears began; she rambled. "You are so pitiful, holding on to them. We are so pitiful. I do want to believe you. I want us whole again."

Jon kissed her forehead and her cheek, punctuating each of her sentences as she continued pleading, "I will try to believe. It's just that we fit together so well. No place else is so comfortable."

She was right. They were comfortable in their own territory: their quiet house, surrounded by the furnishings they had brought together from their lives apart and their joint choices, where nothing came in uninvited, except now an envelope announcing "Dupont on Sheridan," disturbing the quiet of that home.

Still untouched was the eagerness of their bodies. Jon soothed her, holding her tight as he moved her to the bed to slip her under the bedspread with butterfly kisses for her neck, her shoulders, her lips; there would be no facial scrub tonight.

17

Your Hands Heal My Heart With Morning Rushing Water

A Love Letter to Love / Malachi Ajaya

GENEVIEVE – heal my heart

Denise arrived at the apartment late, very late. She closed the front door and stepped into the dark, soundless space, sandwiched between the peachy vapor light of the street lamps flowing through the windows and the blue-silver moonlight peeking into the kitchen. An agonized screech of a cat in the alley below broke the silence.

"Gen," she called, "Gen," moving through the apartment leaving switched-on lights in her wake. "Genny, I'm home," she called again, peering into Genny's bedroom where a miniature bedside light cast a single soft glow in the corner of the room.

Denise heard no response and turned on the ceiling light from the wall switch. Her eyes moved from Genny's rumpled bed, the ghost of her body still imbedded in the yellow and blue stripes of the comforter, to the floor beyond the bed where balls of crumpled papers lay in a mound, like snowballs readied for a midwinter fight. The light exposed her sister sitting quiet and cross-legged in the corner of the room. A blanket grasped from the foot of the bed sheltered her and protected her fragility. "Genny," Denise whispered. "What have you done ..."

She picked up and spread open one of the snowballs. *Come, tiptoe in a little closer ...* she read to herself. Then read again louder to Genny. She opened another, an earlier version of the first, the page filled with doodles and scratched out words, the clumsy path of a poem in the making.

The next crumpled ball unveiled yet another unraveling of the crisis core. "'If you can, if you will, come, tiptoe in ...' Amazing," she said as she read to the final line. "How you find those words? Who else but you would couple 'unto me' with 'wonderfully' and have it make sense? and who would put 'madhouse' and 'bliss' in the same sentence? But then, that's not really a sentence."

This conversation, an attempt at normalcy, went unheeded. Genny didn't respond.

Denise opened a sheet with words filling in all the empty spaces surrounding yet another draft of a poem. "'What I didn't tell you what I couldn't tell you, what I shouldn't tell you what I wouldn't tell you like to sell you might compel you surely fell you ...' This is something different, Genny. It's too strange. What are you thinking? What's happening? Talk to me. Look at me. Oh, Genny." She peered into her face, shocked. "What have you done to your hair – you've cut it – all of it. What a horror. Genny!"

She spotted the discarded email print-out and understood. "Oh, Genny, oh, Genny, oh, how sad, how sad you are," she murmured as she crouched and put her arm around Genny's stiffened shoulders.

18

Fall's screen of golden locust leaves
filters the harshness of afternoon sun
giving us a measured flow —
droplets of fleeting summer light.

Autumn Sun / Jonathan Waterhouse

JONATHAN – a tiny measured flow

"Jonathan, I hope this will be a happier day," Karen said looking out on a bright Monday morning that had begun late and lazy.

A peace had settled over the spartan motel room. The two decided to postpone breakfast until they had put some miles between Toledo and their speeding car, miles between the squabble of the night before and this morning's mildness. Jon was intent on reaching Vermont without further bickering. He had extracted from Karen vows to proceed through the week, trusting him. He was aware that every reference to the destination registered with her while she tried to decipher his dedicated rush to attend this poetry fest. He gave no clue he was traveling not toward a conference but away from Chicago confrontations.

They drove along the level coast of Lake Erie, then through the Maumee Valley and arrived at his sister's home, tired and reserved. The house was bursting with energy and teenage commotion.

"Why are you suddenly coming East?" Janice asked when the bustle of unbending from the car ride and Jon's astonishment over the growth of the children played out. Confusion over the hastiness of the trip underlined her happiness at seeing her brother. "And why when our papa is away? He'll be home Friday. Why not stay with us for a while?"

"This was all your brother's idea," Karen said, taking no responsibility for the spontaneity of the visit.

"And you're going on, into Vermont? How come? What's the big enticement?"

Handy with excuses, Jon said, "You know what a colorful place Vermont is. I haven't been there in ages and this poetry gathering we are headed for is a writer's dream destination. You've all vacationed there. You're probably used to its beauty. But we're from Chicago, remember? It's a little flat where we come from."

His eyes sent off a warning scowl to Karen. *Don't disagree with me,* it said.

"And, uh, it's our insatiable urge to explore," he said. "Karen could get the week off. I'm always off. The conference is conveniently happening this week, the only one around worth going to. You know how I need a destination when I get into a car. Woops ..." He turned and apologized to his niece and nephews who were quick to raise their eyebrows at the slur. "Not that Buffalo isn't destination enough."

"Let me show you some things about Vermont," he said as he took the kids, their mother following, into the family room with its computer.

"And then I'll show you our town's new face," Janice said. "and its better grub palaces."

Karen stayed behind, pouring a fresh cup of coffee, nursing her unsatisfied curiosity. Jon had invited her to join but she declined, offered instead to clean up the mess of munchies they had created. "You take them. Your sister deserves a break from the extra load we are inflicting." Cleaning up messes in a kitchen was an easier assignment than straightening out the mess of her relationship with Janice.

Jon sensed the real break needed was between him and Karen. Away from her, with the family gathered around, he was so convincing about the pleasures of Vermont, he almost picked up a couple more riders.

The enthusiasm didn't spread beyond their circle. As promised, Karen restored order to the kitchen but she was gone when the eager group returned from touring and dining. Jon found her in the guest bedroom, manicuring her nails.

"Couldn't you have done that at home, before we left?" he asked, "and joined us?"

"Yes, I could have," was her frigid response.

Jon didn't answer but retreated into their bed, into sleep to escape a reprise of yesterday's icy atmosphere. Throughout the next day, her sulkiness being ignored, Karen had no other recourse but to participate in the family's boisterous activities, wearing herself and her resentment out. By Wednesday morning, as they packed up and continued the journey east, she was more acquiescent.

Vermont and the B&B lived up to the promises made to Karen. She gradually became more pleased with the snuggery and attracted to the diversion of the locale.

Jon divided his time between selected programs and playing tour escort to Karen, pointing her toward boutiques and galleries, or studying the leaves, bridges, barns, and street wanderers with her. Their time together and apart passed in more tranquility than anticipated.

He left her each morning after gracious terrace breakfasts under skies the color of electricity to catch what he could of readings and lectures. With little other choice, Karen strolled through the town by herself, finding her excursions a satisfying reward for the distance and days it took to bring her there.

In the evening, the sun set the trees ablaze as they wandered in and around the quaint community pausing for sweet and fruity local wines and mellow cheeses, content both in and out of each other's company. Jon filled up on poetry; Karen filled baskets and bags with maple candies, brown breads, a bottle of "Evening in Paris" she unearthed on a musty shelf, and for him "Tired Old Ass Soak" mineral bath salts. He talked her out of a rocker displayed in a country store and into a hand forged wine rack that meandered over a planked wall.

On her own she found a garnet ring and graceful skirts to augment her loaded closet. They nestled in each other's arms each night, reveling in their finds of the day – hers, new kitsch to surround her, his, new poetic voices.

One of the voices that sparked his final morning was familiar, coming to Jonathan via an overheard conversation in an antique book tent. He turned to see the face he and Genny had toasted with such abandon just a week before.

"Hey, it's Lenard Lavinski, isn't it?" he asked. Lenard Lavinski it was, but a blank face stared back at him. "I'm Jonathan Waterhouse – from the library sessions on sensory poetry. Last summer. In Chicago."

Jon watched him reach into his memory until his eyes lit up with a connection found. Not remembered, thankfully, was Jon and Genny's non-attentive appearance at the Saturday reception nor was Jon's recent pleading phone call for help, dismissed without any indication of interest. The memory that surfaced was of Jon at a library table.

"Sure. Jonathan. Yes, Jonathan. Good to see you here – it's the place to be. How's your writing going? Seems I remember you as quite the master with words."

That he recognized him at all was a wonder. Their contacts had been so superficial. That he associated quality writing with Jon's face was the advantage Jon needed to support continuing the conversation. Crowds milled around them. Other conversations washed over them. Jon pressed on. With attempted optimism he answered, "I guess you'd call it going painfully. Some of it is flowing pretty well. Some needs some real reconstruction work. But I keep putting my mind to it. I hope being here will light some fires."

"It should. I'm glad you're still writing, Jonathan. Look over your stuff. See if anything is ready for the world. My publisher's looking for some new blood. I told him I'd keep my ears open. One of the reasons I am here. And here you are – ready to go."

"Almost ready to go."

"Well, get ready," he said, shuffling through the pockets of his rumpled linen jacket. "Here it is – my publisher's card. Oh, and here's my agent's card. Give her a call. Tell her Plathouse is looking for new faces. Tell her I say you may be one. Go for it." Then he was off, pulled away by another budding poet who recognized him from a reading or lecture or book signing.

Stunned, Jon stood watching him mill through the crowd, glad-handing everyone but not handing out business cards to anyone else, putting the presumptuous thought in his mind, *how good is this moment that I am here.*

They routed themselves home in two days via a more southern path having had enough of Buffalo, Lake Erie, and Toledo. Jon was eager to fuse again with his city life and to fit Genny back into that life. He had already put out a lure.

19

May I be well, and happy.
May I be peaceful, and calm.
May I be protected from dangers.
May my mind be free from hatred.
May my heart be filled with love.

Buddhist Loving Kindness Meditation

GENEVIEVE - peaceful, and calm

Genny began tamping down her emotions during the week. Midweek arrived, and Denise took Wednesday off to be with her grieving sister.

The weather was balmy, and warmer than expected for late September. A steady rain fell, relieving a very dry autumn. Denise had a plan for the day. Genny didn't. A precious free Wednesday, and Genny had no plan for it. She had only a memory.

Denise's plan included an early appointment for Genny with a perplexed hairdresser charged with organizing her head. She sat in the cushioned chair while the beautician spun her around, studying the shameless sprouts coming out of her scalp. They were dark, and glossy, with no pattern to their length, like the fur down the spine of a frightened feline.

"Can I ask how this came to be?" the young beautician asked.

"Guess." Genny teased because she had no credible answer. As the locks had fallen to the floor last weekend, each clump carried a slice of sorrow. Then, she had felt a freedom with each clip. Now she just felt foolish.

"Okay, let me see – you were trying to catch a helicopter ride to Hawaii, and jumped too high."

"No."

"Then, let me see – you were whipping up a batch of banana bread, and you tried to smell the batter."

"No, not really."

"Well, how 'bout – your lover escaped to the Caribbean with another woman while you were clipping your toenails."

"Close." Too close. Genny changed the subject to exploring what could be created out of what was left.

"Not much, but I have some great ideas," her hairdresser said, and since you are starting from nowhere we can only improve. I saw a cute little do in last month's 'Style Magazine' I'd love to try out on you. Are you willing to put yourself in my itchy little hands?"

Genny nodded an acceptance, and closed her eyes to remember the hair he had run his fingers through, murmuring his pleasure. Gone. Gone the hair. Gone the pleasure.

Back home, Denise greeted her with enthusiasm. "Much better, so much better," she said. "Much quieter, and very flattering. You have a nice neck. No one ever saw it before, and look, a forehead! Turn around. The back is fantastic! Who wudda thunk?"

Genny was grateful for her assessment. She hadn't checked the back in spite of the hairdresser's plea for her to take a peek. "You will be so pleased," she had said. But Genny doubted that. Pleasure could never be a part of this package.

Denise had the remainder of the day planned. "Let's pack up all our pretties, and send them to Utah," she said. "Then Mom can get them all pressed, and waiting, ready for us to step into when we need them in December."

A very bright plan, it would fill up a potentially treacherous day. Her wedding dress would go west once she had her final fitting, putting "dress" in the "done" column. Together they had chosen Genny's dress, and all its accessories. Making sure the outfit was complete, they put it all aside.

Practical Denise decided to add her summer clothes along with a growing pile of delicate underpinnings. They spent the remainder of the morning organizing the scarves, nightgowns, panties, bras, teddies, and hosiery Denise had gathered, lining them up in piles like an ice cream parlor display case.

They wrapped, and packed everything into corrugated storage boxes, taped them up, and addressed them to Denise in Utah.

Outside at the intersection, they hailed a cab to cart them over to the post office where the line waiting for service snaked around the lobby. While moving toward the counter they reviewed, and previewed all they had accomplished, and all that was left to be done. Getting married was a complicated endeavor. Planning it with her sister provided a balm for Genny. More than that, it had become a loving farewell project for the two.

With patience, their turn came to stand before the clerk who took the boxes off their hands, and sent them on to their temporary Utah home.

They emerged from the post office into a gentle rain. And Denise suggested they walk the mile and a half home. Their jackets and jeans were impervious to the mist. Their hair, what hair Genny had, could be revitalized. Their faces would benefit from the refreshing splashes of raindrops. A walk in the rain would nourish them with uninterrupted moments together.

"So, soon you'll have a month with nothing to do but party and prepare," Genny said. She was beginning to feel the separation. She wanted to hear how Denise would handle it.

"Party and prepare ..." Denise mimicked Genny's gay tone. "It sounds so shallow," she said. "I feel more is happening. I feel like I am changing my whole life, my whole being."

"You are, my dear. Is that big news to you?"

"I don't want to change anything. I just want to add David to what I already have."

"You know you can't do that, Denise. You won't be here. You won't be in Winton. You'll be someplace new. You'll be someone new. You'll be little Mrs. David now." Genny reminded her that after her twenty-nine solo years she was moving on to a new set of relationships, changing best friends as surely as she was changing addresses.

"What about you?" Denise asked. "How are you going to get through this Mountain Man thing without my steady advice? No more shoulder."

Genny scoffed. "He is beyond advice, Denise. Despicable. He's been despicable. I'll just dwell on that despicable behavior, stamp out whatever else comes to mind. The best advice you can give me now is to tell me to get out of town too."

"Not a bad idea," Denise said. "Not bad at all. How about Denver? There's plenty of room for you there., and I'll bet there are even some mountain men for you to play around with."

"Please, not another Mountain Man," Genny said. "Just what I need to push me over the cliff. But I'll tell you what I'm really hoping for."

"A penthouse apartment in New York," Denise butted in. "A year-long cruise on the Queen Mary. Walks in the rain with someone other than me or Jonathan ..."

Denise could run on with a few more preposterous candidates but Genny interrupted her. "No. A promotion. I handed in my application for a team leader position yesterday."

"How's it look?" Denise asked, attempting to bring Genny to a positive place with her optimism.

"Eh – so-so. I didn't see any wild exuberance in Chris's eyes but she said it was good I was applying. Why good, I don't know."

"That would be a great step up. Pretty soon you'll be president of the company, and then get your penthouse apartment in New York."

"New York is nowhere in my plans," Genny said. "Moving up a little where I am, is."

The rain was attacking them now. The wind had picked up, and the temperature dropped. What was soothing at the beginning of the journey home became challenging. They were too close to home to flag a cab, too far to be comfortable with their present situation. They quickened their step.

"I wonder what this winter will be like in Winton," Genny asked, a little out of breath. She knew the December wedding date was a gamble. But then, any wedding date was a gamble to Genny's way of thinking. Any wedding was a gamble. Period.

"Well, we know what it will be like here," Denise said. "Frigidly cold. I wish that man would reform, and come around to keep you warm after I go."

"It would make more sense to buy a space heater."

Picking up their pace another notch, they marched along the quiet tree-lined, house-lined streets of the neighborhood back to their apartment. The heavy rain had intruded into the stillness of the afternoon. Genny heard it splashing off roofs onto cement walks and patios. She heard their shoes making sloshy beats against the pavement. She swiped the hood of her jacket off her head and let the drops soak her cropped head of hair. She felt it washing away the pathos. She lifted her face and caught the drips from her nose with her tongue. She discounted a renewed life with Jonathan Waterhouse.

"I don't want that man back, Denise. I want his poetry. I want his help with mine. That's really all., and maybe I don't need any of that anymore."

"What's it like for you, Genny, with him gone?" Denise persisted, making Genny face what her tomorrow might be. "It worries me to see you alone, without him, without Brian. Alone." Denise had been non-involved with Brian. At best she had been nonchalant toward Jonathan. The onset of Genny's interest in Jonathan had been so unconventional Denise hardly saw it as sincere romance. As the intensity increased, her interest had increased so this final collapse had come as a Pearl Harbor sneak attack.

"Without him, Denise? Without him, a suffocating sadness comes over me. It's like a huge plastic Christmas bag is tied over my head, capturing all the glimmerings of holiday tinsel. I can see gaiety through it but inside I'm losing oxygen. I find it harder and harder to breathe. Every survival instinct in me fights to break me out, to slice away at the plastic sheet, to stab holes in it. Then I do. Then there comes a time I feel free, and full of freshness, and hope. That's all I feel. For a moment. Then loneliness."

"But should he come back," Denise asked, trying to absorb the descriptions of Genny's feelings, "you'll think a little this time before you take him in again?"

"I'll think. I'll forget the suffocation. I'll remember the kisses and see the blue of his eyes. Maybe he'll be more available."

"Oh dear, I hope so," Denise said. "I did like you being in love. I liked the two of us in love at the same time. It was so sisterly. But for you, you need it. For you being in love is inspirational. Love is good for poets."

"Is that what I am?" Genny wondered out loud.

From: jonwat
To: gennydu
Date: Fri, 01 Oct 2004 22:39:06
Subject: wordfest

Festival is wonderful in spite of the short duration. Listened in on a range of talent – some students just beginning their journey into poetry – all the way up to established masters. Some beautiful stuff flowing out of the tents. Very alive. Lavinski is here. But you aren't. Makes the event incomplete.

The road trip has been fabulous, up the coasts of Lake Erie and Ontario over to Vermont, and now about to drive home in a dash. Hope you are well.

Genny didn't consider herself well. She was discarded and desolate, and dour. She was grounded in a grey reality. She had four productive ten-hour days with her clients and her co-workers and her airlines. No one spoke poetry to her. She spoke to no one unless her responsibilities required communication.

Even Deets, the closest thing she had to a best friend, sat motionless across the desk from her, sensing discomfort. He kept his eyes on his screen. He could have provided the distraction she needed if she had let him in. When his eyes looked over at Genny, they seemed to be all pupil, so black and deep were they, buried in his glowing olive skin stretched taut over narrow bones, wide cheeks, his sharp incisive nose. The eyes seemed wise and old in contrast to his young face, joyfully topped with a crop of corkscrew curly hair, the color of Kansas wheat. The color wasn't natural; the curls weren't natural; chemicals created them both. But his eyes were real. They consoled her.

The week was busy. Corporate travel ran high. Genny sent her clients out to negotiate contracts, to inspect plants, to attend meetings, to do what they were paid lavishly to do. She did what she was paid miserly to do. The system worked well enough. Genny would be well enough. That was the minimum she hoped for.

She ignored the email.

20

Free of the herd,
With no supporting choir, no softening harmonies,
You, the black beauty of the boundless field,
Bless this empty ground.

Crows / Jonathan Waterhouse

JONATHAN - this empty ground

"Your coffee's almost ready, Jon." Karen stood at the kitchen counter, waiting for the final drip, watching him, wishing out loud that she were he. "What a life, still in your pajamas, with no apologies." She had said that before; she said it again this morning while he planned his agenda of leisure, in his playground of words, enjoying a day she had been invited to enjoy with him but declined.

This coffee ritual began Karen's day, her first chore of the morning, one of the many wifely chores she accepted as the price of security. From creating a home resonating with colors and proprieties to providing a welcoming retreat for Jon's sexual desires, she had adopted them with enthusiastic skill.

Today he needed their coffee after a hurried trip home, a steady and tiring trip. Through Saturday and Sunday Jon had commandeered the wheel maintaining a two-day reprise of the festival by listening to CDs he had purchased. Not able to dispel the aura of the past days, he distanced himself from Karen and filled the car's interior with spoken poetry, poetry set to music, and music inspired by poetry. He extended the mood as long as Karen remained tolerant. Either she was too tired to fight this competition, or maybe becoming used to it. Jon had accustomed Karen to expect silence and distance when he was in his singular world. She would wait for him to return to her. He always did, to her and the reality she represents.

"And what will you be doing today, lazy one? Can you take a look at the back stairs? They're getting creakier. They're beginning to scare me." This was Karen's reality.

"I can do that," he said feeling he could do anything this day since in his pocket were names: a literary agent's name, a publisher of poetry's name. "I should get to my writing, see what I have to offer that publisher out there waiting so eagerly for me."

Karen smiled a mocking smile but admitted to being pleased for him. Her pleasure was not enough today. Enough would be getting back to Genny with news of his prospective connections. Genny and poetry. The two were synergistic.

Because nothing had come back from his earlier message, he sent a follow-up in an attempt to massage into life the cushion of memories she purported to hold so dear.

From: jonwat
To: gennydu
Date: Mon, 04 Oct 2004 10:39:58
Subject: return

*Of the oddest components of my return home was
finding buried in my socks drawer a red and brown
Slipping into Third bookmark — with a lipstick
imprint planted on the back.*
    Should that remind me of you?

Nothing came in response to that question either.

21

If yours is the singular dream
To question the things that don't seem
So well understood,
Just pull on your hood
and head for the fair academe.

Academe / Rory Ewins

GENEVIEVE - academe

Genny stood before the counter in a room that was angular, surreal, a Salvador Dali canvas. It ended in a point created by bare windows that framed a park beyond the aging
building. Buses, taxis, and automobiles were sending their flap
and fumes up through the panes opened to the early autumn
heat. Genny waited. Cop whistles and an occasional shout
from a raspy-throated beggar invaded the silence of the room.
Some drumming rapped in the distance. Somewhere else a
muffled phone rang but went unanswered.

Colleges with downtown campuses didn't have the
glamour of the open-field campuses surrounded by greenery
and filled with stately halls.

Two blue-jeaned women sat cross-legged on the floor behind the counter, ignoring Genny, gathering up and organizing files and papers that seemed to have cascaded from shelving above them. To disturb them would have been an intrusion. Genny stood still, respectful of their attempts to create order.

But there was no order anywhere. Notices hung askew on the walls, secured with scrubby masking tape. Doors opened into offices bursting with piles and papers.

A small, dark-haired woman exploded through one of the doors, startled by Genny's presence. She glanced from Genny to the women on the floor. "Yes, yes, do you need something?" she asked with a befuddled expression that hoped this intruder did not.

"I am here to see Marlene about registration in your literary program," Genny said.

"Marlene. Marlene Jacobs? She's not here. Not in this office. She's down the hall in room 312-A. Do you have an appointment? She's only available by appointment."

Genny sensed envy in her tone. Her splattered Jackson Pollock environment was in such contrast to Marlene's precise Norman Rockwell only-available-by-appointment style. Genny thanked her and left the trio to their disarray.

Marlene Jacobs was instead in room 312-B and prepared for Genny's visit. The sophistication of her office was better suited to interviews for corporate employment. Genny might have been a more comfortable interviewee for such a job, more at ease with the business world she serviced with expertise. Marlene greeted her as Genny tapped on her open door, rose from behind her orderly desk and came to Genny with hand extended.

She was wearing spiked heels and a dress that flowed from her shoulders, snatched at her waist with a band of mesh. She was color coordinated to her office décor, slate grey accented in white. A touch of scarlet peeked out from a hip pocket and another from a pillow on the sofa across from her desk. She invited Genny to sit on it and joined her. Fingers of doubt tickled Genny's resolve.

They plunged into the purpose of the appointment. Marlene discussed the broad base the school could provide and the philosophy of the faculty. She had Genny review again her academic background. Genny found herself apologizing for the detour she had taken since her graduation. "I come from a small town – not much mentoring or guidance. I did seem to find a niche in travel. I guess I buried myself there. It should have inspired some poetry."

This docility prompted Marlene to say, "Then I would suggest you enroll at an undergraduate level. We can prepare you for the demands of a Master's curriculum." The syllabus was in her hands. "While you're here we'll get you ready to study the likes of Yeats, Frost, Eliot, some Ginsberg, and Ashbery." Her voice took on a rhythm. "Looking at the Romantics, delving into Milosz, Neruda, Soyinka, and of course Shakespeare. Cubism, Futurism, Imagism."

Genny's head began to reel. If Marlene's intent was to dissuade her, she succeeded in making serious dents in Genny's determination. Credits needed for an advanced degree. Fees per credit.

Genny nodded her appreciation for her time, gathered up the printed material, the applications and course descriptions, and backed out of the office. She was not so sure now if the travel industry wasn't her calling.

At the hallway elevator, Genny's mind wandered, taking her away into a new semester. She envisioned herself working toward an advanced degree, maneuvering her book-laden body down the crowded hall, slipping around young and enthusiastic students beginning their new studies. She was a step ahead of them, picking up again intellectual pursuit. Maybe not so young, but she matched their enthusiasm. In this vision she saw herself finding the classroom with ease. In this treasured building with its history of educating the sons and daughters of the urban masses, she was at last home. She fit. She knew her way around its corridors. The door to her assigned room was open. She saw the cliques of young men and women who had studied together in the past reacquainting themselves with each other, enjoying a new semester with old friends. Not Genny. She was a stranger. Then she noticed, standing behind the lectern was a Jonathan Waterhouse surveying his class. Her mind created this Professor Waterhouse to be one of the more esteemed members of the literature faculty. She knew his work. She owned every small book of poetry he had published, had memorized every phrase and stanza that reflected her life. It was as though he had lived it, felt her joys, collapsed in her anguish, so appropriate were his words to her emotions. She saw the class begin. She saw him surveying the room, matching faces to names, stopping at her name. "Do I know you?" he asked. She raised her eyebrows in response to an unanswerable question and pursed her mouth. "No," she indicated with a turn of her head. She was new to him and to everyone in the room.

The faces in this vision faded into beige blurs. Except his. His face remained in sharp focus in her mind as the rest of the daydream disappeared. And then she lost even that face as the elevator doors opened.

22

Ink runs from the corners of my mouth.
There is no happiness like mine.
I have been eating poetry.

Eating Poetry / Mark Strand

GENEVIEVE – eating poetry

It waylaid her, Marlene Jacobs in her proper downtown office with her papers in organized piles at the corners of her desk, her notices arranged in parallel lines on her bulletin board, her sureness of the importance of what she was doing.

Thirty-six wayward years may be too late for Genny to become anything resembling her. Nor would a Masters' Degree in Literature bring her the freedom the Mountain Man lived. Something less compelling would be adequate. Something more fun and something less expensive.

She studied varied course advertisements that filled Saturday's newspaper, directed at those who missed the fall semester enrollment deadline or shirked at a commitment to study.

The choices focusing on poetry were enticing. The internet brought her into The Graham School and into Newberry

Library, both offering examinations of the craft. Genny pulled up the Truman College and the Poetry Center sites. There for the pickings she could delve into the traditional forms that had overwhelmed her, modern poetry, maybe a better fit, experimental. It was all experimental to Genny.

She discovered more as she dug into what comprises poetry – stanzas, meters, syntax, sound, schemes. She wondered at her place in this arena. In innocence she had started out, a little gathering at the library, a little dabbling with words, a little tumble with a poem, and then with a poet. Her downfall, her little tumble with a poet. That experience opened Genny's mind, her heart along with her mind. Now she considered taking on the inner workings of stanzas, meters, syntax, sound and schemes even though nothing was left in her to expose, nor was anyone in her life left to receive it.

Hooked by Mountain Man's craft, she sought to fill the void he created and committed to a six-week non-credit course downtown. She'd study under a woman with seven books of published poetry under her belt, three awards and a full professorship, with the lyrical name of Shannah. This was a poet beyond her ken, all set to take on Genny for a season, for a fee – Genny and a classful of others at one hundred and seventy dollars a head. Genny plunged. At this price she now had to be good. She would be good; she knew.

Sometimes they sat at a big round table with easy eye access to each other. Sometimes they sat in rows while Ms Seven-Books-and-Three-Awards lectured about the ways of a poet, what goes into the making of a poet, how life interacts with poetry. Her most dramatic presentations centered on how to read poetry. As a bonus, they would learn to create poetry.

Tonight they sat in a circle, lounging on the floor. Shannah had warned the class they would be testing out their experimental skills. Genny was unsure how to dress in an experimental atmosphere. Sensing casualness, this night she chose jeans.

Shannah also wore jeans. Shabby and chic, they might have taken her through college and the years after. A pastel linen urban cowboy shirt topped them off. The pastel of the cloth matched her smoky blonde hair that reached her shoulders in cascades of crinkly curls. Her eyes were soft with heavy eyelids suited to the mood of an after-hours bar. Freckles covered her nose, in support of her name, and a constant high color tinted her cheeks. She smiled often; her enjoyment of poetry was obvious.

Nothing in the room echoed Genny's first experience in an adult poetry class. She searched the circle for any clarity of eye, for a resonant voice, for a lean body. She tried to relive a memory. No one in the room suggested the characteristics of a Mountain Man. None showed interest in her beyond the poems she contributed. No one wrote poetry to touch her nerve endings the way the Mountain Man did that first night in their downtown library.

Yet, without that inspiration, Genny produced well beyond her expectations. She rewrote, reworking the poetry she had been writing under his influence. She realized its original weaknesses but recognized a core of strength. She stripped the poems down to their core and rebuilt them. Now they were better. Now they were louder, deeper. Her new poetry satisfied her.

They satisfied Ms Seven Books, too. She called Genny mid-course and asked if she would bring copies of poems she hadn't yet shared with the class.

"I have stacks, Shannah, but they aren't polished enough for you to look at."

"Maybe you are too critical," Shannah said. "Maybe you don't know enough yet about poetry to know how good or how bad they are. Could I see them and help you judge?"

"Of course. Of course, I'm just a little nervous about them."

"And that's why you are in this class, I hope," Shannah said, "to discover what is poetic and to do more of what pleases the poet in you. To be wise enough to drop the habits that get in the way of flowing ideas."

Genny nodded her head in agreement, thinking how easy she made being a poet sound.

Shannah then opened up another door. "I'm editing an anthology of students' work that I've gathered over the past several years. I'd like to see you in it. The sestina you brought in last week, would you be willing to work on that a little more – remove some of the strain?"

Genny answered an enthusiastic "yes, oh yes" and Shannah answered her with, "Good. Work on it. Bring it to me as soon as you become satisfied. Bring anything else you think might work for me. Anything."

An anthology to include Genny's sestina. The hours she spent on it now being rewarded. She was breathless. Yes, she could do more than send clients to Amsterdam. Maybe her words would find print. She held tight to her heart to keep it from bouncing out of her chest.

23

Nothing in the world is single;
All things by a law divine
In one another's being mingle -
Why not I with thine?

Love's Philosophy / Percy Bysshe Shelley

GENEVIEVE – I with thine

Back in Utah, local plans were gelling without any Chicago assistance. The two sets of parents, long awaiting this project, engaged the country club for a midweek evening in late December, the only available choice, and settled on food and flowers and all the fill-ins to color an event gracious.

David attacked his Winton responsibilities with gusto. He nailed the church for the date the country club offered. With his bride over phone conversations, he filled out affidavits, license applications, name changes, banns of marriage, and newspaper announcements.

Mom and Mom-in-Law probed nearby dress shops then moved on to Salt Lake City in search of complementary outfits, complementary to each other and to the season.

Before she moved out of their apartment, Denise relished her last days as Genny's roommate. In return, Genny took Denise into their shared kitchen to her heterogeneous collection of treasured cookbooks. "Anything you want. It's my final contribution to your nuptial stockpile."

Genny didn't cook but her kitchen thought she did. Maybe someday she would. In the meantime, the books and the pots and pans gathered in anticipation. Genny spread her arms before them. "Whatever you can use is yours. There are some treasures here – I'm sure they'll find a happier home with you."

Denise tried to say "Thank you" but the two syllables caught in her throat. Genny rushed to hug her before they both became teary. "Genny, this collection has been growing for so long," Denise whispered into Genny's shoulder, "how can you part with any of them?"

True, the shelf widened over the past dozen years, since her job allowed her to take up traveling in earnest, bringing back cookbooks as remembrances. To Genny, they were more significant than photographs. Cookbooks spoke of the land with pictures more tantalizing than any photo she could have taken. Much easier to carry home than masks, art canvases, glassworks, packaged foods or any of the other artifacts that tempted tourists.

Her pet client Stan often sent her cookbooks he had picked up in obscure villages, often written in foreign languages. The words weren't important; he knew she didn't cook; the pictures were the essence.

Genny's collection was curious. Many of the books were in mint condition. Many pages contained specialty recipes that no one except those reared in the culture would have had a taste for. Her entertaining rarely ventured into culinary surprises and certainly not when cooking for Brian or for Denise or herself alone.

Standing before the volumes, Denise's eyes widened now with domesticity closing in on her. She took down "Best of the Greek Islands" and Genny expected great spanakopita and baklava from her. She pulled down "English Royal Cooking: Favorite Court Recipes," thinking no doubt of her mountain castle. She spotted Genny's Australian find with its steaks and chops and specialties from the Outback. The pile grew. Genny could not imagine Denise's first meal in Denver. The Australian book would suit her best as she settled in beef territory.

Genny's eyes moved down the line coming to her Celtic cookbook with all dominions covered – Brittany, Cornwall, Ireland, Isle of Man, Scotland, Wales. Before she added it to the rising pile, she hesitated. This was invading her land of dreams.

She had often planned a quiet, just-we-two dinner for Jonathan. The inspiration had always come from this book: appetizers that Emily Dickinson might have eaten, entrees to tempt Blake, something Genny's Swinburne would linger over. The menu never materialized. Her kitchen was not the Mountain Man's room of choice. Genny let the book go, leafing through its pages one last time. The messages had stopped. No need for tasty dishes.

The same reticence overcame her with "Let's Go Dutch," filled with recipes for puddings and sauces and even an unexpected potpourri. The book had come from Stan after one of his many Amsterdam trips. That book she kept; some memories must remain. She couldn't divest herself of every link to love. Maybe she would try again to create the potpourri she once considered sending to Stan as a gift. What stopped her was the required pound of flower petals needed as a base.

Genny brought her mind back to her kitchen library. "Here, take the 'Old Havana Cookbook' someone smuggled off the island for me along with a few cigars. Does it still smell like Cuba?" Denise held the book to her nose, but the rich and robust aroma had dissipated.

Together they flicked through the pages of "Edible France" when Denise, startled, said, "Pictures! We don't have a photographer lined up. Who do we know in Winton who's good?"

"No one," they realized. Genny said, "How about someone here who might want to make the Utah trip with us and capture the glory of this event? Someone who's crazy to create a portfolio?"

Denise had a couple of artsy friends, mostly working in oils but her memory landed on the name of Jeffrey who had been hanging around their kitchen as long as they were neighbors. He lived upstairs. He was a pest, wanting to borrow props and accessories for his shoots, wanting them to stop in at his exhibits, checking their frozen pizza supply. But he had an eye; he did take fanciful photographs.

"Let's ask him," Genny said.

Denise was enthused. "Great idea. He's probably never been out of Illinois and would drool at the chance. If we paid his airfare."

"Dad will," Genny said. "Or maybe Delta will if I can pull a companion pass for him." They were another step closer to the perfect wedding.

24

Yonder see the morning blink:
The sun is up, and up must I,
To wash and dress and eat and drink
And look at things and talk and think
And work, and God knows why.

Yonder See the Morning / A.E. Housman

GENEVIEVE – the morning blink

"I am surprised, Genevieve, to see you applying for this position," said the department head, looking straight into Genny's eyes. She moved around her desk to bring Genny into her office. She was taller than Genny, larger boned and darker skinned. Genny cowered under her gaze, wondering *why surprised?* and waited for an explanation. None came. Instead, the woman returned to her chair indicating that Genny should sit across from her.

She said, "You seem to be more in sympathy with your fellow agents than in agreement with management and its decisions."

Aha! thought Genny, *there it was!* Her team had squabbled some with the higher-ups about who gets the plum hours and days, had complained about the lighting in the rooms where they sat at computers, the chairs they sat on, about breaks. All were minor tiffs with Genny always on the side of the agents. After all, those were her days off being tossed around; the glare bounced off her computer; break time was undependable after long, weary sessions tied to a telephone cord. Of course, she was simpatico with the gang that worked around her, suffering the same discomforts.

"Wouldn't that be an advantage? To understand the stresses of the front line?" She asked the question but it was as though no words came out of her mouth. No response came across the desk. She accepted the silence as the extent of any explanation. It floored her.

First, she didn't realize an "us against them" relationship existed at this company. She thought they were all in the travel game together. Opposing management was the reason for turning down her application? If that was what was happening, it never had entered Genny's mind. Perhaps her corporate mind wasn't well tuned, maybe; perhaps she hadn't mastered all their formats and programs, maybe. But to be in sympathy with the agents, that she was. They backed each other up when they needed to switch schedules. They pulled each other out of jams when their computers acted up. When one agent blanked out, someone else contributed to the inventory of common knowledge. Indeed she was in sympathy.

"We just don't think you are ready for management responsibilities. Could be a little adjustment in mindset is needed here," the department head said while Genny gathered her defense.

"I was ready for every other responsibility you threw at me," she countered. "Remember, I came here as a two-bit rookie from the boonies. But I was as good as the rest of the domestic agents. When you needed me to go international, I picked that up. I can get you from here to Ankara to Bangkok to Auckland to Helsinki and back to Chicago through Vienna, if that's what you want. And in a New York minute." She accelerated her pitch as she added, "with minimum discomfort. And book you for a shower in London."

A smile broke on the face sitting opposite her as she allowed Genny to continue with her case. She eased out of her chair, fingering a file that held the agent's future. She stood over her. Genny was uncomfortable under her stare.

But Genny continued, "When you needed a troubleshooter to clean up local office messes, I was there, too, ruffling as few feathers as possible. I even took on the night shift when there was a hole in that schedule. And those guys, the guys who call in at two in the morning, are the worst. They're either drunk or doped up, or so disorganized they don't know if they are at home or in Honolulu. Doesn't that count for anything? I am versatile, flexible, educated, in control. Aren't those management skills that a travel manager needs?"

"Of course," the frozen face answered, with the assurance of a mind made up. Her lipstick was meticulously applied. Her suit collar lay flat. The lapel pin she wore was of subtle stones, abstractly balanced. Even the pen she held in her manicured fingers glittered with a metallic glow. She was assembled with style, in control of everything about her. Now she was in control of Genny.

"You are well aware of your assets, Genevieve. So are we. You are a valuable employee. We receive more kudos on you than anyone. You are gracious and a first-rate problem solver, a natural as a client contact. We hate to move you from that. Sometime soon we can put you in a management training program perhaps. But not now. Not for this opening. We need proven experience here."

Genny had no backup attack. Her face was bare; she had forgotten the belt to her slacks; her fingernail was broken. The department head had called her in before she had expected a response to her application. She was neither ready to present nor to defend herself.

The interview was over. She said, "I'm sorry, Genny. We'll get you there. Sometime soon."

Yeah, Genny thought. *That's something I can build my life around.* She walked back to her desk disgraced. She felt overdue to move up or over or someplace else.

Deets was on a client call, concentrating on his monitor when she sat down. She was quiet. He knew where she had been. Had the interview gone well he knew a smile would decorate her face and that she would plug into the stream of calls coming in, answering with her cheery "Hi, this is Genevieve, how can I help you?" The afternoon could proceed at its productive pace.

"Not good news?" Deets asked when he finished up the travel arrangements with his caller. "Don't fret – there's more where that came from. Don't you read the 'opps' page?"

"Not too regularly," Genny said. "I thought I was content in this spot. Yet 'supervisor' seemed an obvious next step, and now I've got a 'moving right along' bug."

"Look around, notice who's not here anymore," Deets said. "You think those jobs came looking for them? Nope. They were the hungry masses yearning to breathe free – checking the job openings religiously – and doing something about them. Opportunities page, old buddy."

Searching for the company site on Deets' advice, Genny mumbled to herself, *restless, restless, restless. I need to accomplish something big. And fast.*

Deets's "Good afternoon. This is Demetrios. How can I help you?" ended any job counseling coming from across the desk. A clicking in Genny's ear piece warned her of her own call coming through. No time for commiseration. No time for opportunities. Time to recalibrate. Recalibration tired her so. She mustered up a cheeriness and answered, "Hi, this is Genevieve …"

A dim lamp lit Genny's living room sofa. She had trouble focusing on the print in the book that rested on her knees. She had read the same stanzas over and over with not a line registering. None of these bunches of meaningless words said anything to her. Yesterday she would have understood their message. Tomorrow they could penetrate. Tonight though was another night alone, remembering other times, alone.

She was thirty-seven and she was alone and stuck. She did the same thing today that she did yesterday, the day before, the week before, that she did the month before that. The same thing: "Hi, this is Genevieve …" She would repeat "Hi, this in Genevieve" again tomorrow. In the background of her ennui, a bright spot: she had Shannah and her anthology and the encouragement they offered. It was a buoy taking her to an island of satisfaction while she turned away from the mainland of silent security.

The silence and its pain fed her poetic urges. Balancing them was the flurry of wedding activity with Denise living up in an atmosphere where Genny only visited. Denise's comings and goings to and from Utah since David put the diamond on her finger left Genny behind, tending to her Chicago duties. Her fingers grew numb addressing wedding invitations with a strained and stylized calligraphy demanding a precision she should have been adopting in her life.

Emails continued to clutter her PC bringing her nothing she wanted to read. Then, after weeks of silence, the conversation began again. Three weeks of waiting produced this:

From: jonwat
To: gennydu
Date: Wed, 27 Oct 2004 08:15:16
Subject: talk

> *I am writing. About you. I find you on my mind and then on paper. What we talk about. What you say. What you don't say. You inspire me. I remember a thousand kisses. The lemon essence of your skin. Small doses of your voice. We talk in small doses. We lived in small doses. I can see no conclusion. I try to write conclusions and I can't.*
>
> *Will you meet me today? Are you home today?*

Today. Wednesday. Genny thought of his yesterdays and Mondays and Sundays and who filled them and whose snatches of talk and scent and life took up his yesterdays and tomorrows. Genny wanted those days too, all of them.

No, Wednesday again became Genny-day. Mail poems to arrive on Wednesday. Have fun on Wednesday. "Wednesday's child is full of – woe" was the childhood verse that warned against any salvation. She would not be where he wanted her to be on Wednesdays. She would wonder though, and the wonder would turn to poetry, her most dependable outlet for her confusion. *Wednesday's child is full of woe.* Wednesday's child …

He comes holding out to me his heart / Fingerprints of another embedded in its flesh / Wednesday again, full of woe, is mine / Flanked by time full of her…

189

Genny settled into her aloneness, coming closer to the truth, aware of her hollowness, accepting it. Surrounded by the quiet comforts of her room, within the protection of her somber walls, her words made more sense. They became important to her healing. As her mind composed, she transferred them to her computer screen. Let loose, they flowed, flying beyond her intentions. They stabbed and they pounded at the pain, pulverizing it. They were her mighty words, elegant, her new hope.

A weekend trip to Winton, catching up with Denise, removed Genny from her job disappointments, her Mountain Man enigmas. She was again in her sister's bridal world, full of flurry and joy. The diversion was invaded when the two returned to Chicago together.

From: jonwat
To: gennydu
Date: Mon, 01 Nov 2004 06:07:57
Subject: Yellow morning

> *Grey as it is around me, I wonder if your bedroom is glowing with your morning light. I wonder if I will this morning run into you on your beach. Around 8? That would be too serendipitous. No, that will not happen. You seem to be gone from me.*

Jonathan was right. "That will not happen" because Genny remembered the pain. "*Grey as it is ..., glowing with your morning light.*" *What sublime words*, Genny thought. She wondered if she could use them somewhere. She ignored the email and readied herself for a day like any other day.

From: jonwat
To: gennydu
Date: Mon, 01 Nov 2004 14:59:41
Subject: grey

Your beach was wild and windy. Desolate. Empty. And you were not there. When I stared up at your windows I saw no echoing motion. The time of moonlit rooms felt distant. I think this period of grey can pass, soon dispelled by a not distant bright day.

From: gennydu
To: jonwat
Date: Tues, 02 Nov 2004 05:46:01
Subject: Re: grey

I am my beach, not to be shared. Its wildness is mine. Its windiness is all mine – don't impose on it. And I am long gone. Blown to new places.

From: jonwat
To: gennydu
Date: Tues, 02 Nov 2004 11:23:14
Subject: Re: grey

So you are alive. Are you well? Will you tell me why you have been so distant? Distance disturbs me.

Distant? Genny wondered. He disappeared from her screen for weeks. She searched for his name daily, twice daily, hourly as the time dragged by. He turned up celebrating with poets in a state with maybe two airports, with planes that never come to Chicago. He left her alone, watching a disappearing future where words were their bond, their base, the blood that ran through their veins. Where words would be their purpose.

He asked if she were well.

From: gennydu
To: jonwat
Date: Wed, 03 Nov 2004 05:40:59
Subject: Re: grey

>*Not distant – removed. I feel the need to protect myself from the pain you cause by your absence. Your abrupt and unexplained absence. There may be better ways to do this but my way has to be – removal. That week of pain while you went east forced me to think you through and the expectations you fostered. I need to be away from them, from you. And now, I, too, am leaving town.*

United Air was rewarding Genny for work well done. Well done with pain, she wanted to enjoy her world again. She wanted to write out of joy, not despondency. She wanted to create images of radiance and beauty. She wanted to be free.

From: jonwat
To: gennydu
Date: Wed. 03 Nov 2004 08:16:23
Subject: Re: grey

That pointedly explains your silence. It does
nothing for my need to see you. Have a good trip.
May you be happy; may you be well.

From: jonwat
To: gennydu
Date: Fri. 05 Nov 2004 11:30:52
Subject: Re: grey

Read your email again and I realize what I have
done to you. You, who I admire so. Who I was so
immediately drawn to at the Lavinski sessions — so
direct, so individual, so sensitive with all the traits of
the poet I strive to be. I didn't mean to be a potential
for pain for you. I just hoped for your company. That
we could find fun together. Is that possible anymore?
That we can find that fun again? Could we meet
when you return for an unpretentious glass of wine
and maybe determine what room is left for friendship?

Fun and friendship — what jolly words on her screen.
How light and frivolous her life could be if she could start
again in the library and say "How do you do, my name is
Genny, let's be friends."

At dinner that evening Denise sensed a return of strained
silence. The email Genny read as soon as she returned home
late Sunday afternoon froze her spirit. She hadn't wanted a
friend. Not anyone who condemned her to pain with a single
phrase — "what I couldn't tell you …" She hadn't wanted a
friend whose absence reduced her to meaninglessness. She had
enough friends. Friends didn't punish her.

Denise broke into the constraint and Genny showed her the latest emails. She had been in and out of so many, too many moods this past month while Denise remained in the constant bliss of wedding plans. These moods confused Denise; Jonathan confused Genny; his emails confused both of them. They were unlike any correspondence that moved between Denise and David.

"I wish I could be you and he could be David," Genny said, words she couldn't imagine herself ever saying. "You seem to know where to put all the pieces. Everything fits so well. It's like I picked up the leftovers from a jigsaw puzzle factory. Nothing belongs to anything else. Brian doesn't belong. Jonathan doesn't fall into place. I don't fit in at the office anymore. Even here in my own home, I am on the outside looking in."

Denise's face clouded. Genny was stamping out her brightness like campfire embers. She was bringing her into the greyness of her own life. But they were sisters and Denise tiptoed into the gloom.

"Genny," she said without following up with additional comment, with only concerned love. She didn't have any helpful words. She knew loneliness when she was in Chicago without her David. She knew frustration when he was reluctant to move in the direction she always hoped he would. She knew uneasiness when their time together was strained. She had been displeased and disgusted and distressed. Nevertheless, she was always guided by hope, a hope now materializing in her December wedding. She had confidence in her future.

Genny felt she had no future.

"I wish he were a better man for you," Denise said. "You seem to be so energized when he is around. Don't give up that energy."

"When he is around." Genny laughed out loud at those words. "He is around so sparingly. Late at night over email. Wednesday mornings when I am free. Where is he on weekends? Where is he when I want to show him off at evening events that we can enjoy together? With his muse," she spat out the name, "Karen, no doubt." Karen, a nymph she could not touch. Her presence surrounded them without sound or form. Seldom mentioned and then dismissed without a ripple of interest.

"I am not going to be his friend," she said to Denise. "He wants me to be his friend, his kissable, huggable, make-love-able friend. And that's it. A friend, and nothing more, I guess. Not a damned thing more."

"You don't know that," Denise said. "You can't be certain that something might just pop and wham, someone's in love with you. You never know. Good things happen in time. Or your own David will come along and Jon will have prepared the way for him."

Denise, she was the goddess of time and fortune. The good thing happened to her years ago and she nurtured it into this wedding date.

Genny didn't have that kind of time. "I don't have that kind of patience," she said. "I see what I love and it belongs to someone else. She's got a better grip on it. I have nothing except his wish for fuckin' friendship – kissable, huggable, fuckable friendship. I don't want it." Genny had lost control. Denise shrank away from the fury.

"Can't you make rules?" she asked, attempting to tone down the conversation.

"What kind of rules? That I will write and he will read? No more, no less? Would that be painless? That the friendship ends with the last stanza? If I could just convince myself that poetry is our only link, sure, I could try again with that kind of friendship. I could try."

Genny then made a promise, only to keep from further darkening Denise's happiness. Painless friendship with all its superficiality. A possibility. She threw down all her shadows, letting them scatter in the happiness that surrounded Denise that eventually even Genny would not long resist. With new-found acceptance, she was better prepared to receive his next peace offering.

From: jonwat
To: gennydu
Date: Wed, 10 Nov 2004 07:32:35
Subject: Re: grey

Do we ever share again a glass of wine? Are you a Humanities Festival devotee? It's happening this week. I am free through the weekend and going to a whole slew of things solo, starting at Northwestern's Thorne Auditorium at noon today. Will I bump into you?

The autumn humanities festival, was she a devotee? Not yet. Its gamut of intellectualism was intimidating, a Chicago gem beyond her experience. It was another discovery in the culture of Chicago she was unearthing, thanks to Shannah. Early that evening her teacher presided over a poetry presentation with Genny reading her Einstein "slipping through time" piece.

From: gennydu
To: jonwat
Date: Wed, 10 Nov 2004 22:14:12
Subject: Re: grey

I doubt it. I did some poetry readings for Shannah's program on the other side of town tonite. Haven't paid much attention to what's on the rest of the docket. Nothing looks tempting.

From: jonwat
To: gennydu
Date: Wed, 10 Nov 2004 23:07:52
Subject: Re: grey

Tempting? You want to be tempted? How's this?
Saturday
10AM - at the Chicago Historical Society - 1789 REVOLUTION
2PM - at the Cultural Center – HIP HOP
3:30PM - Chicago Historical Society - 1848 REVOLUTION
Sunday
12:30 - CHS - 1968 REVOLUTION
2:30 – ART AND MUSIC (I have a ticket for you)
Consider the possibilities. Join me. Please.

Possibilities were all around her: the optimism that Denise had left behind again with her happy weekend comings and goings. A Mountain Man weekend with another new beginning. Genny with the will to end her desperation – with new rules?

She sent the email back into her computer and tried to weigh the consequences. She asked, *this time would be different? What could make it so? Was he ready to comprehend her need for him? Was she ready to expose it? Would that pressure send him fast back to Karen who, in her security, probably had no needs? What was the "or" in this "either/or" dilemma? A future without Jon? A life without poetry?* No, not that, never that.

She didn't answer any of these questions but would join him Saturday at ten as instructed. Without any forewarning, she would appear. No email would prepare him but he was not surprised. Her decision to go had been made after two days of resisting the invitation, of intending to dismiss its existence. He expected her appearance.

Genny awakened early. She made pancakes. She organized her closet. Still early, in an impulsive move, she dressed and walked out into a bright crisp morning.

The reunion was faltering. He had put on a little weight; his polo shirt was snug. Genny had lost a couple of pounds and inches of hair. Her skirt hung but her hair didn't. He ran his fingers through what was left and sighed.

"This is good," he said. "It's good to have you with me again."

She wanted to turn and flee from the lecture hall. The scars erupted. She wasn't as strong as when she boarded the bus that brought her.

His voice was soothing, quieting her anxiety. "I have missed you."

He stepped back and studied her. "You have so pointedly avoided me." He took her hand, hesitated, and said, "I couldn't let our separation stand without an effort to put a stop to it." This was not an apology, nor an explanation, nor a plea. It was Jonathan moving back, claiming his territory.

Genny should have brought up his disruptive disappearances, but she couldn't and didn't. She allowed him to lead himself back to her.

They sat together through the revolutions, through the music of today and yesterday. Through a glass of wine, and another. His freedom extended into the night and through the day following. Genny gave in to it. No new rules. No rules at all. She was at his side in the auditoriums, in and out of the auditoriums, walking along the breezy streets of Chicago his arm around her waist, on and off the streets. They shared lunches and dinners, her bed. Inevitably, intimately, under her comforter, his arm cradled her head. Breakfast.

He asked for more poetry. She created lines and stanzas for him. She loved him; he made love to her. She noticed the difference but put out of mind his week away with his poets, with his muses, the loneliness, the fear, Karen. She forgot how he shielded himself behind a computer screen.

This weekend he was at her side. This weekend was different. It was full, beyond fun. The sensation of plenty possessed her again. Inspiration flowed again – poems about spirits in revolt, about the expression of youth, about color. Ideas were rampant throughout the weekend – uprisings in politics and music and his thoughts on them, inspiring her again.

His infusion, her addiction, the emerging poetry, how to maintain the electricity?

25

A poet is someone
who can pour light into a cup,
then raise it to nourish your beautiful,
parched, holy mouth.

A Poet / Hafiz of Shiraz

GENEVIEVE – parched, holy mouth

The agency was quiet. The afternoon air was still, filled with the oily odor of microwaved popcorn. Genny's compatriots sat motionless, their eyes intent on paperback novels in their laps, florescent lights washing their disengaged faces.

The intervals between client calls gave her time to pull up her personal email again and again. The usual political pleas, ads, and cultural announcements kept popping up. She deleted them as they appeared. She was in no mood to write her Congressman, lose tummy fat or to pass messages on to friends. However, she ran through a few laughable jokes, a few salient quotes and a cheery note from her father who seemed to be surviving Denise's whirlwind wedding preparations, writing checks on demand.

No afterthoughts from the Mountain.

Shannah's classes had ended. Genny's confidence in her poems waned without professional support. She pulled out her notebook where the weekend's raw poetry lay with revisions and edits scribbled over all available whitespace.

No, they're good now, she persuaded herself. *When he reads how they've turned out he'll say they're good, or he'll tell me again how to make them good, or even great. Or maybe they're great now. Maybe they're not.* She copied them again on clean sheets of paper, changing a word, repositioning a phrase.

She slipped a page over to Deets. "What do you think, my fine philo?" Genny was nervous. Deets was aware how immersed she was in poetry and, not knowing how else to react, found it amusing at this point. He had never been around poets. His response to Genny's seriousness was strained. They were both in uncharted territory: Genny sharing and Deets evaluating.

Deets focused on the sheet. She watched as he turned somber. Would this be Jon's reaction to these latest renditions?

A call came into Deets's line. He answered with an apologetic glance at Genny and booked the air and hotel requested with efficiency. As soon as the particulars of the trip were secure, he turned back to Genny's poem and concentrated on the words again.

"Wow," he said as he came up a third time. "You sure got that guy's gig. What'd he do that made you write that?" Deets was hooked.

"If I can get that out of you, Deets, I'm golden. I'm a comer. I'm a work in progress." Deets's reaction bolstered Genny but so far her real poet hadn't shared any next-day considerations. A hasty note saved a disappointing day.

From: jonwat
To: gennydu
Date: Tue, 16 Nov 2004 13:19:03
Subject: tomorrow

Did we make plans for tomorrow? Can we? I need to mingle the musky air of the country with the ambrosial scent of your skin.

From: gennydu
To: jonwat
Date: Tue, 16 Nov 2004 13:45:31
Subject: Re: tomorrow

Can they include a new batch of poems if I bring a haystack and a bottle of cologne?

From: jonwat
To: gennydu
Date: Tue, 16 Nov 2004 13:49:53
Subject: Re: tomorrow

We haven't finished with your old batch. Slow down.

From: gennydu
To: jonwat
Date: Tue, 16 Nov 2004 14:02:39
Subject: Re: tomorrow

*I think the old batch is cooked. I reworked them. You
helped, remember? I'm pretty pleased. Ready to move on.*

From: jonwat
To: gennydu
Date: Tue, 16 Nov 2004 16:19:21
Subject: Re: tomorrow

*I'm thinking maybe a ride to the Arboretum, just
we two – but you can bring your progeny if you want
– we'll dissect them on the road. What kind of music
for inspirational background?*

From: gennydu
To: jonwat
Date: Tue, 16 Nov 2004 16:32:32
Subject: Re: tomorrow

*Jazz – these are flying high pieces. I am so happy
and pleased and glad to be with you. I love what you
do to my stuff – you give me structure, new words and
thoughts, rhythms.*

Genny added another "I love what you do. I love ... " She
stopped at the repeated "I love." She couldn't write "you" in
an out-loud love list. It was an emotion they didn't share. He
was kind to her, affectionate, attentive but on a schedule to suit
him. Genny tried to bring him to a place of love, but when she
stepped through the door and turned, no one followed. She
stood alone. She was afraid to ask why.

If not in love, they stood together in the creation of poetry. Such a solid team – Genny leaped off mountaintops; he reassembled what landed in the valley. After she exhausted her original creative passion she was freer to accept help putting sense into the lines.

In the morning Genny waited for him in her building lobby with a packet of four poems in her pocket, four good poems about to become better. Her eagerness for the sight and touch of him matched her anticipation of the blossoming of her creations.

He pulled up on time, leading her to believe he welcomed the day which began with a prim curbside kiss. Genny expected better kisses to follow.

"How many today?" he asked.

"How many what – kisses? Many, many."

"That's good to know but I was asking about poems."

"Oh. Four," Genny said. "One about the miles to Utah and one of last night's moon. Did you see it? A sliver. Like a closing parenthesis enfolding clouds."

She stopped herself from continuing the conversation, halted by his lack of enthusiasm. He may have viewed the dim light as it danced around the clouds, but with whom? She could ask him. They would be in the car together for an hour with no escaping the question or Genny. There would be no answer so she continued, "one about the day my father married my mother..."

"Where did that come from?" he said. "That must be a bad day in your life, your father marrying someone who's not you."

Jon had often joshed Genny about what he called her incestuous passion for her father. To him – incestuous passion; to her - high regard, a sentiment unknown to Jon since his childhood tales related rather distracted parents who let him grow up without anything akin to emotional support.

"No," she said, "it was a very merry day. Even without me. It was merry in spite of the fact that he was off to do battle in a war that made no sense. I made it a very idyllic occasion. I want it to be sentimental." She paused to remind him of the coming marriage. "I'd like to read it at Denise's wedding."

"Well, let's hear it then. What's the last about?"

"I'm not sure I'm ready to expose it to your discriminating ear. It's about a small child discovering an imaginary friend."

"You?" he asked.

"Maybe. I'm not sure." Genny was sure. She was the child and the imaginary friend was the Mountain Man. He disappeared in her poem as all imaginary friends do when children grow older and wiser, when reality smacks them in the face.

"Shoot," he said, cruising down the expressway at seventy-five miles an hour, Lionel Hampton's vibes providing the backdrop. Genny began with her parents' merry wedding.

His hand was beating out the Hampton beat against the steering wheel. The pounding overrode the deliberate meters she had constructed into the poem. She considered stopping the recitation but wondered if her silence would be noticed, as noticeable as his many silences. Genny didn't have the courage to experiment. She read on, the merry poetic words now reduced to background sound.

Tomorrow would be Thursday. Perhaps he listened with more intent to words whispered to him on Thursdays.

Holidays broke the rhythms of life. Throughout the seasons, families prettied up their houses in celebration. They rang bells. They polished their silver and donned their party clothes. Roses and chocolates filled their spaces with sweetness.

They wore the green. They hid colored eggs. They breathed the smoke of barbecue grills and waved flags. They came bearing gifts. They blew out candles. Always they gathered their families together.

Now, the Thanksgiving weekend was upon the Dupont family, time for all to give thanks. Genny would try.

She and Denise boarded another Delta 737 for a holiday trip west that would disrupt the rhythm of Denise's propulsive plans for her marriage day and Genny's spiraling descent into unrequited love. The long weekend would be punctuated with reminders of their blessings.

Blessings. A week passed without any cyber comments about poetry or fun or freedom, about the day spent in nature where everything was verdant and alive except Genny and Jon. She had learned to hang tight during these times of dead space. But, like the center of a tornado, they sucked the air out of her. She reminded herself to refill her lungs.

"Did you bring your notebooks with you?" Denise asked, noting the minimal luggage Genny toted as she stuffed a carry-on into the overhead bin.

"Nope, no need, I'm taking a word-break." Genny considered packing some books and blank-sheeted journals. The week had been so empty of inspiration she was more inclined to extend her languor into Utah. No muses whispered in her brain. No words of encouragement came through her computer. She left them behind.

Even the weather was placid. Autumn was ending along with her expectations of his further involvement in her poetry, or her. Winter was beginning. *So get on with the cold,* Genny urged. *Be done with it. With patience, another spring would follow.* On the plane, Denise read bridal magazines. They provided enough fluff to keep the sisters in conversation throughout the flight. Denise was pleased with the plans in place. The staff they had collected was functioning at high peak: David, the two sets of in-laws, Jeffery, their eager photographer, and all party planners they had enlisted. Much in the magazines discussed the stresses of weddings. "We've avoided all that. Good for us." Genny could entertain only one stress at a time.

Their parents were both at the airport to greet the young women. Genny's mother thought she appeared wan. "Genevieve, what are you eating? Any vegetables or grains in your diet? Or are you living off coffee and yogurt again?"

"Mother, that was a high school craze, twenty years ago. I think I have more nutritional sense now."

She marveled over Denise's hearty presence, "I see *you* haven't been bitten by the skinny bug."

Their father smiled his encompassing smile that told Genny that she was healthy enough for him and every bit of Denise was just as beautiful as befits a bride.

Once settled into their Utah home Denise and Genny used their time meeting the demands of the impending feast. Some last minute shopping guaranteed the pantry had all the ingredients needed to prepare the family classics. The table was bountiful and festive. Genny had hustled up some juniper branches with their dusty bittersweet berries to dress the napkins at each place. At David's place she put a little paper mache groom found at the dollar store.

Since the departure of their offspring, these parents had gathered new friends to fill in for their wandering daughters. The new cast included a widowed woman Genny knew only by sight. She wouldn't have recognized her now for all the weight the woman had added to her girth. An empty-nested couple, new in the neighborhood, made its first appearance at the holiday table. The pair reveled in their emancipation, adding vigor to the room. These were people whose lives were in flux, who found stability in the easy pace of the Dupont home. They etched a new facet to the Thanksgiving traditions.

Beyond that, this expansion of family alliances gave Genny a wider and softer cushion for her tottering life's collapse, if it did or when it did.

The evening darkness outside slithered into the home as the dining ended. The guests joined the family in the living room to let the meal settle. A fire crackled in the fireplace, filling the room with the warm, rustic smells of earth.

Genny and her father took on the kitchen chores. He was being kind to her mother, rewarding her for the successful dinner. Genny was restless, unable to commit herself to the quiet around the fire. Together they tackled the kitchen chaos: the stacks of dishes, the hordes of leftovers, the glassware, silverware, the pots and pans. Lingering were the scents of cinnamon and clove from the remains of the pie, sitting, waiting for late-night snacking. The pot of spiced apple cider with its anise and citrus overtones simmered on the stove. The oven still emitted the buttery fumes of the turkey. Genny could have reingested the whole meal just by inhaling.

"Dad, how is Reggie doing?" Genny brought up the name of her former travel agency boss. The question ended a pause in their conversation, growing stilted because of her unwillingness to touch on her disappointments.

"The travel business is not the easy money it used to be," he said. "But Reggie knows how to charm recluses onto cruise ships. And we got a lot of those types around these parts."

"Oh god, remember the promotion parties he'd have, enlisting the most uncanny people into those armies shuffling aboard those boats? Or I should say navies. Then, remember the time he sent me on one of those cruises as a reward for bringing in the most sales? That ship – the average age was seventy-seven, an AARP recruiting vessel if ever there was one."

"As I recall," he said in his usual optimistic way, "you found a sun bum half that age on St. Thomas to counterbalance the geriatrics. We worried a little about your steady head over that one." He chuckled. "Thought we might lose you to a better climate. For my part," he said, "I was kind of pulling for you, thinking how nice it would be to go visit you when the temperatures dip here."

"My steady head," Genny said. "Where did that get me?"

"It seems to have gotten you a pleasant existence in Chicago – with a job, and a Brian, and a view of the lake that you keep raving about," he said.

Genny didn't want her dad to suspect the job was at an impasse. That Brian was passé. Only the lake sustained her. "My pleasant Chicago existence – I am wondering if I could replace it with a pleasant little life here," Genny said.

Her father jumped at that thought, a little too fast for Genny's comfort. He started itemizing all the new modern condos in downtown Winton to consider, and the new restaurants to sample, the local theatre developing in the neighborhoods, and the adventuresome adult education classes being offered by the high school.

"They are getting beyond "Computers for the Confused," he said in a final effort to bring her home.

"I'm a beer and pizza girl, Dad. I don't need all that. I don't take full advantage of what Chicago has to offer. Except for the classes. And my beach, I do need my beach." She wanted to add she needed her poet to walk her beach with her but she held back. Instead, she said, "Maybe I will stop by to see Reggie and open up some options. Denise's moving back here has unsettled me."

"That would please me," he said, "and a couple dozen bachelor doctors, lawyers, and chiefs that I know. They keep asking about you."

"Who? Name one."

26

Unborn babies are not aware that
their fathers work overtime through the night, that
their mothers rise pregnant from sagging mattresses
to bring their husbands home, feed them
and send them off to work again.

Beyond the Womb / Jonathan Waterhouse

JONATHAN – through the night

"Oh lordy, lordy, Jon, look at the time," Karen said. She slipped out of bed and shook off her dreaminess. Behind in her morning schedule, she readied herself for work, blaming Jonathan for the early morning seduction that had ended with that outcry.

Jon remained wrapped in comfortable blankets and said, "It's Tuesday, how heavy can traffic be on a Tuesday? You'll be at your office in no time."

As she scurried into the bathroom he called after her, "Aren't you glad you have someone to take your mind off your morning drudgeries?"

"No, I'm glad I have someone to muddle up my morning," she said. More than that, his bedside encouragement reestablished her feelings of security in her career and her oneness with him.

Soon she was gone in a rush of tweed, bobbing hair, and clicking heels out the door, her footsteps sounding out the seconds that brought him solitude.

Lingering in the fog of Karen's leftover love, a ring of the telephone pulled him into his undemanding day. He squirmed at the displayed name. Now he was tired, tired of others imposing on his comfort, tired of needing others to add to his down-filled status quo, tired of the restlessness the need begot.

"Hello Jonathan, this is Genny," she said in response to his foggy greeting.

"I know. My phone announces you."

An embarrassing quiet followed, fed by the dozen days that had passed since she had shared her poetry with him during the long, sometimes silent ride to the Arboretum with his mind on poetry he wasn't writing, on her retreat into a holiday gathering, and on the discomfort of her sharing the front seat of his car. He stumbled into the conversation, "How was your Thanksgiving?" he asked.

"Reserved," Genny said, "just like everything else in my Utah. I just got back yesterday and couldn't even unpack I felt so out of place here without Denise. That's why I'm calling you."

He shifted the phone and swung his legs out of the bed knowing she was waiting for some explanation of his inattention. Nothing. He stood, walked to the window as he attempted to make some feeble comment about Utah or Denise or the sun attempting to brighten the day. Any comment other than about them.

"On the plane back to Chicago," she said, breaking into the impasse, "I started writing some poems about the people I'd just left, about Denise and David, even about the man next door, and some old friends. Anyone who came to mind figured in a poem. They just burst out of me all the way home. I sent them to you. Seven of them. They're rough. I want you to read them and tell me what you think. I still don't know how to judge my stuff. They're not Shakespeare or Angelou but I like the way they sound. Seven new poems. I'm so excited. When you get them, please tell me what you think."

She stopped talking, out of breath, out of anything more to say without an encouraging response.

"I will, I will. Seven, huh?" was the only support he provided, grateful Karen had left for work even though a reverberation of her presence remained, grateful that no one was listening to question his meager end of the conversation. "I'll go pull them as soon as I hang up."

With that extracted promise, Genny ended the call with a hasty, "Gotta get to work."

He placed the phone back in its cradle and held it there, settling the urgency that seemed to emanate from the plastic. *How cold. Was that as cold as it felt?* He was not adept with early morning social disruptions. *I've got to be ready for her cropping up in the wrong places.*

Seven poems, huh? his mind echoed as he headed toward the bathroom and then to the coffee pot where Karen's morning brew was still hot, where the kitchen table was set with a plate patterned with the colors of fall, a laundered napkin, silverware, each piece matching the other, and a crystal glass filled with orange juice holding down a message of fealty. Her usual slip of paper – this one with only X's and O's in red marker – was an echo of the morning's love.

Later, showered and dressed, he sat at his computer and logged into his email expecting what waited on his screen: gennydu, gennydu, gennydu, gennydu, gennydu, gennydu, gennydu.

Absent was a message from "Prairie Poets," the publication still sitting on his last submission. This daily ritual, searching for any word of praise, any promise of consideration giving him the exposure he needed to impress Lavinski's agent, was becoming more urgent now. Nothing. He might have found in his stable of poetry others to work over but instead brought up Genny's new poems as inspiration.

With her first entry, he found neither introduction nor explanation preceding a poem standing on the screen unadorned, untitled. It consisted of three stanzas of three lines each, nine lines of elegance, shocking him with their simplicity and effectiveness. He was awestruck as he pulled up the next "gennydu" to find another, unintroduced and unexplained, neither needed, this one longer and stronger with a note of bitterness shot through it.

He read through the seven, finding each one different in tone and message and style, finding her a lion as promised, pouncing on prey, devouring emotions to satisfy a hunger. He returned to the first, copied it to the file labeled 918 and printed it out, returning to each, copying each, printing each out. He deleted the emails, turned off the computer and sat reading the pages the printer had spewed. Their effect was puzzling. *What now, what's in store for her? Where am I in her?*

He brought the sheets back to the kitchen and poured himself another cup of coffee. This would be his morning's diversion, to analyze the effects of the words she had chosen, to ferret out weaknesses and make her poems stronger, if that were possible.

Each time he read the poems through, their powerful consistency became more striking and the flaws minor and correctable. He tried to rearrange the images, to rewrite the words to reflect his voice, but they resisted change. To manipulate the flow was to destroy the power; Genny had taken charge of her own mind and her own direction. The agility he found in her work was breeding an envy expressed in the questions: *Why is it so easy for her? Why not me?*

The phone rang again with an urgency that roiled the mood. He relaxed when he noticed the call was from Karen, picked up the instrument and cooed "Hi, sweets" into the mouthpiece. He played his dutiful role to perfection in spite of the distraction of Genny's work.

Karen's voice was not so controlled. It sounded high pitched and tense. This alerted him that a savory soup should be simmering on the stove when she arrived home.

"Hey Jon, it's me."

"Yes? What's wrong? You sound breathless."

"It's mom again. She's whining at me. Something is bothering her again. This time it's her liver she thinks, or some other organ that she can't identify. I've got to drive up there."

"Right now?" Jon asked, realizing the absurdity of his question and of his mother-in-law's request. The woman kept Karen on call twenty-four/seven, a watch he avoided by ignoring her bleatings, unfeeling.

"Right now, as soon as I can get away. I'll finish out the day here. I promised her I'd get on the road first thing tomorrow morning. Can you handle the rest of the week? Do we have enough food?" she asked.

He laughed at her concern since he was now the keeper of the house with time to spare and the classic homebody itch for escape, but not to Wisconsin. He had victuals aplenty.

"Whatever I need to eat I will find, somewhere, I am sure. How about you, do you need anything for the trip? I'll gas up the car this afternoon. You didn't drive to work this morning, did you?" He had no memory now of her leaving, so much had filled the time between her departure and the phone call.

"I took the bus. That would be wonderful. Do you have some twenties handy? Otherwise, I'm okay. No imperatives through the week that I can think of. I'll try to be back by the weekend," Karen said. "Four days of sympathy should be enough to hold her for a while."

"A daughter's gotta do what a daughter's gotta do," was his insipid reply, feeling grateful she wasn't asking him to chauffeur her into Wisconsin but rather rushing off to clear away her workload.

A sickly mother and a dutiful daughter and an unscheduled week ahead of him put a smile on his face.

From: jonwat
To: gennydu
Date: Mon, 29 Nov 2004 11:04:05
Subject: time on my hands

The poems arrived. Enviable batch. Got anything going this week? The pressures of my non-productive inactivity are closing in on me. Help me dust off my brain. Any ideas?

From: gennydu
To: jonwat
Date: Mon, 29 Nov 2004 11:57:27
Subject: Re: time on my hands

Jealous of my productivity? Or just clairvoyant?

Eerie. I just won a twosome trip to Paris, ala Air France, promoting their new US connecting flights. Trouble is – gotta leave during the week and gotta come back through Cincinnati. Chris pulled my name out of the blue. Not really out of the blue – out of a very chic blue and red Air France carry-on – which I also won.

Latch on to this offer before friends come crawling out of the woodwork to join me. Want to get in line? Everyone else does. Genny

From: jonwat
Date: Mon, 29 Nov 2004 11:59:16
Subject: Re: time on my hands

Nothing wrong with Cincinnati that Paris won't fix. Didn't I always want to be your friend? Now hear this: I AM YOUR BEST FRIEND with the right to accompany you to Paris. Isn't that what friends do? Matter of fact, I am already packed. Years ago I packed my bags for Paris, just waiting for you to ask.

Jon stretched reality with his profession of "best friend" but the offer opened the possibility and promised rewards.

From: gennydu
To: jonwat
Date: Mon, 29 Nov 2004 12:21:21
Subject: Re: time on my hands

*I guess that is a yes. I will book us for Wednesday,
returning Sunday. Quick trips are my specialty. I can
steal a couple days from this place. It's business, you
know. A couple of days is time enough. Too many
hours in Paris tend to bubble up the brain, not good
for poetic productivity. Or is it the absinthe?*

Yes, a definite yes, to the inspiration the city of lights would bring him. He remembered the advice of Lenard Lavinski: take a trip, plunge into romance. What other than a "yes" to cement an alliance with the woman who brought words of love to life, who asked for nothing except they blend their thoughts into word symphonies. What magic she performed whether on the beach or in his arms in her candlelit bedroom or laying down explosive words on paper or leading him aboard an airbus to France. He could not envision the breadth of it as he contemplated the overnight journey to France, and the days and nights on foreign turf with her.

Through the afternoon their emails carried babble back and forth. "Have you been to Paris?" Jon asked and she responded, "Of course, again and again. I'm an international agent for god's sake if I didn't go to Paris where would I go?"

"Where will we stay," he asked. Her advice was to leave that up to her since she would check out what freebies she could snag. The weather worried him but he planned his wardrobe knowing that autumn in Paris would not be the same as April, only better.

Then soon enough, before his questions began to rattle her, she created the itinerary putting them on a plane out of O'Hare at five-thirty Wednesday evening, arriving at de Gaulle the next morning.

"Bring books," she said, "coach flight is tedious. No business class on this deal." Jon would bring Albert Camus, adding to the absurdity of his traveling to Paris with Genevieve Dupont and the three nights, mornings, and afternoons they would have together, together in Paris, every moment promising to be idyllic. He would bring Francoise Sagan for Genny to set a model for behavior.

"Who do you want to be on this trip?" he asked.

She confessed she wanted to be exactly who she was but would dig back into her college literature classes. She lit on Gertrude Stein, "And you?"

"I'll take F. Scott Fitzgerald and hang with Hemingway."

In a more practical exchange, she asked if Jon could pick her up in a taxi. "Deets had offered to drive us but he's working Wednesday. He's free Sunday though, free to meet the plane. See, I give you Paris *and* an introduction to Deets. A double treat you don't deserve."

As a surprise to her, knowing she was so at home in Paris, Jon planned a path following the literary greats taking them to the cafés, the book haunts, the parks, the cathedrals, and the restaurants that had found their way into the literature of the age. The effort took up his afternoon and almost obliterated his duties to Karen, her car, and her money.

Karen drove away in the morning. Later in the day, Jon attempted to nail down her plans for return. "Most likely by Sunday," was her best guess. "Let me know if you'll be out. But how far can you go without wheels?"

That admonition started him thinking about the contents of a note she would read should she precede him home, words that would prepare her for the news that he had left town. Throughout the entire day he mulled over how to answer any undue questions that could arise.

After she had arrived at her mother's and settled into her daughter role, Jon sensed from the tone of her voice she was resigned to her task. The following morning's phone call found her absorbed in her duties as nursemaid. He told her, "I will see you after the weekend. Relax, soon you will be back, then I can stop missing you."

Coming into Chicago on a flight from Cincinnati solved his problem. The content of the note flowed: Dear Karen – with you gone and me rattling around, an invitation from an old teaching friend in Cincinnati fell on very receptive ears. So I am flying over for a retirement party his school is throwing for him in spite of the fact that I vowed never to be around academics again. I will be arriving back at O'Hare about five on Sunday and if you are home by then, plan on a quiet dinner at the Edgewater to celebrate our safe arrivals back into the nest. If you are staying beyond Sunday, then this note is irrelevant and will be trashed before you see it and I can tell you instead all about the glories of Cincinnati which you may never have known existed. XXOO Jon

ps – Shaggy old Wallace is next door with the Aherns and will need rescuing – the neighbors, not Wally. More XX.

With that propped on the kitchen table, with another phone call to Wisconsin, with his passport, and most casual clothes packed in something less than a new blue and red Air France carry-on, with two and a half days of sights worth seeing listed on a sheet secured in his jacket, with traveling twenties aplenty, the day of departure came as did the taxi, making the adventure real.

The O'Hare-de Gaulle flight was long and uncomfortable but the two amused themselves by creating ditties, by reading esoteric magazines, drinking bad wines, by digging into Camus and Sagan and having a quick conversation that he began with "Can I interest you in membership in the Mile High Club?"

"Jonathan," she said, "here I am, taking you to the most beautiful city in the world and you talk about contrived sex. Think of love when you think of Paris. Think of succulent sauces, of dark red wines. Think of fountains and lights and music in the streets. Think of poetry." She paused. "Go to sleep."

He did, and was groggy when the early morning coffee and croissant appeared, the beginning of the ritual of preparing for landing.

The plane touched down with a jolt. They pulled their bags from the overhead bins and waited to disembark. With each facet of their arrival, anticipation of the escapade grew.

A long train ride took them into the city and a cab to their Left Bank hotel. They arrived at a welcoming bed filling a major portion of the dark, cramped room. Falling into it together, flinging their clothes, they made quick groping love, an urgency having seeped throughout their bodies for the whole of the long flight to Europe. They relaxed then and followed the gymnastics with long and tender touches leading to an explosion of emotion. Then sleep fused them into a cocoon containing them through the remaining days. Theirs was now one shared Paris experience, one blossoming passion, their minds and hearts joined.

"I am tempted to not move from this spot," Genny said over a mid-day café crème. "I wonder what was in my upbringing that makes me such a Parisian."

"I am thinking that I left Genny back at O'Hare and worried that this Genevieve sitting across from me will disappear during the plane trip back. I don't want that to happen. I want you to be a Parisian forever."

This incredulous remark startled Genny. He compounded the effect with a declaration, "I need a Parisian in my life." They both drew in their breaths, wondering at the commitment. "But move into our Paris we must. This afternoon," Jon said, "I'll take you to the viscera of the city."

As promised, he spent the rest of the day guiding her underground through the elegant Metro stations he had researched. They rode up and down the rails of the number one to the Bastille, Concord and Louvre stations with their art and beauty for the transient. They transferred to the nine to Trocadero. Then the thirteen took them to Varenne to check out its Rodin sculptures.

Genny joked with him about the pace they were keeping. "Is it time for champagne yet?" she kept repeating.

On and off the silent trains, they tramped up and down stairs, sampling foods from street vendors where the combined aromas of ginger and garlic proved irresistible. They heard the music on the station platforms of Algerian, Portuguese, Asian, and other ethnic Parisians who contributed to the city's essence. They inhaled the acid and dust fumes of industrial Paris. Still, everywhere was the beauty of public art.

They arrived at Place des Abbesses and the distinctive glass-canopied Metro entrance, art nouveau at its purest. There they found a tiny park where "I love you" was captured on a wall of glazed tiles, written in hundreds of languages, "Le mur des je t'aime" appearing the most frequently. Together they stared holding on to their separate thoughts. Genny repeated the words; they went unheard. Neither committed to the emotion, so much love around them but none allowed within. The words stuck in Jon's chest.

A first-night-in-Paris supper in a smoky bistro surrounded by boisterous renegades from foreign lands capped their day.

The music and the exuberance of the languages surrounding them kept them quiet. The silence between them was testimonial to their comfort with each other.

The conversation on the walk home was dreamy, reliving the joy of this elegant Thursday. The day had been full, full of Genny and her submission to Jonathan and his plans, full of the perfumes of Paris, full of his eagerness to write down the poetry he felt welling up within him, and full of the hope that this was a breakthrough for his craft.

"I am so very grateful to you, sweet Genevieve, for bringing me here to this place. It's triggering my imagination. Only you and only this place ..."

"You belong here," Genny said. "I expect great things now from you. Let's race to see who can create the finest beauty out of this weekend."

He accepted her challenge. Later they composed couplets as they relaxed into sleep. Each one was more graceful than the preceding. No one took notes. The words were lost forever. Jon's imagination was fed by the confidence Genny had in him but at the moment he appreciated more the lumpy bed that supported their physical contact and the scented air feeding their entanglement.

The two were late in rising for their first full day in Paris, but in spite of their weariness they pursued the path Jon had outlined when he first learned they would be here together. Well-prepared for the weather, they donned heavy sweaters and waterproof windbreakers, not the fashion of Rue de Rivoli, more akin to the mountains of Genevieve's Utah.

The agenda he designed began with croissants and strawberry jams eaten to the outbursts of a robust accordion player, leaving them little space for morning talk, none necessary.

Genny constantly devoured his face with attention, absorbed his eyes, craved his mouth, said all the love he wanted to hear from her. He loved her back in silence with his fingers, tracing the life lines in her palms, the contours of her nose, her chin, her shoulders ... He wondered, did they really want to begin the route he had laid out, with the day promising such dampness and cold?

The misty green of Jardin du Luxembourg was within sight and drew them into its vastness where they found themselves gazing into the reflecting pool at its center. To peer into it with their images peering back confirmed the fit of them. Jon was first to notice. "We are good together. Look at us, a veritable Robert and Elizabeth Browning."

She coaxed her shoulder into the shelter of his arm. "We are good. I thought we would be. The moment my name was drawn I saw us in Paris together, looking this good."

"I wish I had something to do with your good fortune. I'll do my best here to keep us looking good. I can keep my arm around you; I can never leave your side; I can invade your brain with poetic quotes as they come to mind; I can pour champagne down your lovely throat. I can make us an unbearable couple."

Genny laughed at his preposterousness but Jon was transformed. Chicago and Karen were gone from his focus. He moved to the land of id wanting to stay here on this ground forever, their bodies fused, his arm holding her tight, soaking in the shimmering image of them together.

A child rushed up beside them flailing a pole, slashing at the water, diffusing the image and the reverie. Other distractions pulled them back to reality. Skimming over the water were model sailboats controlled by eager children on outings with their nonchalant nurses. Silent games of chess created domes of concentration about the players. The weathered stone busts of the writers of Paris who used these gardens as inspiration were tucked into the plantings and trees. People of style sauntered around them gazing at the tourist couple as Jon and Genny gazed back at them. People watchers, all of them.

"I know traditional sightseeing isn't primary on your Paris list," Genny said, "but let's compromise and pay homage to the Palais." Its magnificent facade was before them, unavoidable. They walked past its massive splendor, straining their necks to take it all in.

"If we lived in Paris, Genny, which of those thousands of rooms would you want?" Jon asked.

"I want the room where Napoleon slept. I'd want to be his Josephine under that roof."

He ignored her obvious insinuation. "Or do you want a whole floor? Or a whole wing? I think I'll be happy with my little bungalow back in Chicago. Imagine the costs to heat that monster." With that comment, Jon stripped all the majesty from the building.

They moved through the arcade out of the other-worldliness of the park finding fine Parisian food at La Cremerie where Kerouac, James Joyce, and Hemingway had given life to their literature. The street and its offshoots took up the rest of the day, strolling where the ghosts of Richard Wright, Longfellow, Whistler, and Oliver Wendell Holmes walked with them, where Gertrude Stein and Alice Toklas had held court amid their collection of modernist art.

Dinner at Café Les Deux Magots was Jon's special surprise for Genny. Amidst the smoke and noise, they drank of the wines that filled the bellies of Sartre and Beauvoir and then walked along the boulevards to bring them back to their hotel.

"Could you live here?" she asked, conjuring up an image of her future. "If I hadn't found Chicago such a welcoming place, I think I might have tried Paris on for size. Pretty big dreams for a small town lady, no?"

"What good are dreams if they're not big?" Jon asked.

"I know what your big dreams are. Maybe this weekend will be the beginning of them coming true." As Genny voiced these words, she added "and the same for me."

"My dreams," Jon said, "can only come true in the offices of a publishing house with eyes opening wide in astonishment."

He left no place for Genny in that vision but she pressed on. "Would you tell these astonished editors that you have a friend who also writes poetry? That you could send on to them? Would you tell them that hers is poetry that will burrow into the hearts of all who read it?"

The enthusiasm in Jon's eyes faded and the answer was apparent.

Saturday, a new morning in Paris. They used it to visit the Church of St-Etienne-du-Mont, St. Genevieve's church where they paid their respects to the patron saint of Paris.

"I come here whenever I am in Paris," Genny said, "to thank her for giving me my French heritage. Every girl should have a French papa."

A quiet overtook them. A whiff of myrrh leftover from earlier ceremonies brought memories of childhood church services. The heavy presence of burning candle wax touched their skin. Jon sensed the holiness in the stones surrounding them and tried to absorb the mystical aura, hoping to capture it in some future words he would put to paper.

"But enough of this sanctity," he said as he took her hand and walked her away, out to the street and life beyond St.

Genevieve's. There they found Ernest Hemingway's house. In those surroundings he understood the more optimistic Hemingway quote, "Every day above the earth is a good day." Jon said, "Yes, this is a good day."

"And what does that consist of?" Could Genny be part of the mix?

"Good is pretty much what is now. And yesterday, and tomorrow. I take it as it comes. Make the best of it."

"I hear the philosophy of Czeslaw Milosz," Genny's said. "With no incentive to manipulate the now?" she asked, to no avail. Her attempts to have some part in his life were becoming more fervent, this trip to Paris being her most aggressive maneuver to date. But she abandoned the inquisition as he moved her on to Picasso's studio, on to Booth Tarkington's, Faulkner's, and on to Ezra Pound's homes. Jon was relentless in his search for inspiration.

They hurried away, back to the banks of the Seine where the sky was darkening into a smudgy grey, back to the Quai where the bouquinistes should have been but weren't. The chilliness of the day had closed down the vendor booths early.

Jon found the iconic Shakespeare and Company bookstore, a primary item on his agenda. They spent time browsing around books that have been on and off the shelves since the 1920s, capturing the vibes of the writers and readers milling around the stacks.

While Genny moved into sections that contained books of interest to her, books about mountains and waters, Jon found a notice board with sundry messages that carried stories of their own. He penned this: Genevieve - I think I love / the way you lie beside me. / I think I love your hands in mine, / your bones and flesh astride me. / Genevieve - I think I love / our sense of déjà-vu. / Genevieve - I think I love / you.

He posted the poem, found Genny, and hurried her out of the shop with promises of Ionesco and après at the nearby Hotel Vieux. All of Paris would now read the thoughts that wrapped themselves around him, strangling him into inaction, thoughts denied Genny.

"The Bald Soprano," presented for decades at the Theatre de la Huchette, enraptured them both. She followed the storyline with her enviable understanding of French. Jon was satisfied to be sitting in the minuscule enclosure with its theater of the absurd devotees, wallowing in the beauty of the language.

"You really should study French," Genny said, switched over to it and began a conversation that could be a recitation of the Psalms, not that it mattered, so musical was the flow of her words. "Then again, maybe it's best you don't. This way I can say anything I want to you without your having a clue. I like my men clueless." Then she added, "Since I am so regularly in that camp."

He tried to contradict her last thought but didn't want to break the spell she had begun weaving. He waited for more of the one-sided conversation but it ended.

The play, dinner, a stroll back to the hotel, their last of three nights in Paris was as fulfilling as their first.

Genny, having requisitioned the aisle for the flight home from the Cincinnati stopover, sprang up on landing to open the overhead and pull out her carryon. She maneuvered her way toward the exit, checking with Jon as he attempted to join the impatient passengers.

They proceeded through the jetway with her still in the lead. Jon savored the view of her long legs carrying her fast and far, her slim hips slipping back and forth beneath her delicate wool skirt. Whereas he would have wished to escape with her forever in Paris, she seemed eager to resume their risky lives in Chicago. Jon had created a confidence and recognized the challenge to sustain it. Memories of their weekend would feed it.

At the security post, he stopped to offer words of encouragement to the guard whose sour face glowered at the passing passengers, and heard "Jon, Jonathan" coming from the crowd. Genny heard it too, stopping at its sound and turning back toward him. He returned her gaze with the widened eyes of a cornered raccoon, both of them recognizing Karen's voice. She rushed up and clasped him in her arms, nuzzled her face into his neck where she whispered "I am so glad you are back I missed you so much I couldn't wait an extra minute to see you. Thank you so much for letting me know when you were coming in."

Over Karen's shoulder he watched Genny's face harden, her eyes narrow to slits. He saw her shudder as a resolve washed over her. She turned away, rushed toward the airport exit, to the curb where Deets would be waiting, to hear her story of treachery.

Karen and Jon started down the concourse, Karen's arms encircled his waist, capturing him. A halting stiffness limited the speed of their getaway.

27

The Lord is near to the broken-hearted
and saves the crushed in spirit.

Psalms 34:18

GENEVIEVE – crushed in spirit

Deets lived in Evanston, about a mile or so north of the Mountain Man's house, which was a mile or so north of Genny's apartment. The road was a mystic drive on an ancient route that followed Native American pathways through virgin forests up into fur country. Now with its interstate designation, it skirted the waters of Lake Superior and Lake Michigan and plunged south two thousand miles, ending in Miami. For centuries, moccasined feet trod upon this path. Now Genny drove it in anticipation.

She was meeting Deets for a Saturday dinner at a new sandwich shop in his neighborhood.

She spent the afternoon reworking some stanzas on the ancient phantoms who stalked the path she would follow. Printed out in what she hoped was their final form, they were solid, long and languid, like the smoke rising from nearby buildings, like the smoke that had risen from gatherings of native tribes.

Resurrected spirits were all Genny concentrated on this crisp Midwest afternoon. Memories of Paris were too enigmatic. Her mind wouldn't attend to them. They had fallen around her like confetti. She could not sweep them away nor could she scoop them into her hands and examine them for their colorful beauty. No messages from the Mountain supported their existence.

Genny stuffed the sheets of poetic lines into an envelope and headed to her Deets dinner with an intermediate plan. She needed to establish her relevance to Jon, to secure her position with him, to plead for acknowledgment, to beg. She turned down his street noting addresses. "Fourteen seventy-one, fourteen seventy-one," she kept repeating, searching for his number on the porches.

There it was, spotted on a classic bungalow, fronted by a scrubby lawn. Somewhat surprised by the dilapidated feel of the structure, she pulled her car to the curb across from the house.

While she gripped the steering wheel, Genny forced strength back into her will. She pushed aside the library books collected on her front seat to unearth her cell phone. Then breathing again, she gathered her courage and began tapping in his phone numbers.

Noticing movement along the side of the house, she shut down the phone and pulled air into her lungs, picking up a book to hide her face. She caught sight of a young couple struggling to pull a stroller through an adjoining backyard gate. Her cheeks puffed as she released her breath.

Neighbors, lucky neighbors to live next door. She sat back, composing herself. *I've come this far*, she reasoned, *I might as well see it through*, and plugged in the numbers again.

His "hello" was hesitant but her exuberant "guess what!" overrode his lackluster greeting. Genny didn't expect an answer yet he humored her with a few succinct possibilities. None of them close to the actuality, none referring to Paris.

"I'm parked in front of your house with a bunch of poems that are my claim to fame," she said. Even though she had practiced words she would say as she drove to his street, they toppled out, sounding anxious. They carried the mixed flavors of tension, insecurity, and obsession.

She wished her opening had been a more controlled *Hello, Jon. It's Genny. Just passing by and thought I'd see if you're available.* A poor choice of word. Availability was not his primary asset.

The interior of the car throbbed, like the green room of the "Tonight Show." She wanted to recall each tentative word back into her phone, back into her mouth, back into her brain. The sound of her blood pulsed off the upholstered padding of her car.

Genny's hopes: an invitation into his home, an elegant glass of French champagne, a tour, hesitating before his bedroom where she would hustle away knowing Deets was waiting in an Evanston restaurant. Then taking him to Deets, what a party they would have. Three generations – the unfettered enthusiasm of a youthful Deets, her entrancing mature solemnity and the wisdom of Jon's majestic years – all wrapped up in one gabfest over supper.

In reality, Jon said, "I'll be right out. Wait there." He hung up the phone and slid into the passenger seat within minutes.

He was ready for his own party. He wore an oxford dress shirt, an artist's palette of a tie loosened at his throat, and razor-creased suntans. Wide red suspenders peeked from behind a denim sports jacket fresh from the cleaners. He was scrubbed and polished and smelled like he had been rubbed down with spices. He looked brand new. Genny felt an urgency in his voice, the tightness of an actor in the wings.

"Poetry. How sweet of you to hand deliver these. Are they products of Paris? Ah, Paris," Jon said, "Paris" but left no room for remembrances. "I could have picked them up later. We could have met for coffee Monday," he said.

"I work on Monday," Genny said. He knew she worked a ten-hour day on Mondays. "I was passing by. I'm meeting Deets for dinner. I thought you might want to come along and meet this imp I spend my days with ..." she relaxed ... *since you missed your previous chance at the airport,* a nagging voice thundered in her head. Her intent was weakening. His tense reaction was whittling away her conviction that pressing herself upon him was wise. Now in his territory, the fun and freedom of her neighborhood were not tangible.

"Oh that's really not possible tonight," he said. No regrets at missing Deets again were apparent. Genny had the good sense, or was it the frozen atmosphere that surrounded them, not to ask why.

He continued without her prodding. "We're – I'm due at an alum function downtown in about a half hour. Otherwise ..."

She didn't hear *Otherwise I'd ask you up for a quick drink before you go to Deets,* nor *Otherwise I'd have you call Deets to cancel and feed you myself,* nor *Otherwise we can sit on my stoop and watch the moon move across the sky and wonder over your poetry.* And certainly not *Otherwise we can hold hands and re-live Paris.*

She heard him instead adding a perfunctory "Otherwise I'd love to ..." as she was saying "That's okay ..." when in truth, it wasn't. Genny hoped she didn't need to say anymore.

Her mind erased the scene she had wanted to evolve with all the clever repartee they would have exchanged.

He brushed her cheek with a kiss, not unlike a thousand others, and caught himself bringing his hand to the back of her neck to pull her closer.

"Wednesday, then?" Wednesday, a day for bike rides, walks through the park, excursions into the country, coffees, and lunches. This was Saturday. A day for Karen. He opened the car door, turned his eyes away from hers. She saw them no more.

Without waiting for her okay, he walked toward his front steps as he tucked Genny's envelope into his jacket pocket. He never looked back. The scent of ensnared animal remained.

Genny lost her appetite. But Deets waited with his unending enthusiasm for food, drink, and chatter. Genny needed all three. In a conversation she could not keep herself from having, Deets asked, "What did you think he'd do? Take you downtown with him? You're hardly dressed for polite society."

Deets was right. Her scrappy jeans, comfortable and colorless from years of washings, with a vintage cotton knit sweater, once bright yellow, now also washed out, gave the impression nothing important was to happen. At least she was clean, also washed up, and out.

"No," she said, "of course not. But he said 'We're due' – a 'we' that he changed to an 'I' as soon as it was out of his mouth. She's in there, Deets, firmly entrenched."

"Just because she's 'in there' getting ready for a downtown date doesn't mean forever."

Genny wasn't swayed. "No, not forever. Just every weekend, every evening. He's only been with me twice on a weekend, only a couple of times at night. And then Paris. Does she dissolve? Where does she go? How was he free to leave for a long weekend? How does he get away from her? And why? I never ask; he never says."

Pretending Saturday had never transpired, Genny waited for him Wednesday, pacing the running path that separated the beach from the park.

While she scanned the surrounding trees, shadows of other attachments emerged: love poems he had shared that had references she didn't recognize, agonized poems brushing against the kind of passion he might have known in another time, words written for others. Genny had read them as creative exercises.

The thoughts scattered as she watched his determined approach, striding as if he hadn't brushed her off, as if he hadn't left her sitting in her car before a doorway that didn't open to her.

"Where'll we go today?" he asked with an eagerness in his eyes and a casualness in counterpoint to her tautness. His innocence befuddled her. The weekend now archived.

The question went unanswered. Instead, he rephrased, "Where can I take you? My grimy car awaits. Maybe a hearty breakfast for a change, more than coffee? Or just a drive? Would you like that? We could find some back roads. No destination. Let's just enjoy some music and sweet air. I have some Beethoven piano sonatas in the car."

Genny still did not respond.

"Hey, smile. We are free for the fun of the day. Want some folk? I got that too," he pressed on. "What kind of music would grab you this morning?"

This morning, bright and crisp. They stood on the beach and faced the sun as it escaped the clouds in the east. The wind whipped off the lake. It made Genny's nose run and her eyes water. She clutched the handkerchief balled in her fist and brought it to her face. She would have been cold but the Mountain Man's arm was around her shoulder, pulling her as close to his vibrant warmth as was physically possible, divided as they were by two down-filled parkas.

"Where'll we go?" he repeated. Genny studied him, not able to absorb his untainted attitude toward the day. She waited without reward for some mention of Saturday's rebuff or of the pages he had carried off. Nothing was offered. She resigned herself to less than she needed or wanted. Memories of other wants crowded in.

"I want to have breakfast in your kitchen," she said. She had never been in his kitchen. Not in his kitchen, not in his home, only once on his street – recently – disastrously.

To that suggestion, his torso tightened. He released the pressure of his hand on her back. Those blue eyes hardened. The reaction confirmed a recurrent thought about the freedom he preached. *Freedom for the fun of the day* reverberated in her ears.

"C'mon." She soothed her voice into a seductive coax. "You've seen every inch of my apartment – even the places I don't dust. I want to see where you write, and eat, and sleep, and brush your teeth." She wanted to see where he made love. She wanted to see whose pictures were on his windowsills. She wanted to see what filled his closets.

"We can't, dear heart. I'll take you to a wonderful Viennese café on Halsted. No, you need a raspberry tart – let's go over to Sweet G's." Entrapment swept over his face. Genny had seen that look before. He must have felt it because she saw it wash away the cheeriness in his eyes. She shivered from the cold that encased them.

After she put down any hopes she held, she pulled her head tall and steeled herself to say, "You are married."

It was the oft-uttered statement she had rehearsed in the quiet of her room when his phone went unanswered. It was a statement she practiced after last-minute calls came asking her to stand-in during sudden free time. Sometimes it became a question, sometimes a pleading lament.

This time, "You are married" came flatly out of her mouth as a condition to be verified.

"You are married," she said again. No more than that. She didn't fill the silence that followed. She closed her lips tight, letting the silence hang, leaving a cavity in the air for a denial that would have eased the tension. There was none.

As they stood face to face she felt the answer moving into his throat. "Yes." He said "yes" without a stammer. Genny gasped. The cold rushed in and kept her from uttering any-thing plaintive: ... *along the shore, through the rags of fog* – an Adrienne Rich poem moved across her mind – *where we stood, saying* – what? — *saying I.* With this Genny's "we" became "I". "We" gone.

"Yes. Karen and I – yes we are – we are married."

Genny's continued silence forced more out of him. She heard little of it, "... met her after a confusing marriage ... unex-pected upheaval ... needed peace. She ... my home ... peaceful. Years of peace. I am content, in control, like never before. I have made peace in my life – like never before. With Karen."

Zap.

"Peace," Genny whispered.

"You don't want that, Genny, to be peace. You are a burning soul. I come near you because of the pull of danger and heat. You counterbalance my life. But what I need is cool peace, ultimate peace."

The words were controlled, spoken in the deep, mellow voice that first drew her to him. They made no sense. They were unapologetic. She stared at his peaceful, contented, unapproachable face, now fading into strangeness. The angles she had traced in darkness, in silence. The words she wrote to that face. The joy she felt memorizing every wrinkle, every pore.

She expected his face to contort with anguish over what he told her. He must have known she left him with this confession, taking the fire with her. He must have known the poetry went too, that hers was the poetry that enhanced his own. She brought the words he could not say, words he did not feel. She laid before him sounds never imagined, of unrest, of purity, of power. In his eyes she saw his peace moving inward, away from her pain. That peace would protect him as he wandered in his empty fields.

"Genny, don't ..." he said as he faced and steadied her with a grip on her shoulders.

Don't what? she wondered. *Don't vaporize?* Is that what she was doing? *Don't turn to granite?* That is what she felt happening to her.

"Don't turn your face away from me." His hold grew tighter.

She stared down at her feet, at their feet, each foot next to the other, his right, her left, his left, her right, side by side. They made little impression in the solid sand.

"I need to see your face. I need you to know that if Karen wasn't my wife, it would be you, only you. How faithfully and tenderly we would love. What poetry we would live. If Karen weren't my wife ..."

He paused, spent. Genny then heard three muted words, "But she is ..."

Trios of words through the ages mark milestones for the young growing old. You and me. I love you. I thee wed. It's a girl. Alone at last. In her life, Genny had heard too few, those too shallow. Now she heard, "But she is ..." Those three would mark a diffraction in a life left for her to reassemble.

With those three words, an iron gate crashed down between them, unmovable, impenetrable. She could stand with her face pressed against its hard coldness and plead for re-entrance to the sunshine and the warmth. She could sink into the sand, and pray for mighty cold waves to toss her back and forth along the surf, annihilating her. Or, she could turn away, as she did, and walk west into the city's distraction, and into the endless possibilities promised when she first chose Chicago. To another love. To another wasted emotion. Endless possibilities.

"But she is." So be it.

28

Keep silence now, for singing-time is over,
And over all old things and all things dear.
She loves not you nor me as we all love her.
Yea, though we sang as angels in her ear,
She would not hear.

A Leave-Taking / Algernon Swinburne

GENEVIEVE – singing-time is over

Genny's veins emptied out. Her bones stiffened. Her heart hardened. A falcon-like reality swooped through her, merciless talons splayed, gripping her guts in an unbreakable clutch. She walked past the tall condos, across the boulevard, and moved away from a sun that brightened the branches of naked trees, that skipped off the glass of windows closed against the cold, that lay a shadow ahead of her. She followed it west until the buildings flattened and broadened, from high rise to courtyard apartments and clapboarded city homes. The sun shone on their crispy lawns, layered with morning frost. She walked, the sun at her back.

Her head throbbed with pleas to gods that no longer governed the fate of living creatures. She wanted the day to be gone too. She walked.

And then words began to echo off her footsteps. … *what help is here? / There is no help, for all these things are so, / and all the world is bitter as a tear.*

Swinburne. He was there in her head, enriching her again, keeping a cadence with her. With each footfall, she heard *There is no help, for all these things are so.* The Swinburne words offered no relief. They only verified the reality of this ache.

The pounding rhythm of the poetry mimicked the rhythm of her step. She turned the beat into her own poem of anguish. Words fell into place. Lines moved into her head from pages of dusty books, precise words she borrowed. She marched into the shadows passing bushes, fences, and the merriment of children's chalk drawings. She walked away from the sun, away from the mountain of her love. Alone. Making a poem out of pain, into the city's distraction.

Returning home Genny was more ready to rid herself of Jonathan. She went from the street to her computer to say goodbye as he had said hello – via email. She tried to use Swinburne to express her heartbreak. Some gender changing made old poetry fit into a fine finale.

To: jonwat
Subject: a leave-taking: Swinburne

Let us go hence, go hence; he will not see.
Sing all once more together; surely he,
He too, remembering days and words that were,
Will turn a little toward us, sighing; but we,

We are hence, we are gone, as though we had not been there
Nay, and though all men seeing had pity on me,
He would not see.
I am gone

Genny

She didn't send the message. He wasn't worth the words. She sent only the final line.

From: gennydu
To: jonwat
Date: Thu, 16 Dec 2004 02:19:52
Subject: a leave-taking

  I am gone
Genny

She moved into Swinburne's soul, heard classical sonatas, heard the dear old Victorian murmurings he hummed into a love's ear. Did she listen? Did she listen as Genny had listened to the Mountain Man's beloved Beethoven and shared the best of her Springsteen as they drove around the streets of Chicago in his battered sedan – their private listening booth? Had any of them been listening to anyone?

Springsteen was the music Genny played now, eighties superhits. "Goin' down, goin' down, goin' down," those twangy rock lyrics reminded her of their summer days. How they shared the vast waters of the lake, stood watching the storms of autumn when sand whipped around their feet, and the horizon was black and white with water and waves. They didn't know they together were as vaporous as the wind and as unsteady as the sand or the waters. Genny couldn't have guessed love would be so rootless.

Maybe she suspected. Was it blindness not to sense that he flicked off her suggestions of love as dust on his shoulder? Sawdust. Worthless. Never a mention of love? Never a mention. The concept of love was hers alone.

He would not love. He would not care that he didn't love. She should have known last summer when Jon's smoky blue eyes first looked at her. They might have said *beware.*

"And how was your Wednesday, mighty mountain climber?" As Genny entered the agent floor Deets's shout boomed across the room with morning enthusiasm. She cringed hearing the term "mountain" broadcast for public consumption, was unwilling to acknowledge his remark. On the agent floor only Deets knew of the Mountain Man.

Genny let the greeting drop. Since they all spoke in code, the other chattering agents took little note. Genny's life could have been everybody's focus in their closely-knit team. Many lives were. Genny's wasn't.

Daily Deets saw her face beyond his computer, a face that reflected whatever joys or pains Jon had inflicted. He deserved to know how her Wednesday had been.

Genny walked toward him with paced steps, knowing what their initial conversation would be. She stared at him as she removed her hat and gloves, took off her coat, arranged her tote bag under her desk. His frozen expression indicated he knew the answer would be dramatic. Her calculated control gave no clue to the intensity of the drama.

"He's married, that's how my Wednesday was," Genny said as she lowered herself into her chair. Deets knew "he."

"Married?"

Genny shushed him with narrowed eyes. He toned down his voice and said, "He can't be married. He's been courting you for the last five months." Deets was simple, and young, and single. Maybe to him things worked better if older married men romanced their wives and left the vulnerable alone.

"You know, Deets," Genny said, "some men can't stop courting. It's up to us, the courtees, to figure out if the courtiers are legitimate or not. I chose not to ask." In her defense she added, "I did once ask if he had children." Then she recalled that he never answered the question.

Her continued composure belied the scope of the confession, confounding Deets.

As Genny settled before her computer, he rolled his chair over close to hers, moving easily over the tight carpeting. He was beside her as her monitor lit up. Genny was eager to log in, to get into the business of the day, to bury the day just passed. But Deets was her buddy-boy and he now functioned as the best buddy-boy a female could have.

"Not fair," was his initial assessment as the import of her response penetrated. "Know what you should do?" Deets lifted her hand to his lips. He emanated the aura of a deep scholar, his settling tone spoke with the voice of the ancients. She would never have anticipated "Go for his brother."

"Oh, Deets," she said," you with your twenty-year-old outlook. I'm a little beyond ..."

"Twenty-three, closer to twenty-four."

"You with your twenty-four-year-old vision, your barely bearded face, your untouched heart, there is no brother. The Man is a rarity." Lyrics raced through her mind: *The mate that fate had me created for ...* Not quite.

To distract him, Genny glanced at the clock that oversaw the room, closing in on seven a.m. "Plug in time," she said. She wanted to bring this conversation to an end, perhaps forever.

"Listen Genny," Deets said, "I've been in love. I'm Greek. We know about love."

"This isn't any kind of love you'd know about. It's adoration. It's obsession. It covers me. It's nothing I can transfer to anyone else. It's nothing I can step out of. I really need to go away. I need to get rid of this city and everything he is part of. Leave town. Get as far away as I can afford. Maybe Australia? Maybe Finland."

Deets picked up on her ruefulness. "You want to go someplace else? Go to New York. There's an opening right now on the Regeants Park account for an international agent. More money too, because it's New York." He pronounced it "New Yawk" with a flourish.

Deets pushed her chair aside and pulled his into its place. His fingers flew over the keyboard until a listing of company job openings sprang onto her screen. "Is that far enough away?" he asked as he pointed to a Madison Avenue address.

"What are you looking at the 'opps' listings for?" she asked. "Were you planning on leaving me here all alone, without your camaraderie? What kind of desk mate are you?"

But the thought of New York settled well on her mind. An opening she was trained to fill wasn't an impossibility. She could handle New York. She had heard similar suggestions before.

"Just an idea," he said. "Job Opportunity listings. They're there as dream fodder. He shut down the page. "Couldn't you use some dreams?"

"Regeants Park. I haven't heard of them. What do they do?" Genny asked.

"Interested, no?" Deets pulled up the Regeants Park Inc. home page. "Just an idea," he said again, "one that has been flying around my brain pretty regularly. Some sort of import outfit. It's a new account Betty Lisson is heading up. You

know her. She's that skinny blonde broad that came whirling through here last year heading for the big time. Go for it."

Genny remembered Betty. One night last spring, sipping Chablis high over the city in a bar with a view that took in the spread of Chicago, she tried to entice Genny out of a Brian-boredom rut.

"The East Coast," Betty encouraged her, "that's where you want to be."

Maybe Genny did; maybe she didn't. Then Betty spun off to turn up in New York City. "Maybe I will; maybe I won't," she told Deets. She knew then she would go.

With that, Deets scooted his chair back around the desk. As an afterthought he called over the top of his computer, "What about Paris? What did he do to deserve that? Or how's he explaining the champagne extravaganza last month?" Deets knew too much.

Champagne needed no explanation. It was a celebration of her Swinburne-like sestina. For five weeks she manipulated the original draft and more hours to make them sensible. She was proud she had tackled the challenge, prouder she had produced something with meaning and import.

When Shannah had asked to see this complicated poem for her anthology, Genny worked on it with her for another six weeks, readjusting the lines, perfecting the words. With that, she stepped through a door into her glory.

The Mountain Man was proud of her and in awe of the poem, with its intricacies. It was he who announced her achievement to his writers' group she had been attending in spurts. The poets-in-waiting had lounged around the laminated library table staring at her, their faces a mixture of hope and envy.

She tried to be humble. But she was now something more than a dreamer. It was he who later pulled a bottle of champagne out of his backpack, not for the group, for them alone. They drank alone in her moonlit bedroom.

"I love, really love, what you are doing for me. My personal promoter. Every poet needs one," Genny said. She remembered his response. "What fun we are. And now you, a success." Genny gave him the word she wanted him to use, twice, "love, really love." It died in the air between them. Instead, his response, "What fun we are. What fun."

So her answer to Deets was, "'No thorns go as deep as a rose's, and love is more cruel than lust.' More Swinburne," she said. "Some of us love. And some of us lust."

29

Some nights an unborn poem, heavy in my belly,
drags me, startled, from full-dream sleep,
the way the moon magnet drags the helpless tide,
whipping the sea to tumultuous crescendo.

Beneath the Waters / Laurel Yourke

GENEVIEVE – tumultuous crescendo

Genny dozed through most of the three-and-a-half-hour Christmas flight to Salt Lake City. Jeffrey, loaded with his camera equipment, was with her, but she avoided being drawn into his enthusiasm for their photo project. Drifting off was the best way to protect her isolation.

Through the week she had slept sporadically, reading instead, writing, listening to music, whimpering, researching, and thinking through a personal life reconstruction plan. By the time her parents met the pair at the airport to drive them back to Winton, she was recomposed.

They rushed to their daughter at the carousel as she waited for their luggage. Chattering travelers and clattering luggage carts

mingled with expressions of joy as families and friends came together up and down the carousel. Genny stood at the center of
the commotion relaxing, pleased to be back where she began.

The melancholy she tried to disguise as solemnity gave
her a grace she hadn't possessed when she left home three
years ago. Jumping back into those years helped suppress her
sadness. Whatever ingredients went into the impression she
brought to the wedding, her father thought she was prettier
than ever. He said it out loud and often. He hugged her often,
smothering her underlying discomfort.

Her mom took little notice of her homecoming, much
less of her pain. Genny made no demands for her attention,
nor for her sympathy. Bad enough Denise was beating her
down the aisle; she could not add more fuel to her mother's
vexation. Genny's pasted smile was satisfying enough.

"Where's Denise?" Genny asked. She knew she and David
had been on a marathon, finalizing the minor details that
would perfect their wedding day. No surprise that they were
with a real estate agent signing off on their Denver apartment.

"We'll be meeting them for lunch at the Monaco. We
thought we'd start the celebrations in grand style." So like her
father to make elegant plans for Genny's arrival.

Denise was long gone, caught up in a flurry of pre-nuptial
partying in Winton, when Jon admitted his "Karen as wife"
arrangement. It was Genny's silent bile, not a pre-wedding
topic. Genny had so few moments left with her before she lost
her to David and Denver, she could not waste them on the
Mountain Man's marital status.

Denise's only reference to him was a tossed-off comment, "So you really won't bring the Mountain Man to the
mountains? I kind of thought you'd relent. Thought you'd

ask him to come along, just to make the romance around here explode."

"Explode? You don't know the meaning of the word," Genny said to cover her discomfort. "I never got around to inviting him. I thought he might get in the way of the real romance you've got brewing. I think he was beginning a class at the university this term. He wasn't ..." She stopped making excuses. They were feeble, unbelievable. She didn't want any more Mountain Man talk.

In a softer tone she said, "This is our ceremony, remember? Just us Duponts – and David, of course. I guess we have to include David, and his parents, and the rest of his family, and his friends. This is getting to be quite a crowd." Genny proceeded far enough away from the thought of the Mountain Man to be comfortable and safe.

Once settled into her old bedroom, Genny ventured out and became caught up in the hustle of small-town activity. The sisters made the rounds. They did some last minute shopping; they stopped at cafes; they dropped in on old friends and neighbors; they walked through the park. Everyone complimented her city style.

"Ohmagod," a high school crush said on the streets of Winton. "You look as hot as you did at the prom."

Genny didn't recall he had been at her high school prom. By prom time she had been heavy into some jock-type and no one else existed. Everyone in town, including the jock-type and his yoga-type wife, was home for the Christmas holiday, welcoming her back.

Her former Winton travel boss said, "I didn't know Chicago could turn out such lovelies." He still resented her deserting his local agency for the mega operation she preferred. He didn't suspect she almost returned to him a month ago.

Genny checked the appraisals in store windows on the way home. It was true. She did look fine. Inside she was bloody and ravaged but she contained the damage. She looked fine. Denise and David looked fine. They all looked fine. And acting happy. Some of them were happy. Genny mimicked them, matching their joy with processed happiness.

Her previous shopping sprees, with and for Denise, up and down, on and off Michigan Avenue, the city had outfitted her in classic Magnificent Mile style. She wore a hunters green crushed velvet suit for the rehearsal dinner where David's friends courted her with jovial exuberance. Older women have their appeal, she suspected. The following day a lustrous raw silk pillar of a dress, the color of candied walnuts, took her down the aisle preparing the way for her sister's bridal entrance. All fine.

Amusing Genny was the memory of the saleswomen bent on sending her and Denise to bridal departments in search of a fluff of a maid-of-honor dress. "But I don't want to look like a bridesmaid," Genny argued. "I am thirty-seven years old. A little beyond maiden days."

"What color is your bridal gown, dear?" The woman directed the question at Denise, ignoring Genny.

"Ivory with bronze-y accents," Denise said.

Genny had wished she had said cow pie brown with orange feathers. Her attitude implied what business was it of hers what the bride's sister wore in the wedding. "All right," she said later, "it was her business."

The saleslady wasn't listening to Genny anyway. Nobody was, not through any of the four lunch hours devoted to outfitting the thirty-seven-year-old bridesmaid. When they graduated from the bridal shops with their unacceptable offerings where nothing suited her, they found themselves in the more sedate surroundings of upscale boutiques. No strobe lights, no blasting music hurried the decision. "If you have anything in a deep color," Genny asked, "something appropriate for a late afternoon march down an aisle, something that makes me look serene, appropriate to my age. Anything like that? Can you show us anything like that? If not, we really must move on."

Move on they did, and on, until they found a handsome dress, a fitting reinforcement to the splendor of Denise's gown. A yin to her yang. A fine dress. Everything fine.

A latecomer to the festivities was Genny's Aunt Betsy, the best thing the Dupont family had to offer, next to Genny's dad, alike in their appreciation of Genny. She was due to arrive at the Salt Lake City airport from the West Coast early the day of the wedding. Genny offered to meet her. Out of the house and away from the happiness, the gloom began surfacing again. Betsy stamped it out the minute she appeared at the baggage carousel. Throwing her arms up in exaltation she shouted, "Genevieve, darlin'!" as Genny rushed to her. She was an antidote to this precarious mood.

"Look at you!" she said. "Look – at – you," as though Genny were a product of the Hollywood magic Betsy knew so well. She put her hands on Genny's shoulders and pushed her an arm's distance away. "Look at you, so svelte. Really, you are too skinny. You need a little flesh. Are you happy? How long has it been?" She took an overdue breath. "When did you leave Utah – it's been that long. How is everything in your new life? Oh, darlin' we must talk. It's been too long since we've had a Gennysession."

All through her aunt's exuberance, Genny kept repeating, "I am so glad you are here. I am so glad to see you. I have missed you so much."

Genny had missed her. Her Aunt Betsy, truth be told, was the mother she should have had, the lady who could have taken her by the hand and exposed her to all the possibilities of life, who could have offered her something other than wife and motherhood as life's only options.

Betsy had pleaded for her to come to her Los Angeles booking agency the minute Genny had her college degree in hand but the jump from small town was too frightening then, even under her adventuresome aunt's wing. They substituted with Genny's visits to Los Angeles and Betsy's visits to her brother, Genny's dad. This favorite aunt wanted to pull her away, always urging, but Genny stuck close to home.

When her engagement fizzled, Betsy was the first to hear the details of the failed romance. Picking up the anger in her voice, she didn't hesitate to reprimand her. "You are wasting a lot of energy with all that howling, little lady. Can't you take up boxing or something to work the venom out of your system?" Genny took up Pilates instead.

After Genny had chosen the Midwest rather than Betsy's West Coast, guilt smothered their relationship. Betsy had let her go.

"Let's have a cup of tea before we barge in on the family," she said. "Everybody at your house is probably much too busy fussing over the bride to fuss over me. And darlin' I need some fussing over."

"I'm so good at that," Genny said. So fuss she did, listening to all Betsy's triumphs and pratfalls – the ones that got away – ooohing and ahhing in all the appropriate places.

They had ducked into the closest pub and were drinking a midday brew. The ambiance was sterile, with a hint of decadence, but quiet and cordial at that hour of day. Betsy began to relax and adjust to Genny and Utah when she noticed that Genny was not adding much to the conversation. "And you, Genevieve, is life good?" The pain swelled throughout Genny's body again and she lowered her head. "Genevieve, not good?"

"Not good."

"Can I help? You can still come to LA. Can you tell me?" This is where Aunt Betsy shone. She knew how to cut to the core.

So Genny told her, holding back tears. Betsy nodded her head in sympathy with nothing to say. Genny stopped the narrative, realizing the obvious. Betsy was still single. She had been through the territory Genny was emerging from. Her familiarity with aloneness was in the eyes now so intent on Genny's face.

She took Genny's hands in hers and talked about love and the adventures love had carried her through. "All of it valuable, Genny, you will see. Disaster teaches you how to survive. Wisdom comes from wounds. It is all valuable to whatever you choose to do."

Enough soothing, she skipped to practicality.

"But you need a sunnier city to do it in! And what are you doing now darlin', other than booking flights?" Aunt Betsy suspected they had overstayed in the lost love conversation as she took Genny out of her funk to bring her more in line with the gaiety of the household they were to join.

She was impressed with Genny's travels but said they were not enough to make a life. "You have to light somewhere, sometime," little knowing how ready Genny was. "We will talk later."

The wedding day into evening proceeded without a flaw. From the moment the notes of Pachelbel's "Canon in D" reached the vestibule, a calm settled over the whole family like a shower of feathers. Genny centered Denise's cascade of cymbidium orchids at her waist and reminded her to smile before she stepped onto the aisle. She put on her own smile.

She was the first down the aisle, steady and dignified, clutching a ribbon-wrapped stalk of pale green orchids. A long interlude followed. She was alone and very aware of the eyes of the community on her, they wondering why she wasn't the bride?

On cue, the father and the bride entered the aisle as Genny reached the halfway point when eyes shifted to the rear of the church. She heard murmurs of approval. When she approached the altar she gave her mother a wink, but those eyes were on Denise. David was waiting at the altar and validated her with the wink her mother withheld. Then his attention turned to his bride.

The well-rehearsed ceremony unfolded. Soon Mendelssohn's "Wedding March" set the pace for the church exit.

At the country club reception the food, more tempting than tasty, coupled with the multitude of toasts offered by the bridegroom's entourage, filled the evening. Not quite ready to draw the focus to herself, Genny rose. At first, she was unable to find her voice but recovered and raised her glass of champagne, "To my beloved Denise, and her beloved David, to the joy they feel and bring into our family, I offer this Hungarian truth: In dreams, and in love, there are no impossibilities." She quoted a Janos Arany poem she hoped spoke truth. She had the dreams, half that promise intact.

The dancing through the evening seemed eternal. Genny checked in periodically with Jeffrey at significant times, noting that his photos ran the gamut from ethereal to amusing. She was satisfied. They would provide such an afterglow to this event for years to come. So pleased, she made plans with Jeffrey to put them in order to have them waiting for Denise when she returned from honeymooning in Aruba.

The party simmered down to its end and Denise began life anew. With New York in mind, Genny made promises she would do the same. By the time she arrived home, Genny had survived six days without cracking open. Weddings and Aunt Betsy made solid glue.

"Hello Dad?" Genny tried to steady her voice but her throat muscles quivered. "Daddy?"

"Genny-girl, are you okay? You got home all right?" He sounded urgent, feeding her pathos. Genny saw him bolting up in his lounger, his feet hitting the floor, ready to spring. He was her protector. She should have released him from that responsibility years ago as she grew up. But he never let her grow. Genny still needed his protection.

"Oh, I'm okay Dad. It's just …" and then her mind went blank. What brought her to this state, squatting against the hall wall of her apartment still in her overcoat and boots? She had just returned from a celebration that marked one of the happiest events in a family's life. She and Jeff had just flown back first class thanks to Delta's appreciation of the seats she filled, well attended by a cheerful cabin crew. "I dunno. It's just so lonesome here. I am so alone now. It's so quiet."

Not so quiet. Her neighbor upstairs clicked around on her hardwood floors in heels that must have been four inches high and a half a centimeter wide. Clack, clack, clickety-click. That she moved around so merrily annoyed Genny. What right had she to be so happy? Water rushed through the pipes in the wall for someone else's shower. Someone was getting ready to go out into the town for a pleasant rendezvous. Here Genny was alone while Denise and David honeymooned on sandy beaches – a trip Genny's own computer arranged.

"We can come see you, make a lot of noise and take up your extra space," her father said. With a more serious tone he said, "We are kind of rattling around here too after all the hoopla. Would you like that? For us to take a trip to Chicago?" Then he slipped back into absurdity. "Or maybe we could all meet halfway in Denver. I'm sure Denise and David would be thrilled to have us drop in."

"No, that's not it. We needn't do that." He was getting ridiculous, her dad's way of skirting over the rough spots. "It's just that there are no plans anymore, nothing to get ready for. and no one to talk them over with." The conversation didn't ease her lonliness.

"Okay, darling. Then we won't travel to Chicago or Denver. Darn. Want to talk to your mom?"

Genny didn't, so she sent her perfunctory love and told him, "I got home okay, Dad. It was a smooth flight. Everything's fine. It was a beautiful wedding."

He was interjecting "good – good – good" between her comments and ended with "yes, it was." Genny sent kisses and hung up the phone. She pulled herself up off the floor, turned toward her bedroom to unpack her suitcase, or to write a letter, or to climb into bed and pull the heavy down comforter over her head. She had no plans for what she would do once she arrived.

Genny's sister had been her personal aide and sidekick since she had realized she was a little person just like her. When she learned to walk Genny led her to all the places of delight she had discovered in a full ten years of life – the swings in the park down the street, the ice cream wagon that appeared on warm days. When she learned to talk Genny shared all her little girl thoughts with her knowing Denise would agree with them whether she understood them or not – the discomfort of tights, the barbarism of little boys. No other sibling joined the family. Those two only, with a parent for each to push them along. They grew together, Genny leading the way, Denise taking advantage of all Genny's missteps, making a complete life for herself. When Genny moved to Chicago, Denise was quick to follow, leaving her David behind.

"What will he do without you?" Genny asked when she expressed her plans to join her.

"He'll probably jump on a plane and come marry me," she said.

"Is that what you want?" Genny asked.

"Gen, I've been dating that guy since kindergarten, it seems. Sure, I want to marry him, but we became so settled in our settled little life in that settled little town, I think marriage would disrupt him. I need to shake the ground a little."

So Denise joined Genny in Chicago where she had settled into a nice little life with a nice little job and a nice little lawyer boyfriend. It wasn't much different from what the two sisters had left except for the potential, the endless possibilities that the city held out.

As Genny unpacked her suitcase, each dress plugged her into a diorama of the events that comprised Denise's wedding. "Probably the most lavish wedding the state of Utah has seen this season," her father had complained. Complained? Bragged.

She pulled her bridesmaid's dress from its protective tissue and there she was, standing before Denise, arranging every curl under the burst of net and lace while the bride studied the bridesmaid, "Gen," Denise had said, "you make me wish I were the maid of honor instead of the bride, you are so poised, all burnished and brown." Denise said that to Genny, Denise with her petal perfect cheeks, her eyes in shades of milk chocolate, her column of a neck Lladro might have sculpted. She had said that to Genny. Genny had wanted to cry.

"Denise! This day is about you. And look at you!" She turned her around to face the mirror. "Where in this room, on this planet, do you see a lovelier creature?" So true. Her whole face radiated her happiness. The hair Genny had fussed over shimmered. Her tiny torso, encased in the delicate eggshell satin of her wedding dress, rose out of the bouffant skirt, a living Madame Alexander doll. Her eyes rested on the image. She smiled a sweet smile of agreement. She was now the bride of those longing years.

Genny was close to her now as she had always been: behind her, urging her on, next to her, faithful and strong, in front of her, making a path. But Denise had bolted to the head of the line emotionally. She was so sure of this marriage, so sure of what she needed to be complete. She designed this life she was stepping into.

Standing in this silent moment, Denise moved away from her. Genny couldn't hold her. The diorama darkened. She buried her face in the cloth she held in her hands. Her tears, she realized, were spotting the shimmer of the silk. "That's okay. The day is over."

She sat on the edge of her bed and began writing. Suitcase emptied with its dresses, shoes, and laundry heaped up on an empty chair, sun disappearing, darkening her room, Genny wrote. In this loneliness she could write words that expressed

the loss. She was writing poetry that was the face of her aban-
donment.

Genny woke up at two forty in the morning with words
pressuring against her skull, forcing her eyes open. She needed
three more hours of sleep to hold her through the long day
coming of itineraries, computer formats, details that travelers
expected from her. Instead, she was awake, crouching on the
bench at the foot of her bed letting the words escape again.
Word after word fit together into a compact whole, easing the
pain.

She promised herself when she emptied her head she
would climb back into her bed, to sleep. Her eyes burned.
She wanted to shut them tight so they would stay shut, to
stretch out full length, her toes wrapping around the edge of
her mattress, the palms of her hands grasping the sides of her
bed. To stretch out full and fall asleep. Just a few more words
fitting together, saying what she wouldn't say in the sunlight.

At three-thirty she would return to bed. At four. She
needed sleep.

Genny slept, at last. At dawn, the hours stolen from her
night dulled her body, while shadows of the words now on
paper faded from her head in the chill of her morning shower.
The palpitating water washed away the night. Her skin was
new. Her spirit was new. She was normal again. Her attention
turned to the mundane, to her orange juice, the morning news,
to the button that needed replacing on her sweater.

She didn't remember the words of the poems she created
in the storm of the night. She refused to read them, frightened
by their urgency. What replaced them in her interest were the
opportunity pages, Regeants Park and New York City. She
applied for a transfer.

30

Which I wish to say is this
There is no beginning to an end
But there is a beginning and an end
To beginning

Stanzas in Meditation / Gertrude Stein

GENEVIEVE – a beginning and an end

Taking up the spaces vacated by Denise, and her marriage, and the Mountain Man, and his marriage were the papers flying around various offices regarding Genny's proposed relocation to New York. She stood at her boss's desk who was saying, "If you really want it, Genny, it's yours."

Mine. Something good that is mine, Genny thought. "I want it. It's time. Yeah, Chris, I would like to try the East Coast." With that Genny committed herself to another upheaval. A lateral transition, yes, but she saw it taking her up and out, a productive choice.

"Okay then, there are some things we need to go over. Sit for a moment please." Genny lowered herself into one of a pair of mesh ergonomic side chairs, poised for the blueprint of her future.

Chris picked up paperwork on her desk that she was marking up with a highlighter. Genny strained to see what had her attention. Messages from Regeants Park, papers had been flying.

"You will need to be on the job in New York by the end of the month but stay with us here through some of January and then take off. Even though the Regeant's New York travel department is short-staffed right now, they plan to put you through some quick training before you take over the client calls. So let's get you there reasonably soon."

None of this surprised Genny. Deets had shared the drill with her.

"Once there, it'll probably be a couple of weeks learning the ropes, their ropes. There will be an increase in salary due to the cost of living and all that. I'll have to find out the exact figure they've settled on. You should know that before you accept." Chris glanced up from the papers to catch Genny's reaction. The figure wouldn't matter; in her mind she had already accepted.

"I'm sure they'll be fair," she said, indicating that money wouldn't be an issue. No issues. She didn't have the energy for issues. She would be going. No reason to stay behind. "Is everything in place with Deets? When's he leaving?"

"He's all set," Chris said, "I'm pleased that arrangements are so near completion."

Deets was the "settest" person Genny knew. His mind probably solidified his New York plans the moment Genny had expressed a need to escape Chicago, as though he were only waiting for someone to accompany him on an adventure. She welcomed his assuredness, needing some direction in her flailing life. He had been there whispering "New York, New York" at every opportunity. Soon she was responding, "Of course, New York City."

Made in the USA
Lexington, KY
06 December 2019

Chris reached behind her to the credenza where a similar file labeled "Demetrios" rested. "Yes, Deets and I have worked through all the complications," Chris said. "He'll be on his way as soon as we get you nailed down. He said it might be a twosome when we first talked. So we've tried to get you scheduled together." She checked through his folder again. "Yes, he's all set."

"I guess he's surer of my future than I am." Genny sounded more wistful that she intended to appear. But Chris knew Genny's weak spots, knew that her sister had left the city. She suspected that there were man complications in her life since she had heard no recent chit-chat about Brian, nor any replacement name. Mountain Man was a secret Deets had kept well. He had kept mum about the original infatuation, kept mum about the poetry that came out of it, and was keeping mum about Jon's undercover wife. Neither would talk about any of it anymore.

"So we will proceed, Genny?" Chris asked.

"Sure, pedal to the metal. Nothing tying me down. I don't have a lease. Never got around to signing one after our second year." Genny rummaged through the pockets in her sweater for a notebook to write down any information she needed to tie this transfer up.

Chris said, "A very understanding landlord, no?"

"I think he smelled the vagabond in me," Genny said. "He maybe figured out I might not be in that apartment long with Denise leaving. I guess I suspected it too. So my apartment is no problem. I can just pack up and go. Like a nomad."

"We can give you the time you need to relocate," Chris said. "If I can push all this paperwork through, you should be able to check into Regeants mid-January. Great way to start a new year, I am thinking."

263

Chris's optimism enthused Genny.

"You know, don't you Genny, how much we are going to miss you. You have been valuable to us. We all have enjoyed working with you. You're such an asset to this office and to the company. Lucky New York to get you.

"Before I forget, Genny, we have people in New York who can find you an apartment. Get in touch with them ASAP to tell them exactly what you want. You probably won't get it, but they will try. Here's their card. Call as soon as possible."

Genny clutched the card in her hands like a Tiffany gift certificate.

Chris had more advice to offer. "I think they are on Deets' case already. They can set up your furniture move too, if you want to use them. We'll be relaxing your hours at both ends a bit while you are getting organized. We're not giving you much time to relax." Genny answered her supportive smile with a small bow of appreciation.

Genny didn't need much time. Denise had carted away much of what they had in the apartment. Most of it she had bought with a home for her and David in mind. Some of it had come from Winton and they split that down the middle. The rest was ripe for a rummage sale. Little else remained for transport to New York. She thought it would be invigorating to start fresh in a new town.

But when she started organizing what filled the closets and shelves, she was amazed at what she wanted to follow her. She packed up all the books acquired with each poetry class. She packed up the files of writings, poems, essays, reports, research. Such a scholar. In a corner of the room, she set aside the remaining furniture, what was left of the kitchenware, the

Chicago clothes that had long ago squeezed out the Winton wardrobe. She was ready to revamp.

In side-table drawers, she found notes of encouragement from her father, new correspondence from Aunt Betsy reiterating her invitations to the West coast, scrawled lines of poetry along with pages of memos from Denise keeping her abreast of the status of the December affair. Buried with clippings of wedding planning advice was a quiet ivory-toned card with a scripted message: "Dear Genevieve, thank you for your sympathetic thoughts. Your beautiful words touched my heart. I feel I know you well. Stanley talked so often of you, the fun he had with you, sharing your antics and your poetry. I wish you well in that endeavor. Poetry is so important in our lives. With love, Adelaide"

Now Genny knew her name. A sense of intimacy overwhelmed her. All this now became precious, a snapshot of love.

Then, unable to avoid hidden recesses, Genny approached the corner of her closet where Mountain Man residue lodged. Printouts of his emails, copies of his writings, his edits on hers, smart-ass notes on coffee-house napkins, the Beethoven CDs he had left behind, the Dickinson anthology, brilliant pictures Genny had snuck of him in the sunshine on the beach. The photo of them together taken at Levinski's book signing surfaced.

She stared at that gray photo and wondered why that man couldn't love that woman. He stands behind her, his long slender fingers draped across her bony shoulders, a puppeteer controlling her movements. Those same fingers that later that evening played across her naked flesh like a master pianist creating chords that resonate inside her still. She sits there in the picture with the light picking up the planes of her body, two slashes across her collarbones, a dash down her nose, glints

of light at her cheekbones, cascades of light falling from her scalp outlining the ebony hair caught at the nape of her neck. Why couldn't he love her? She sits on the granite gallery bench, her head twisted around to gaze at him, bathing his face in adoration, his eyes gazing past her to land on the face of the camera woman whom he has charmed into taking their portrait: "For the jacket of the book of poetry we will write," he said as explanation.

He should have loved her.

The picture was a mite out of focus, grainy. It gave off an aura of transience, as if it were disappearing, as if when next she picked it up, the image would be gone. She captured it now in protective tissue and buried it within the pages of Dickinson.

This assemblage of pain, she didn't know what to do with the mass of it. She couldn't leave it behind. She couldn't pitch it down the garbage chute. She couldn't pack it up and send it back to Winton to be filed away with all her adolescent memorabilia. She didn't want it in New York. She closed it again behind the closet door.

Deets rang up. He was bringing over some CDs of Genny's he had found mingling with his, borrowed, never returned. They relaxed with a couple of beers for a small moment.

Then, sitting across from Genny at the kitchen table, taking a deep breath and biting his upper lip, he said, "Gen, can I ask you a personal question?"

She was not prepared for any conversation of consequence. With "I don't think so," she tried to evade the topic she was sure he had in mind.

"It's about the Mountain Man."

"I figured. Shoot."

"When did you first meet him?" Deets had a calculating scowl on his face. He had cleaned out his apartment, now he wanted to clean out the mess of Genny's life.

"When? Last summer, the middle of July. Why?" Deets was not answering her questions. He was on a path of his own.

"So you met him in July and you dumped him in December. That's five months, Genny. Five lousy months. You're looking like hell worked you over because of five lousy months?"

"They weren't lousy," Genny said and added, searching for a reflective surface, "I look like hell?"

He ignored that question too. "Middle of July, is that when you first went out with him?"

"Oh no," Genny said, "not 'til much later."

"How much later?"

Genny couldn't figure out what he was driving at, but he had been through so much with her, she guessed he deserved answers. "Sometime early in September." *Some time*, Genny chortled at that answer. She knew the exact time, the month, the day, the hour.

"So from the middle of July to the first of September, what was happening? That's a month and a half for god's sake."

Genny's answer was honest and ridiculous. "I fell in love. He was emailing me almost daily towards the end of that month and a half and I was falling in love. Eventually, emails came sometimes twice, sometimes three times a day. Every one of them, sending me deeper into love."

"And what was he doing in that month and a half while you were falling in love?" Deets pushed his luck.

"I don't know. Washing his car, cooking dinner, rubbing his wife's back, buying her roses. Who knows?"

"And did he ever cook you dinner? Rub your back? Buy you roses?"

"Yes he did," Genny said. "Not dinner, but he bought me roses. He brought me single roses and once he brought me tulips and once he brought me a tiger lily he stole from somebody's alley. To make up."

"And how many times did he need to do that? Make up? How many times were you mad at him?"

"I was never mad. Disappointed, never mad." A clarity developed. What little right she had to be so forlorn.

Deets persisted. He raked his fingers through the curls of his shaggy hair. "How many times? For how long?" He became relentless, eager to make his point.

"Jeez, Deets, I don't know. What are you doing this for? It's bad enough that it happened the way it happened without you dragging me through the whole horror all over again."

Genny turned around in her chair, wanting some escape from this disquieting conversation. All she saw were snapshots on a refrigerator door. Hanging off a door hook was the scarf Jon would wrap around her chin when the cold overtook them. Spaces on a shelf where cookbooks had been. She didn't want to review her summer and fall. Deets knew the answers to all these questions. He was making Genny hear them.

"I don't want to hurt you, Gen. I just want you to put it all in perspective. I want you to start out New York fresh, no baggage." He was trying to make it easy for Genny to pack it all up for New York.

"All right. Maybe I only had only a couple months of the good stuff. Maybe the rest of the time we were out of sync. But when the wheels were meshing it was glorious."

"A couple of months," Deets said. "More than a month of that was spent in courting you by computer. I was there, remember, when those words on fire came through. I felt the excitement."

That was an unbearable truth. Genny had shared her delight with Deets every time she had snared an email on her office computer. She had captured them, printed them out, reread them until she could repeat them word for word without the scripts.

Deets settled into the kitchen chair, taking another poke. "And then there was that month when I couldn't mention his name without you snarling?"

"Yes, there was that. It was a very rocky time. I should never have let him back in."

"But you did. So what do we have here?" Deets was winding up. He needed another beer and helped himself from the fridge. He offered to bring one to Genny. She refused. She was drowsy from the beer she was nursing and the review of the tragedy of her season in the sun. "Maybe at most a couple of good months when you add up the good days."

"And nights," she had to add. His cold stare reduced the time spent with the Mountain Man to insignificance. She couldn't bear to have that happen. Not yet. Not now.

"All right – good days, and nights. A couple of months out of your thirty years."

"Thirty-seven. Thirty-seven years." What wisdom had those extra seven years given her? She sank down in the chair knowing the answer was *none*.

"So once in thirty-seven years you thought you at last found love – a couple of months of love." Deets's face was adopting that too-wise-for-his-years veneer, his mouth crimped into an irregular line, his bottomless eyes narrowing.

"Love, yes, at last, love," she said. The word became a sound, a meaningless sound.

"You are wrong, you know," he said straightening up in his chair. He took a slow breath before he dared to add, "It

wasn't love. You get nothing out of love. What you found was imagination and inspiration. A kick-start to poetry. What you got, was poetry."

"No. Love."

Deets then moved his shoulders over the table and lowered his head to peer into her eyes. Those dark Greek eyes were brimming with compassion. "Genny, let it go. New York's gonna be a new ball game. It'll be good. You'll see. Everything else will fade away. Let it go."

Deets left satisfied. From the living room window, Genny watched his slender body exit the apartment building, parka resting on his shoulders, hands stuffed in the side pockets, a spring to his step. What remained in his wake was a hollow shell that Genny tried to fill with confidence in a future she could not envision, that she tried to fill with Deets's friendship, that she tried to fill with memories of family love and loyalty. Still, a hollow space remained.

The office party saying adios to the pair departing for New York was rowdy. Get the agents away from their headphones and their dignity evaporated. They took their regular places on retro bar stools around chrome plated café tables and huddled in tufted booths. They danced to wild rock music, drank margarita doubles, hugged and smooched with abandon. In the midnight hours they were booted from the dingy pub that had housed them for years of after-shift drinking.

In the scramble of readying herself for New York, Brian surfaced. He had heard of Genny's departure. They had a "for old time's" pizza when he promised to check in on her up whenever he was in New York. She wondered why.

In a more sedate tone, Shannah hosted a small dinner party for a few students she had tapped for greater glory. She

dressed for the evening in a sweater dress that skimmed her body and touched the floor. Genny had not seen this elegant side of Shannah before. Her curls were gathered up in a thick braid she had wrapped around itself. She wore makeup that gentled the lines in her face and brought their ages closer together.

Seated around her rough-hewn harvest table, they all talked through the evening about the magic of New York. Genny almost believed them. As they separated at the front door, Shannah held on to Genny's arm, herding the others out to the street. "Stay a bit," she whispered.

Back in her entrance hall she leaned against a book-laden table and sighed, a sound coming from beyond her body like wind whistling through winter-barren trees.

"Genny, I know what you are doing, and I know why. I do read your poetry and very carefully at that." Genny's whole life was exposed in the poetry she had created for Shannah's class and shared with her when the classes were done. "I want you to be very careful what you do as the next step beyond lost love."

"I'm okay," Genny insisted. "I am going to New York because it's a great city and a great job. I know the woman I will be working for and she has a terrific reputation for running a great office. I will be fine." A hollow response, but it was all Genny could muster.

"You are already fine and good," Shannah said. "You are thirty-seven and good. I want you to stay that way through thirty-eight, through forty, fifty. To run over this disappointment as if it were but a rise in the road.

"Let me tell you what I took on when I was thirty-seven. I was a new widow, a war widow. I had married a career Army man and pictured myself a soon-to-be general's wife. He was

that good a soldier. But the Gulf War got him before the Pentagon did. I got a folded flag to cherish.

"Taps had hardly faded away when I was on a college campus beginning the degrees that would bring me here. A dozen-plus years later, a Master's degree, a Ph.D., even a new husband. It worked out, Genny. I never looked back. It was much too black behind me. But I didn't have to, my poetry looked back for me. It said all the things too unbearable for me to dwell on. My poetry was sad and angry. It worked out. Loss is not the end of a good story ..." Her voice trailed off.

Genny was ashamed. Shannah had exposed so much of the real pain she had survived where Genny whimpered over half a love. "I am so sorry for you," she said, but Shannah interrupted.

"I didn't tell you that for your sympathy. I want you to see how you can use pain; it's the underbelly of our humanity. Use it to accomplish a good substitute for what you have lost. Go to New York. Write good stuff. Heal yourself. I am watching you. Genny, I can only repeat Plato's admonition, 'The poet is a light and winged thing, and holy. There is no invention in him until he has been inspired and is out of his senses.' Go be senseless." She sent Genny off with a chuckle.

Senseless. Without any sense. The state Genny had been in through the summer and beyond. If there were to be any ultimate reward for her experience, time would tell.

Time. All of a sudden she was out of time. She had so little time to pack up, to wind down. So little time to get from here to there. So little time to grieve. No time to grieve. The wisdom of winter was taking over. The gray, somber season had blown the autumn away.

Genny sorted through her friends. She forced cheerful goodbyes on those she knew would come east to visit. Others she let slip out of her life.

A follow-up phone call from Shannah carried a promise that she would keep her hand at her back, "Please, please, please let's stay in touch," she asked. "We have that anthology to get published." Genny would stay in touch. "And just to make sure I can keep my eye on you, I will find you the perfect poet's group in New York. One that will keep you on top of your game. You are good, you know."

Genny would try to do all Shannah wanted. She needed the hope she offered. and strength to replace the bonds she was unfastening. In that final phone call, Shannah applauded her going, trusting that she would keep experimenting and begin to tether her style. "Remember," she said, "even a broken gladiola stem will still blossom, flower by flower." With that, Shannah said good-bye.

One by one, Genny printed out the poems from the infantile "11 going on 12" to her last middle of the night creation, a poem she could not bear to reread, with all its sorrow. Then one by one, she also saved them to discs. They were all together now, comforting each other.

She packed away the discs, packed up the printer and the laptop after taking one last survey of her email. It was loaded. She hadn't harvested the inbox for a week. She had too little time for that obsessive luxury.

Scrolling down, deleting everything but the personal notes, the name that stopped her heart appeared. The summoned message exploded on the screen. She tried not to read but the habit was too ingrained, the curiosity too overriding.

From: jonwat
To: gennydu
Date: Thu, 13 Jan 2004 15:25:19
Subject: Re: a leave-taking

> *I am missing you. I have no right to miss you*
> *because I had no right to be in your life. And no right*
> *to bring you into mine. But we were there together.*
> *And we felt good together. Fun and passion. A very*
> *fine combination. May it come to you again in a man*
> *more worthy.*
>   *Someday we will be friends again.*

Genny was breathless. *No. Please dear God, no. We will not be friends again. We played at friendship once; I cannot play again.* With that determination, she packed him away. Duct tape surrounded the box that held him. He had no delivery address label attached. Yet there was no place to go with him but to her New York apartment. There she would place him next to an easy chair, cover him with a tablecloth, put a lamp and a bouquet of flowers upon him. Let him serve some purpose. She would plant the fields he left empty. He would not be a friend.

31

for whatever we lose (like a you or a me)
it's always ourselves we find in the sea

maggie and milly and molly and may / e.e.cummings

GENEVIEVE – whatever we lose

Genny moved on. She left a city that draped over her like a protective cloak but couldn't shield her from a one-way love, reaching out, never bouncing back.

Her most wrenching goodbye came with a winter dawn. She awoke before the sun when it was only a hint beyond a charcoal sky. Would she be ready for this goodbye? She had endured such separations before: from her father, from old beaus, was it so long ago from Brian, from Stan's conversations, from her work buddies, from Denise, from the Mountain Man. They left hollows in her heart. Now she was leaving her lake and its beach and its many moods that changed or reflected hers. She could do this.

She rose out of bed, one limb at a time. She knew where to go; she knew what to wear. The air was a record-breaking cold even for the mid-January day, her new day, her new year, her

cold empty new life. She pulled on her sweats. She reached for her ski socks and laced up her hiking boots. Her parka, a scarf, and stocking cap were nearby. Mittens. She stuffed handkerchiefs in her pockets. And a notebook and pen. All this to say goodbye.

The beach was empty at that early hour. Gone were the sun worshipers who had populated the sand and grass through the warm season, ignoring the two of them. Gone the hot sun and the cool waters. Genny walked along the snow-brushed sand and wanted those days again. She tried to strike the images from her memory as a kaleidoscope of emotions scurried between her brain and heart. She needed new images, to leave the old behind. Could rowboats in Central Park, the banks of the Hudson and East Rivers, the excitement of Broadway and Soho replace this lake?

She saw herself in New York – purple. All around her, purple.

She saw Denise's purple face. Purple. Genny is twelve; Denise is almost four. They are walking down side streets on the way home from the candy store in Winton. "You okay back there 'Neecey?" she calls to her over her shoulder, not looking back. Denise is riding in her wagon, happy, Genny thinks, to be pulled all over town.

"Geevee, I'm cold, really cold."

"You're the one who wanted gumdrops, little lady. I would have made you hot chocolate instead and we could have been sitting in a nice, warm kitchen."

Denise's voice turns into a whine that angers Genny. She could be up in her room reading Judy Blume's "Forever." She could be on the phone hearing the newest dirt on simple, sexy Katie Cutestuff, real name Crestoff. She could be sitting in a musty movie house watching "The Muppet Movie."

But she is wheeling her little sister around town on the coldest day of the year finding her green gumdrops because Neecey is about to celebrate her fourth birthday and green gumdrops are what four-year-olds crave for their birthdays. With a stern face, she turns around to make a point and sees Denise has turned purple. And she's shivering, shaking the wagon.

"I'm really cold, Geevee, really cold" she pleads as Genny swoops her up, opens up her jacket and tucks her inside. Too heavy to carry all the way home, she returns her to the wagon, tells her to hang on, bury her face and breathe deep breaths. She runs, the wagon careening behind her. Denise whimpers until she is delivered into their mother's arms and the word "frostbite" rings in Genny's ears.

She will never forget that color or that cold. She will never forget the pain the purple indicated. Her mother will never forgive her. She failed Denise. Purple will always be the color of failure.

By the time the morning light strengthened Genny was at the water's edge, separated from the waves by a crust of choppy ice. The early sun was brilliant. It burst through the clouds in sprays of aqua, magenta, and peach. Overwhelmed by the display, the clouds crept south. This was to be a day when nothing could share the sky with the sun. The ripples in the water caught the rays and spread them over the sand threatening the fragile coat of frost. The whole landscape was crisp.

How long could she stand chilled by this morning before she regretted her decision? She thought of Jon's "But she is …" bouncing off the frozen sand, bouncing around her brain. Its echo left nothing to rethink.

The cold numbed her nose. It paralyzed her thumbs. She brought them into her mittens and wound her scarf tight around her chin.

Genny picked her way across the sand to the breakwater, encrusted with mounds of sculptured ice. The waves rose like crystal whales shattering against the cement. She walked to the end, to the point jutting into the lake. Surrounding her was water so heavy with the cold that as it beat against the pillars it displaced the sound of the city. Genny was lost in it.

Returning to the beach, she walked over a risky ice-coated path that eased into the park. The merciless wind followed her across the grassy banks as she walked south. Hadn't she abandoned the mountains of Utah and survived? She could abandon this terrain and survive. While it nurtured her deepest love, it too served as backdrop for her reentry into a lost world of poetry. Along these waters the most poetic of words were whispered into her ear.

She walked south. The early hour and the fallen tempera- ture guaranteed her the beach and the park to herself. The squirrels still slept. The crows and the gulls were hidden and silent. Genny walked this territory alone. It was here only for her. Quiet sounds accompanied her – twisted branches creaking with the wind, stones crunching under her step. The sirens of the day and night, so much a part of her environment, were still. The morning was brand new, quiet, a brand new year, quiet. Genny would walk into it alone in silence.

She approached a contemplation circle of cement blocks sitting scattered among the trees, waiting for the summer strollers to stop and rest. In warmer weather tree foliage sur- rounded the respites and lush grasses shrouded them. Now they stood stark, cold. The softness of summer was gone. A summer goodbye would have been easier than this hard-angled farewell.

Maybe she should have packed up a bag with a clean pair of socks and a toothbrush and left, closing her eyes to the beauty at the edge of her city, knowing if an ocean bordered the East Coast, if the sun shone on New York City, if breezes blew through Central Park, Genny would find words she could gather into poetry again. Maybe, too, a sensible love.

Yet tears flowed, chilling her cheeks as she plodded south along the cement banks that here again replaced the beach. The graffiti of summer she trod upon was dingy from exposure. "Jon and Genny" was nowhere inscribed on the cement. Such permanency was denied them. They never attempted to add their names to Fran and Bill's, to Jorge and Juana's, to Ted's Ashley, Marcy and Gina. These sun-baked loves surrounded her chanting, "Look at our love; it's eternal, embedded in the cement you stand on." Genny moved to the grass and threw a scowl at them, "Don't bank on it." She and Jon never considered penning their poetry in primitive lettering, dating it, signing it. Michael and Janice did: "I am my beloved's and my beloved is mine." The cement verified that Richard loved Charlotte. The summer world was so expressive. But so was the autumn.

The morning air smelled of ice and snow. Haunting her appetite were memories of summer gatherings around barbeque pits, the jingle-jangle of Manuel's ice cream cart gathering small dark children about it, the squawking of gulls picking at crumbs. This morning no trace of warmth remained, as if no living being had ever penetrated this space. Not true. Genny had been there, leaving traces of lemon lotion behind. They had been there together, leaving the aroma of love behind.

Could she live in this space again?

At the beachside basketball court the hoops stood barren of nets. No balls bounced off backboards. No sweating,

cursing, muscled young men bounded back and forth shouting, blocking, tripping, unaware of their audience.

No lilac blossoms forced their scent into the air. No crabapple petals feathered the trees. Only scrubby natural grasses outlined the sculptured beauty of the golf course. Concave sand traps held banks of leftover snow.

Genny sank into the Peace Garden, surrounded by weathered field stones. The ivy covering the walls was discolored from the cold. The pond was frozen, capturing for the season the autumn leaves that had fallen into the water. Across the ice, lady bugs skate with silver blades on their feet. "Go away. You bring me no luck no matter how many wishes I make." Some sounds of the boulevard found her. The city was awakening and moving to destinations beyond the hidden sanctuary with its peace poles flanking the path. They offered peace to everyone everywhere. Genny added in a whisper, "Peace to me; peace to you; I hope you are happy; I hope you are well."

She arrived at the canopied café, all its windows boarded up against the winter. How colorful it was that splendid autumn day they stopped for lunch. Genny needed to sit at that table again. She needed to feel its reality, yet the café, the table, the chained chairs floated out into the water away from her.

Beyond, the ghosts of boats remained in the marina, buoys bobbing in the frigid water. Her ghost remained too, walking with an arm around his waist, listening to his mellow voice purr his contentment. She should rescue that ghost, seal it within the box of memories; keep it from stalking these shores forever.

Her turmoil matched the bluster around her. All was temporary. Soon ice would melt; she would mend. She would write out the poetry her turbulence dictated. She would bloom

as sure as the trees surrounding her would bloom, as sure as the brown matted grass would perk up green, as sure as the angry waves would subside and caress the softening sand and the children who would come again to splash in them. She would soften and bloom. Someday.

Returning toward home Genny walked the western border of the park and came upon Cricket Hill, the closest she had come to a mountain since arriving in Chicago. A presumptuous little mound of earth in the middle of the park, at its peak were the smells of freedom, unencumbered, pure. She started up the hill but its peak stayed distant. When she arrived to look over the water it had no beginning, no end. They had climbed that hill, brandishing kites that they had no talent to fly. They had kissed on that hill. They had kissed well, better than they had flown kites.

"I feel like butterflies are invading me."

Who had said that? Genny?

"I feel like they are flicking away my balance and certainty." He had said that. Genny had never felt balance and certainty. She had always been in effervescent water, drowning, or engulfed in clotted clouds. Sometimes in air like this at the top of Cricket Hill, Genny would feel his freedom. She had peered around full circle at the water, at the trees, at the skyscrapers, and the ball fields. And back again at his face. She had read a camaraderie there she now remembered. She hadn't seen love.

She wondered then at the lack of love.

And then they had run down the hill, he much faster than she, eager to escape the emotion that had engulfed them at that higher altitude. The looming city now told her to leave before it destroyed her.

Maybe when Genny reached O'Hare later in the day she would turn in her ticket for a ticket west, go back to the high

hills of Utah. There was always a job waiting for her at her old desk. She was guaranteed that when she left and the promise repeated a week ago at the wedding reception. Or go to Los Angeles where her Aunt Betsy's adventures beckoned. Other places were kinder than these chilling streets of Chicago.

If she went west, white. She would be milky white. She would disappear.

"The dress is beautiful," her mother is saying. It's bridal white, the color of choice.

Her heart is not in this search for a dress for her wedding. Truth be told, her heart is not in this wedding. Something is amiss – true commitment, passion. The wedding date is determined and her mother is at the helm directing her to the day. She keeps the appointments her mother has made. This is the fourth. All the dresses are the same to her: shades of white, flounces and filigree, bouncy bouffant, sparkles. She is a trimmed down autumnal animal, tending toward shadowy colors that don't effervesce. Bridal white on her body is an overlay. Like a Halloween costume. Phantom garb.

"Mom, let's put this off a little longer. I'm not ready for a wedding gown."

Her mother is horrified at the proposed delay. "These dresses take time, Genevieve. You don't want to be rushing things when it's time to walk down the aisle."

"I feel like I am rushing things now. I feel like I am rushing him. I feel like you are rushing me. I want to lean back and wait until he shows more excitement."

"Men don't get excited about weddings. They get excited about having dinner on the table when they come home. They get excited about a warm body in bed with them. Weddings are just a necessary step to those things."

The excitement never develops and he fades. All she remembers is the whiteness of the shopping bouts. She failed her mother and those desires to see her daughter in white.

Troubled shouting in the distance broke the stillness, disrupted the images Genny had imposed on the landscape. "Wallace, Wally." A woman's frantic voice penetrated the silence. Pleading, "Wally you come here. You come here to me. Wally, you come here."

The sound grew louder as a bushy dog dragging a leash came romping toward Genny. Alone, tossing a stick into the air, chasing it, repeating the choreography again and again, happy to be free, snorting steam from his nose and mouth.

The problem was obvious. Genny stamped on the leash as he passed her, pulling him to an abrupt halt, to the end of his delirious freedom.

The woman hustled up to Genny panting her gratitude. As she looked up to accept it, Genny recognized Karen's face from her Paris return. Karen's face – the last familiar face she would see in Chicago. In her muted colors she almost faded into the seascape. Her smile stayed in clear focus, the smile Genny had seen her bestow on Jon. Genny was compelled to speak, to give some substance to this encounter, to acknowledge the woman who loved as she did.

Genny recovered. "He certainly has had enough exercise now," she said as she turned over the leash. Her voice was wrapped in vapors.

"Wally? Wally will never get enough exercise. His daddy spoils him with runs through the park – usually the park up north. This was to be a treat for him, to go to the doggy park here and run with the animals. But his daddy is still in bed, still recovering from a Saturday night celebration, so I was elected."

"And you don't need to recover?" Genny could not let her go.

"Oh, I will recover all right. I am jumping right back into that bed and get all the recovery I need."

Genny had stayed in the conversation too long. Bitter juices were surging now through her veins. She began gagging, camouflaging the sounds with a cough. Wally pulled at his leash; Karen offered a water bottle; Genny shook her head no, excused herself and began a turn toward the path. Her eyes stayed on Karen. Genny had to leave. She could not share the space.

This face before Genny was the reason she was abandoning all this freshness and light of her neighborhood, a face so pleased and secure, offering her a bottle of water. A mere bottle of water when she had taken the air Genny breathed.

Forsake this beloved ground? No. She should stay and reclaim her lake, her beach, her park. She should let the winds that wrapped her body in chilling breezes toughen her spirit. What would happen if she stayed in Chicago? Mauve. All around her would be mauve memories.

"You grew this?" The flower he hands her is gargantuan. "It's grey. How can you grow grey flowers?"

"It's not grey," he says. "It's mauve. It matches your mood when I displease you."

"Am I displeased with you now? Is that why you are handing me this giant hibiscus?"

"You are displeased because I was too busy this weekend to take you to your party. There are too many parties on weekends. Parties should be given in the middle of the week when we have nothing fun to do."

He brings his lips to her ear as if to divulge a secret shared with her alone. "Yes, of course I grew it, sweet lady, along with

a patchful of its sisters, all mauve, all beautiful, all reminding me of you when you are displeased."

"A backyard full of mad me's. That must be inspiring. What kind of poems come out of that garden?"

"None." No inspiration. She, surrounded by mauve hibiscuses, failed him.

The day became brighter. The hearty morning runners on the asphalt path interrupted her solitude. Seemingly pleased that they are not alone, they nodded greetings to Genny. She could not acknowledge their presence. She wanted no others on her land, near her waters. Today, and then never again, they were to be hers alone. Her feet were frozen. She headed for home.

32

I find prayer in a thousand places:
on crammed buses
in trashed-filled alleys
in parks and fields
where sunlight flows over crabby grasses.

Prayer / Jonathan Waterhouse

JONATHAN – prayer in trash-filled alleys

"Jonathan ..." his name filled the spaces of his vapid den. "Give it another try, guy. She's gotta be out there somewhere, maybe just wanting the perfect word from your seductive inventory to entice her back."

With that hope, he retreated to the kitchen and the makings of yet another dinner for Karen and some woman she would bring home to meet him, to flaunt before another office friend her domesticated male. He lined up the fixings, sampled the Bordeaux and took a half-filled glass back to the computer.

The cursor sped down the address list to "gennydu" springing out like a red poppy in a field of buttercups. As he

studied it, he mused over the inappropriateness of the name. *Genny do what? Create the silence of a windless ocean, as barren, as endless, as merciless, without a hint of comforting land. Is that what you do?*

Deluded, he convinced himself she hadn't gone for good. He remembered the devotion he had grown to expect, the nutrient of the creative world they inhabited. Another sculpted message would bring her back into their private world of poetry, he reasoned out loud, willing it to come true. "She comes back to my words, to the poems I write for her. She comes back to poetry with images beyond the chimera of my mind. I can use the bewitchment of poetry again."

Yet, what words she would hear, what poem would she read, what sound would reach her ear when she was so deaf to his pleadings? His last email went untended, floating uncaptured in the vast unknown that had claimed her.

He needed to do better. He penned a few thoughts in a notebook only to find them inert, unable to transfer any of his distress. He picked up a book of Emily Dickinson but found nothing that would speak to Genny. If he could not find in Emily Dickinson what he could not find in his own reservoir of verse, there was another hoard – his 918 file where rested every one of the words Genny chose to express the variety of emotions she laid at his feet. Here were words more penetrating than his own, his to use to draw her back.

He read again through the pages she had sent him over the months of their intimacy, ingesting all the elegance, the love and the suffering. He noted the mystery of the words falling into place, expressing her joy and her pains, one emotion following another like tumbleweeds careening across a distant desert. Distant, like the distance now between them, her voice muffled. He remembered well these words. He had

massaged each phrase; they were a part of him. They became droplets of perfection, pinpointing what she felt.

He needed to be with her again to have the challenge she brought to him, her burning drive heating up the space she passed through. He needed her face before him, to see again her tentative smile, never giving in to bliss, to see her guarded eyes, never surrendering her essence. He needed the constant influx of poetry she provided, poetry he appropriated as his own so tied were their emotions, filling his life and recontouring the flatness and emptiness of his land. She had left before, and returned. She would again.

From: jonwat
To: gennydu
Date: Wed, 19 Jan 2005 23:29:37
Subject: Again

"blue ... the color of silence" Those are your words that you left behind to taunt me. My words seem to say nothing that connects with you. So unbelievable that we were so much fun for each other such a short time ago sharing so many precious hours together. So close. You were my fun. Other than that I failed you miserably but I could not let you be more to me. I wish you had known that — because you need more to be more — and you might have brought more to yourself instead of bringing the meagerness of me. All I feel now is that I want you back with me. Is there a way back?

He sent the message as the phone rang, yanking him away from his sacred place. Unwilling to leave, he pulled the receiver

to his ear to hear Karen's assured voice conveying all the certainty of possession.

"I just wanted to remind you, love, that Beverly does not drink alcohol. I totally forgot. Can you bop over to the deli and bring in some nice Ariel Rouge?" He would do that and in doing so would move his thoughts far from computer messages, from walks on breezy beaches, and from poems that perforated his heart.

The email journeyed through the ether and found its way back to him, a destination he had not foreseen. Its sterile message told a truth that unhinged his senses.

> *From: MAILER-DAEMON@computerwizinc.com*
> *Sent: Thu, 20 Jan, 2005 8:35 AM*
> *To: jonwat @*
> *Subject: failure notice To: Genevieve*
> *Dupont<gennydu@*
>
> *This address no longer accepts mail.*
> *—Below this line is a copy of the message*

He found no reason to let his eyes go below to a copy of the message, to read again those futile, foolish words. He moved his finger toward the delete tab as a heavy curtain drew across his life, capturing in its fold her elegant words, her soulful face. All gone.

But the poetry remained. He had the poetry bringing her close again. He had a telephone number. When he dialed, a mechanical voice droned, "No longer in service" stunning him. He slammed the phone down, "goddamn – crap," a ceramic cup of pens exploded against the wall. "Shit – fuck." He stood looking at the damage. That left nothing. Nothing left of her. Except the poetry.

33

Love means to learn to look at yourself
The way one looks at distant things
For you are only one thing among many
And whoever sees that way heals his heart,
Without knowing it, from various ills –
A bird and a tree say to him: Friend.

Love / Czeslaw Milosz

GENEVIEVE – one thing among many

The building was tall; the apartment was small. Those who had lived in New York warned Genny to "kiss your two-bedroom goodbye." Genny had done that, kissed it all goodbye and headed east. New York, new year, new. The words sparked an unfamiliar optimism. New and old, the old catapulting her into the new. She should be grateful but she hadn't touched ground yet. She was afraid of the maybe cold, maybe cruel, yet maybe receptive ground.

A long hall led to Genny's and Deets's shared apartment. An assaulting odor of dog urine hung heavy. The building

buzzed. The outside wind rushed through ventilator tubes, flapping panels somewhere in the structure's system, transforming the damp city air into a stuffy wheeze when it oozed into the hall.

Russet and black-striped carpet traveled the length of the hall with muddy discolorations providing the only patterns on the floor. At the elevator door, the stripes were spotted with the slush stains of years of winter and spring thaws. The stucco walls were a deep gray, rather, a dirty gray upon closer inspection. Layered paint coated metal doors, flat gray chipping paint over chipped paint. Rusty knobs and locks punctuated the symmetry of the corridor. The ceiling had been white but had taken on the mustard hue from years of rising tobacco smoke.

Low wattage bulbs were recessed into the ceiling, their dim light muting the colors, blurring the stark lines of floor meeting wall, wall meeting ceiling. The end of the hall was duskier, the lights spaced farther apart. Perhaps one bulb had burned out. No light illuminated Genny's front door.

Inside their apartment, the former sunshine of her lakefront view gave way to the shadows of Manhattan density. Genny sat against the living room wall, her legs pretzeling around each other. Sorrow had not affected her flexibility.

She then noticed the wall, painted a rain-slicker yellow, glossy, wondering why. Yellow belonged in bathrooms along with the scents of citrus fruits – yellow soaps, lemon lotions, sunshine towels. She would have them all someday. She would paint over this misplaced color as soon as she replenished her stock of money and energy. She would choose white, flat white; too much color and shine exhausted her.

Deets slouched in a chair across the room, smiling at her. Across the room, a mere distance, she could reach out and touch his toes.

"Well, babe, we made it," he said, "intact and inspired."

Genny depended on Deets being in this escape with her. From the time he suggested she go for the Manhattan position, he was part of it. His "multiple opening" remark gave him away. His participation had been inevitable. He had been across the room, across the desk, across her mind for as long as they had worked together at the agency. He had been her little brother, her faithful old buddy. They made a promising team. He patted her back and she held his hand. In their jobs in the Madison Avenue office, the relationship remained the same. Since the demands their clients made on them now were tenser, more urgent and more profitable, their dependence thickened.

Genny reached out and touched his toes. He smiled again. "What a way to start a new year. What a place," he said.

Outside the day was gray. Perhaps the yellow walls were necessary after all, as an antidote to the gray air. The ground outside was gray with droplets of speckled asphalt.

Genny moved to the windows, opening the center pane a crack to bring in the texture of New York: the heavy grease-laden bouquet of oregano and sausage, cars honking angry blasts, a police siren in the distance, a couple spitting venom at each other in an indecipherable language on the sidewalk above her window. Yes, above. Theirs was a garden flat with sturdy bars across the windows, bars that put designs on the walls and floor when the sun shone in. A garden apartment with not a hint of greenery except for the leaves on the daisies Deets had picked up at the corner deli.

With space for both of them, Deets took a room that perhaps had been an oversized storage closet. Genny, because of her seniority, assigned herself the real bedroom with a single window high on the wall. Deets had none. But Deets had his music, bright and vigorous. He needed no outside inspiration.

Genny had a door to lock in the privacy her spirit needed to heal. She needed the slot of a window above her bed to throw to the wind the thorns of the past. They both needed each other's money to afford the space. Right now, they needed each other. They were frightened.

With nothing more to say, "Let's go taste the neighborhood," was a welcome suggestion. They had wanted to be somewhere other than where they had been. Now they were. So they hit the tar-studded streets searching for their kind.

Over the months in their exilic atmosphere, they found their kind: struggling musicians, writers, actors, mate seekers, mate abandoners, rising executives, wanderers. They all passed through the bars and cafés Genny and Deets passed through. Which Beatle said, "How can you dance when you're down on the ground?" Genny could. And did.

Over the months they plumped up their nest. The yellow walls became covered with coats of rich sapphire blue. Deets had pleaded for a wild kelly green until Genny reminded him he was Greek. Deets had a real bed, his first since leaving home, with real sheets, a deep rusty color and a real bedspread to match. He was growing up nicely.

So was Genny. She spent all her time being someone other than the Genny she left in Chicago. She seemed taller. Her skirts were longer. The fabrics were softer. She wore blacks and forest greens and dusty browns, clothes she found in small neighborhood shops with small dressing rooms and small prices. Her hair was flecked with henna and bronze, colors she added herself. Trimmed regularly, no one needed to draw it off her cheek. No one touched it.

Summer came again, as did autumn. The sleepless nights diminished. The wild, furry animals who had attached

themselves to her neck and back in the middle of the night as she slept moved on. The worms of Blake and Dickinson receded.

The words that had come screaming through the walls out of the New York darkness subsided. Genny had been writing them down, thinking they were her inspired poetry. They were senseless. Genny no longer saw lanky men with angular faces avoiding her stare at every corner. She didn't remember that face at all. She remembered his voice.

She had brought in some incidental pieces of furniture. Pillows and lounge chairs, all soft and comfortable. They now had tables to throw their mail on, put their beer glasses on, to hold their framed pictures.

One of those tables replaced the chair-side carton that had stored the Mountain Man. Before she moved it, Genny re-examined its contents to determine if they were worthy of New York space at seven hundred bucks a square foot.

Last in first out were the printouts of his email messages. She hadn't dug far into the packet before she realized she shouldn't be there. *The unavoidable sadness of life. / How will it hold us? / With the wan sunlight of the afternoon? / With blossoms dropping from tulip stems / under the weight of spring dew? / With the endless departures of those we love / from our lives?*

Genny wondered where those lines came from. She had no memory of a sadness in him to inspire them. The poem had been lost in all the intimate messages flowing through her autumn and forgotten in all the empty hours of silence. The "unavoidable sadness of life" that she had packed away was exploding out of its corrugated box.

"How will it hold us?" Genny could answer that poetic question now. The answer wasn't available a winter ago but

now "the unavoidable sadness of life" held her taut with papers now bound up in a duct-taped box. She gathered them
together and headed for the trash chute.

In their journey down to the incinerator, they escaped
their rubber-band binding. When Genny heard them flutter
off the sides of the tubing, a stabbing sensation ripped up her
gut to her throat. She rushed back into her apartment, to her
bedroom and collapsed into a crouch on the floor before she
could reach the bed. Sobbing, it was her first outburst since the
painful day she had left Chicago. To be so braced all through
the months in New York had taken energy.

Deets was at the front door coming into the apartment,
at the refrigerator pulling out a beer, at her bedroom door
knocking, asking, "What time are the Regeants people coming
over, Gen? Do we need anything from the deli?" She rose,
cauterized by the pain. The process was complete - her body
relaxed, her shoulders squared.

34

The profoundest of all sensualities
is the sense of truth
and the next deepest sensual experience
is the sense of justice.

The Deepest Sensuality / D H Lawrence

GENEVIEVE – the sense of justice

Sundays were Genny's "let the old week go" days. She and Deets usually met at their undiscovered pre-pricey coffee shop and lingered. Genny had usually been to church. Deets had usually slept the ten hours he needed to undo the damage of his New York weekends. A late morning coffee break suited both their schedules.

Whoever arrived first brought "The New York Times" to the table and laid claim to its prime parts.

That is where they learned that John Paul II and Betty Friedan had died, that Deep Throat was exposed, that French surgeons had replaced a human face, that Pluto was demoted.

Beyond the front pages, Genny had "first grabs" at the book section. She zeroed in on newly published poetry reviews, on

readings and book signings. She lived vicariously through the success of published poets. From newspaper notices, she would plan her rounds of evening poetry readings to keep her mind alert.

She was not writing much of anything anymore. New pieces she was putting down missed the mark. Since she was not studying anywhere, having no budget for that yet, not much in her world provided incentive.

Genny was absorbing whatever she discovered on the streets of New York. Her mind was filling up again. She was patient. Shannah urged her on from half a continent away, afraid Genny's reimagined life was neither sad enough nor happy enough yet to produce poetry. Genny remained in idle. Aware of where she was: Genny was in a waiting room.

Sticking to a ritual, Genny and Deets didn't hassle over the book section, but every now and then, Deets would insist on going through the pages before turning it over to Genny, picking out tantalizing items to liven up their coffee conversation. She repaid him with a wrap-up of losing scores of Midwest teams.

This Sunday it was his turn to jar her day.

Deets was reading the review of a poetry collection making its debut, mocking it with his pseudo-Bulgarian accent. "Thees leetul book ese editor's selecshun, my chickadee, so you vill pay close attencion. 'The scope of heez veeshun eez unending. He finds power in ze stories of heez efry day life. Efry grain of sand on heez belufid beach eez vibrant. Ze stark reality of heez ceetee eez penetrating. Efry precise line captures ze reethum, and calar of heez emotion.'

"Wanna go on? This man has no equal. He's like 'a child at the fair, rushing from cotton candy to a house of horrors with a side trip on the tilt-a-whirl.' Want more? 'Rare – sharp – elemental. Waterhouse is a poet to watch…'"

Genny's head snapped up at the name. It meant nothing to Deets. Genny had never spoken Jon's name in front of Deets. He was the Mountain Man in their conversations. Deets respected her privacy, enjoyed the mystery, was satisfied enough to follow the theatrics without knowing who played the lead.

"Read that again," she said, "without the local color." Deets did from the beginning of the review where book title and poet are mentioned. "Bed of Crimson Joy." Jonathan Waterhouse. Genny pulled in her breath.

Deets read the opening paragraphs and a quote from Blake, who had provided his title. "The worm ... has found out thy bed of crimson joy and his dark secret love does thy life destroy."

"Does thy life destroy," oh yes. Genny exhaled. Stunned, she asked Deets to read on, through all the rave remarks, all the enthusiastic commentary, recognizing her words in all the excerpted lines.

She listened in frozen silence to her Chicago poetry captured on the pages of Jonathan Waterhouse's book, paralyzed. All the effort over the past months to muffle her emotions was now without effect. All her quelled memories of her creative work and Jonathan Waterhouse's input were revisited. The poetry reading disintegrated her façade. She had been lying to herself. Now she faced that lie. The passion activated into bitterness.

Without a twitch, she asked, "Is there a local reading?" She was afraid of an affirmative answer, knowing she would go. Deets passed the book section to Genny and pulled out the sports pages. She folded it into the rest of the paper.

During lunchtime the following day, Genny found the nearest library to her office. The Sunday papers and alternate publications were on the racks by the time she arrived. She

scanned them all, reading reviews, looking for notices of public readings until she found what she sought: Jonathan Waterhouse reading from "Bed of Crimson Joy" at an obscure independent bookstore in Brooklyn, his first New York appearance. It was to be followed, she noticed, by several other readings in Manhattan and outlying hinterlands, beginning on a sacred Wednesday. Chain stores and libraries had engaged him throughout the weekend to help celebrate National Poetry Month.

Genny called in sick to Regeants early Wednesday morning and bussed over to Brooklyn, to the Centuries Book Gallery. With good connections, she was in the vicinity earlier than anticipated and stopped for coffee in a nearby corner restaurant to solidify her nerves.

Introductions were underway as she entered the Book Gallery. Picking up a display copy of "Crimson Joy," she heard his name coming from the rear of the store where chairs were set up and a small crowd gathered. Unnoticed, she followed the sound. Praises voiced by the proprietor overrode the genteel chatter that bubbled up from the group.

She saw the Mountain Man standing tall and proud. Dressed in a tweed sports jacket, he looked Midwestern, as if he had just come off a wooded campus in some gracious small town that nurtures small talents. He had weathered well since their frozen day on the beach.

A woman sat off to the side of the podium. She was earthy, proprietary, and plumper than Genny had remembered her from the airport and the park. She was smiling at him as he studied the front rows of the audience. He glanced back at his wife and narrowed his eyes. The blue Genny remembered holding the luster of a moonbeam had turned glacial. He seemed confident and endurant. He seemed content.

Genny stood behind the rows of chairs, in the shadow of the shelves. Books others had written by their own hand surrounded her. Her urge was to scream out the injustice he was perpetrating, to grasp these honors away from him and claim them as her own, to throw the love at his face so it hit like projectile vomit. The horror had made her voiceless; she couldn't, wouldn't.

He spoke, reciting Genny's lines of poetry from the book before him, commenting on their origins in the Midwestern environment that birthed them. Had she hired an actor to interpret her work, she couldn't have found better. His deep resonant voice gave meaning beyond her intention when she first penned the lines. How many evils did he embody standing before this audience: theft, avarice, wickedness, licentiousness. How many scarred his past: adultery, deceit, folly. Her pure words were filling the air. Genny could not absorb them. She held the palm of her hand to her mouth. She didn't want to inhale the words, to have their contamination infect her.

As the gentle applause rose, the ladies of the staff prepared books for his autograph. Attention smothered him. Genny slipped out unseen.

Life-sized caricatures of Robert Frost, Ernest Hemingway, Agatha Christi, and Mark Twain were painted on the high-backed wooden bench in front of the Centuries Book Gallery. Dispirited, Genny moved toward the literary foursome, to Hemingway's image. She stared at the massive face framed by his graying beard with his sad introspective eyes. Her arms and legs were limp as she fell into his wooden, two-dimensional lap.

Waves of realization swept over her. The old Genny, the Genny she had left in Chicago, was in that room, between the pages of the books stacked next to the podium. All that love,

and confusion, and anticipation, and struggle now captured on pristine papers held within two blazing crimson covers. "Poems by Jonathan Waterhouse," a new darling of the contemporary poetic world.

Hers. Her beauty. Her strength. Her insight. Her visions. Her words. Her poems. Memories of a thousand kisses. Jonathan Waterhouse inside signing his name to them. His empty fields surrounded her as a seed of festering rage took root.

She rose and walked down a street crowded with shoppers, workers, children coming from morning sessions of school. Her pace steadied and picked up until she passed the Brunswick Hotel. She turned in, found a restaurant and ordered a salad. Her throat was so tight she could not swallow. It took more than an hour to finish.

From the lobby she called Deets, still at his office, and begged him, her voice filled with urgency, to meet her in the hotel bar after his day at Regeants was done. The sun was seeping through the scrolled outer doors of the hotel, carving strong shadows into the granite floor under her feet. The mocking brightness was everywhere. Genny escaped it into the cave-like entrance to the Vertigo Lounge. Deets would come.

Soon, he did, to rescue her from a barstool she was planted on. Her fingers were clasped around a bottle of champagne, near-empty. *"Hell, this was a celebration, no?"* her attitude said, *"her poetry had seen print."* As he neared, Genny freed her hands and with elbows secure on the bar she raised her slender crystalline tulip to him. Bubbles crept up the side, a thousand bubbles, a thousand toasts.

The bartender had been standing at the far end of the bar talking intently to an elderly gentleman since Genny had arrived. He interrupted his conversation only to fill or refill her glass. Genny sensed the two were standing at such a distance

because they smelled an anger that burned their noses. Fresh, raw anger, like the inside of a stewed tomato can, tinny and bitter. Genny would smell better when the anger solidified. It would, when she could say it in poetry not yet written. She would write it. She would get even.

She caught them studying her. Talking about women, maybe about her. Making wagers on when she would fall off the barstool. They didn't know that she was a published poet, worthy of all the champagne bubbles in France. Or California or wherever the hell this champagne had come from. Napa Valley. So it wasn't even the real thing. Neither was Jonathan Waterhouse. Who cared? Who cared, who cared.

Genny cared.

Who cared she was drowning in memories that had made their way into poetry. Published poetry – by Jonathan Waterhouse. Who cared that there stood a woman next to him, who gazed at him, brushed his cheek with a kiss, made love to him under warm comforters. Who cared that she didn't know that Genny did the same, often, and with abandon. Who cared that the bartender had just poured the last of her champagne into her beautiful crystalline tulip and asked if she wanted another when there was barely room in her gut for one more bubble. Who cared that she didn't love anymore, that she may never again feel the surge that pushes poetry out of her. Or that she was crying. Who cared?

They noted Deet's arrival with relief.

With his arm firmly around her waist, Deets led Genny into a dark distant booth, quietly asking "What happened? What's wrong? Genny, tell me. Genny, it's Deets here."

Nothing Deets said registered. He had learned to live with her secrets and resigned himself to another. He asked the bartender as they passed to send over a couple of coffees, strong

coffees. He set her down on a seat covered in burgundy leather. Or maybe it was Naugahyde. It was dark and smooth, whatever it was, Genny slipped into the corner easily and rested her head against the wall.

"And …? Genny, and what?" came from across the booth. Silence followed.

She corralled her emotions hoping to answer him without wailing. "It's him, the Mountain Man."

Deets waited, his eyebrows raised, expecting more would follow. When it didn't, he said, "Gen, I don't know where you've been or what you're talking about."

"That book review you read Sunday. The poet who got all the raves. That was the Mountain Man. That was my Mountain Man they were praising. You remember good ole Mountain Man? But it was my poetry they were quoting. My good ole poetry."

The coffees arrived. Genny topped off her cup from the cream pitcher the waiter had placed before her. Her hand shook as she raised the coffee to her lips and it splashed onto the laminated table top. She brought up her other hand to steady the cup.

"My poetry in the Mountain Man's book. And he read it today. I heard him. I heard him read my poetry. My poetry." Deets moved his head left and right, frowning, trying to negate what Genny was saying, watching the shaking cup.

"What'd you mean, your poetry. Your poetry is your poetry. What's he doing reading it?" Deets wanted to understand. Genny's expression gave him the answer. "You mean he's taking credit for it? How can that be? How does that happen?"

"I dunno, Deets. How does a man who respects words latch on to mine? How come he calls them his own? I've been sitting here all afternoon trying to figure out when I became

the sap. How did he – how did all those poems slip away – out of my life?"

Deets didn't attempt to answer that question but asked, "Did you see him?"

He brought his face closer to Genny's. She felt some trepidation in the question. Maybe he was afraid she would tell him she had run up to the podium and pulled the book from his hands. That she had torn out the pages and scattered them into the audience. That she had pulled the microphone from his delicate hands and stuffed it in his sensuous mouth. That she had shouted "fraud" as she stormed out of the room. Why didn't she do that? She didn't, but she could now. Deets, not one with cash enough to bail her out of jail, relaxed at the coolness of her answer.

"Yeah, I saw him. I saw him and I heard him. And what was he doing this morning? He was reading and signing books. I had to know. I had to find out what he was doing, how he was doing it. I thought maybe, I thought maybe I could ask him, to ask him to explain. He stood up there in front of all those people reading so proudly. All my words. He took all my words. He left me with nothing. I walked out before they were finished with him. And, and, and guess who was there, sitting off to the side. Her. *Her*. His *wife*. Looking like a plump peacock. So proud. Everyone was proud. The book people, everybody."

"I think you should be proud too," Deets said. "Those poems were good."

"*Were* good? They *are* good, Deets. Remember how I wanted that poet for my own, that Mountain Man? Well, guess what, I am that poet, 'sharp – uncluttered – rarely delicious – a poet to watch'." Genny put the cup down, resisting the urge to put her head down beside it. "'Tragic quality' they say. Well, he can take credit for that."

Deets straightened up from the slouch he had settled into. He recognized the praise from the "Times" book section. Anger shot over his face. "And that's what they're calling him? 'A poet to watch?' There oughta be a law against that."

"I suppose." Genny was crying, Chicago tears, the kind she thought she had used up. Deets offered his rumpled handkerchief. The tears watered the growing rage.

Deets splurged on a taxi to bring Genny's limp body home before she would begin the rant that was on the roof of her mouth. Spastic surges of anger shook her body. Deets held tight to her shoulders until they reached their front door when she stomped around the apartment kicking and knocking into walls. Deets made her tea. A hangover headache crept into her head dissipating the energy she spent on her madness. A quiet settled around her. Within, the hotness swelled.

Aunt Betsy would understand. She lived in the midst of California creativity, original and stolen. Deets's "There oughta be a law" rang in Genny's ears and Aunt Betsy provided the confirmation. She knew a little of Genny's poetic productivity. Genny had shared some of her work since they had reconnected at Denise's wedding. Betsy had provided enthusiasm and support that Genny had made little use of, except she remembered now her "wisdom comes from wounds" adage and found it applicable to this painful situation. If the wisdom were relative to the wound, how wise she should be.

Genny called her late at night, late for Genny's Eastern Standard time, Betsy's evening, and babbled. Betsy asked her to "take stock, slow down and begin at a point where I can walk through the situation with you." Genny reconstructed the coffee shop book review and the visit to the reading. She tried to be coherent and objective but the rage reignited.

"Genevieve darlin', if you're planning on pursuing some recompense, you'll need to be calm and deliberate."

In better control, Genny re-examined with her the poetry immersions they had shared over the months, his import, his support, how his influence had dwindled toward the end of their alliance. "He felt he was going cold, he kept complaining to me," she said. "And it was true; his verses weren't as lush as they had been in the beginning. He was borrowing my stuff then and moving the words around. He wasn't doing it any good, I later realized."

"Now, now, don't be bitter. Rancor won't win in court." Betsy's concern quieted Genny's furor. When Aunt Betsy had absorbed the situation, she told Genny, "Wait a bit while I mull this over. Let me talk to some people who have been through it. It's not all that uncommon, especially in these parts. For now though, know you are protected, darlin'," she said from two thousand five hundred miles away and the soothing words relaxed Genny's muscles. Her headache receded. "All you need is proof. Collect it."

"… Love is sweet for a day; But love grows bitter with treason …" Swinburne, Genny's dependable Swinburne.

The Manhattan offices of Jensen, Fulbright & Singleton, Ltd. were not easy to find.

At the designated floor they walked a circuitous path from the elevator bank along three corridors. Genny was apprehensive to enter this alien sanctuary of rights and wrongs, of justice applied. She could smell the decades of bodies that had walked these tiles emitting their frustrations over the outrages their lives had suffered.

She had continued to talk at length with Aunt Betsy. She had consulted with Brian who "for old time's sake" consulted

with his law partners. Shannah had flown in from Chicago to be at her side. Her father had offered to do the same but Genny had declined. Denise, in her waddling stages of pregnancy, was at home with her feet up. Genny felt her arm around her shoulder.

Shannah and Genny had just left Deets in the coffee shop downstairs. They stood before the glass door watching the receptionist beyond while reading the list of specializations: antitrust … trade regulation … patents … intellectual property. Genny focused on the promising words, "intellectual property." Her hand in her pocket stroked the computer discs that held her poetry. She transferred its printouts to her left arm, secured the poisonous book of poetry on top, opened the door and announced herself, "Hello, I am Genevieve Dupont and I have an appointment with Mr. Singleton."

2020 – Aftermath

... we begin to stop
in order simply
to begin
again

Late October / Maya Angelou

GENEVIEVE – to begin again

"Merci beaucoup, Denise, a thousand thank you's for coming all this way. It felt so good to see you in the audience."

"Thank me? Oh, Genny, no, thank you. How could I be anywhere else but here – sitting in this bookstore hideaway gazing at the massive towers of Notre Dame Cathedral – listening to my big sister read her poetry. In French, no less!"

"Indeed, kind of impressive, no? I've got something more impressive – while you're here I want to show you what I discovered while noseying around this book store. It dredged up some memories."

"Gen, I am afraid of your memories."

Denise had every right to be afraid of Genny's memories. They had defined her life.

A loaded decade had passed before Genny learned to live with them. They buried themselves into her bones after she acquired a master's degree in French that led to a faculty position in a Paris study abroad program. She was teaching language and literature in the land of her heritage. Added to that were a few published poetry books with her name attached and a compact fifth-floor cocoon in Montmartre with a tres impressionante view of the Sacre Coeur out the bathroom window. Brushing her teeth she watched the sun play on the gleaming Byzantine domes. How well Genny had learned to live.

Denise lived a different, quiet, competent life. She deserved this extravagant Paris trip far from her Colorado life and her growing girls. While she reconnected with her sister, she had sent them touring their grandparents' hometown under the guidance of her husband David. This spring, though, they would have preferred hitching a ride on the space shuttle. They were adventurers like Genny.

The passing years since Denise left her sister cowering in Chicago had altered her little. She lived in a world of her design. She was a homebody to Genny's high wire act, so unlike Genny, who was the paragon of her youth. Denise opted for love and Genny, obsession. Who of them was more productive? Both would say it's a draw.

"Follow me," Genny said as she directed her downstairs to a back room doorway where a bulletin board in disarray covered a major portion of the wall. Genny dug beneath layers of notices, messages, cards, and photos to pull out a scrawled yellowing sheet.

Denise read: "hmm, hmm, hmm, mmm: 'Genevieve / I think I love / our sense of déjà-vu / Genevieve / I think I love

/ you.' Oh, that is so sweet. Is it dated?" She turned over the note for some indication of its conception. "I wonder what that's all about. And when? This paper is so yellowed and ratty."

Genny teased her. "Wouldn't you just love to know the story behind it? That sweet little Genevieve, how lucky to have a love so tenuous." A hint of rapture spread to her face and tempted Denise with the possibilities of the tale. "Want to track her down?"

"Would that we had the time," Denise, always practical, said. "Something like that would take years. But you could do it, Gen. You are a permanent fixture here. Sweet Genevieve. How lucky *you* are."

"Denise," Genny said, unable to keep the tease going. "C'est moi, that's me. That sweet Genevieve c'est moi. Me." Genny's self-assured stature then slumped, her head lowered as a play-back raced across her mind. Denise stiffened. Her eyes bore into Genny's, who was saying, "Words from the pen of Jonathan."

"No. Really! When was he in Paris? I suppose he could have been in Paris. Genny, you never told me he went to Paris. But when? Who with?"

Genny owed her the story and confessed. "He was here with me, for a weekend, when you were home planning a wedding. I brought him on one of his few free weekends – my travel agent perks, you know. We visited this bookstore."

"That bastard," Denise said with more anger than Genny had anticipated. By now she was so nonplussed by all things Jonathan she was jolted when others still held bitterness.

"How long do messages stay up on this board?" Denise asked. "I am surprised no one has removed it."

"No one wants it. Not me. Not now."

"And him?" Denise asked. "Where's he been hanging for all those years?"

"Around budding poets, I guess. He disappeared from the literary scene as fast as it elevated me. The court settlement didn't include remorse so there's no personal aftermath. But wouldn't you think over the years some other love-starved Genevieve would have taken down this profession of lasting love? Guess not – maybe it's time this sweet Genevieve re-moves it."

"No," Denise said, "you leave it up there for some other Genevieve who may want to pretend it's her Paris memory."

"Couldn't top mine."

Denise turned sharply toward Genny. "You still idolize him?"

"Oh, no." In a soft hesitant voice she answered, "only the experience of him."

About the Author

Mary Gray moved through small town newspaper editing, corporate public relations, and international travel planning before she retired to write poetry, essays, magazine articles, and *Poetic Justice.* The manuscript was a semi-finalist as a novel-in-progress in the 2017 William Faulkner-William Wisdom Creative Writing Competition. She is the ghost writer for two memoirs, Gerald Fitzgerald's *Africa by Air* and General John Henebry's *The Grim Reapers at Work in the Pacific Theater.* She has delivered readings at the Chicago Public Library, The Printers Row Book Fair, the Chicago Humanities Festival, the Emily Dickinson Poetry Series, the University of Chicago, and DePaul University. She graduated from Northwestern University School of Journalism and has attended the Ragdale Writers' Retreat and the Piper Writers Studio at Arizona State.

Acknowledgements

Poetic Justice has a word for all writers who have had their words stolen. Hope. A story lies therein.

This story so evolved from such thievery and I am grateful to Marylee MacDonald whose enthusiasm and suggestions started me on this story-telling process in earnest. Then, pushing me toward the refinement of the text were Eve Bradshaw, Laurel Miller Dryda, Rick Novak, Timm Holt, and Grace Austin whose bi-monthly critiques kept the words and ideas under their scrutiny. A constant impetus to better writing was Julie Ganey of Chicago's Goodman Theatre with her six-week sessions that specialized in forging words into jewels. Thanks to The Village of Chicago for technical help when my computer would take a path different from my intentions.

My thanks to Brittany Bommelman and Joe Baldwin of Noisivelvet for first discovering the original Poetic Justice manuscript and to my Molly's BNSF commuter-train- riding book group who first read the original effort. I send my thanks to Jean Mcphilomy and to Pearl Grau (at age 101), first readers.

From my past, the Ragdale Artists Community and the former Neighborhood Writing Alliance set the foundation for my venture into fiction, memoir, and poetry. My children Tracy, Molly, Jaime, and Margery were steady in their belief that their mother was an author. I flourished under their expectation that a novel would evolve.